BOUND BY HONOR

BOOK TWO
OF THE BOUND BY STARS TRILOGY

A BRAD MADRID STORY

BOUND BY HONOR

BOOK TWO
OF THE BOUND BY STARS TRILOGY

A BRAD MADRID STORY

GLYNN STEWART
TERRY MIXON

FAOLAN'S PEN
PUBLISHING
faolanspen.com

All rights reserved. For information about permission to reproduce selections from this book, contact the publisher at info@faolanspen.com or Faolan's Pen Publishing Inc., 22 King St. S, Suite 300, Waterloo, Ontario N2J 1N8, Canada.

This edition published in 2018 by:

Faolan's Pen Publishing Inc.

22 King St. S, Suite 300

Waterloo, Ontario

N2J 1N8 Canada

ISBN-13: 978-1-988035-85-7 (print)

A record of this book is available from Library and Archives Canada.

Printed in the United States of America

1 2 3 4 5 6 7 8 9 10

First edition

First printing: November 2018

Illustration © 2018 Jeff Brown Graphics

Faolan's Pen Publishing logo is a trademark of Faolan's Pen Publishing Inc.

Read more books from Glynn Stewart at faolanspen.com

CHAPTER ONE

THERE WAS A FEELING OF EXHAUSTION, of bone-deep weariness no amount of rest could shake, that hung over Commodore Brad Madrid. At a glance, there was no reason for him to be so tired. He was young, barely into his mid-thirties, wealthy and powerful. He was the sole owner of the Vikings Mercenary Company, a Platinum-rated Guild company sought after for their reputation and firepower.

He owned and commanded a fleet of six destroyers, staffed by over five hundred crew and ground troops. The tall and gaunt mercenary had the money to afford those ships and those crews, and that gave him a power few in the solar system could rival.

Right now, however, he stood in a small gallery in the Vikings' home office in the Io Shipyards and looked out over his fleet. His eyes were blind to his warships, however, and all he truly saw was the stone plinth behind him, reflected in the glass.

A statue of a burly Viking warrior, the symbol of his company, stood on top of that plinth. It represented Vidar, the old Norse silent god of vengeance. It was appropriate for its current location, since the plinth had been laser-carved with the names of every trooper and spacer who'd died in the service of the Vikings.

Three months earlier, he'd taken his company into combat in the service of the Commonwealth, the government of the Solar System, and they'd added a lot of names to that plinth. One of his oldest friends and employees was among those new names.

There were a *lot* of friends on that list. The Vikings had been an informal organization for most of their existence, though necessity meant much of that was changing now. The same mission that had added so many names to the plinth had ended up adding four new ships to his roster, payment from a Fleet still reeling from the corruption he'd uncovered.

Many of the officers and crew of those new ships were freshly ex-Fleet, released as "excess to requirements" in recent draw-downs. Despite the information Brad had seen delivered to the Commonwealth, those draw-downs hadn't been reversed.

He finally focused his gaze through the glass, looking at his ships for several long seconds. The two *Bound*-class ships were surplus, released like their crews. The three *Warrior*-class ships, though…those were a sign of the favor Fleet held the Vikings in.

They were the newest and most advanced ships Fleet had designed. These three, in fact, had been headed for service in the Earth Defense Formation. The EDF was instead receiving the three ships that Brad Madrid had captured from the Cadre—identical ships in every sense.

Past the ships he could see Io and then the massive bulk of Jupiter. He checked his wrist-comp to confirm a suspicion, and nodded as the computer told him what he suspected: one of the tiny, barely visible stars hanging between Io and Jupiter was Earth.

Not enough had happened to account for the data he'd sent back to Earth with Agent Kate Falcone. An entire major supplier for Fleet had been caught red-handed selling warships to the enemies of the Commonwealth, the pirate Cadre.

And…nothing seemed to have happened.

That was part of why Brad was tired. If that level of treason could go unpunished, just what was the Commonwealth coming to? Just what was the human civilization he lived to protect coming to?

"Hey, grumpyface," a familiar voice told him as his wife, Michelle

Hunt—also the executive officer of his flagship—stepped into the gallery. "Got your game face to hand somewhere?"

Brad chuckled.

"It's around here somewhere, if I need it," he told her.

She stepped up and kissed the back of his head.

"Well, you probably want to find it and strap it on, my love," she said. "We've gathered the team. They're ready for your announcement."

He nodded and ran a hand over his face, rubbing away the mood that had taken him.

"Then I need to go talk to everyone," he confirmed. "It's time to let the Solar System know that the Vikings are back in business!"

———

"Attention! Commodore on deck!"

Brad waved Colonel Saburo Kawa, his senior ground commander, back to his seat.

"Please, Colonel," he told his old friend. "Necessity dictates a degree of greater formality as the Vikings grow, but *that* will never be necessary."

The Asian mercenary, the youngest son of the man who had built Brad's flagship, *Oath of Vengeance*, grinned incorrigibly as he slowly took his seat.

The scattering of mercenary old hands and ex-Fleet officers in the room returned to their seats as well, with surprising grace. Brad was more than a little surprised that Saburo had got the mercs on their feet at all.

He wasn't so surprised with the five ex-Fleet officers who commanded the majority of his destroyers, though. He and Captain Brenda Andre, the senior of those officers in his force, went back a long way now.

She'd once saved his life—but lost her ship in the process. When Fleet had started drawing down numbers, well, COs who'd lost ships were at the top of the list. However good the reasons.

The other four were new, recruited over the last three months. What Brad wouldn't tell any of them was that the Commonwealth Investigative Agency had screened all of them to a level that was probably illegal.

Brad's relationship with the Agency was...complex, but he was technically an Agent of the Commonwealth. In practice, the Vikings often acted as a somewhat-deniable asset for the Agency as they tried to work out just where the Cadre had come from.

"Necessity does, however, demand more formality than I prefer," Brad finally continued, studying his Captains. "All of our new folks have old Vikings hands as XOs, but that's still five of you only recently out of Fleet."

Said XOs sat next to the men and women Fleet had given him. His surviving tactical officers from before they'd fought the Independence Militia were now XOs, but Fleet had found some damn good officers to send him.

He wasn't even sure how they'd justified letting any of his four new Captains go. They were certainly men and women he would have fought to keep.

"We don't play by Fleet rules in the Guild or the Vikings," he told them all. "But you know that. Even Keala has had a whole *two weeks* to get used to being a mercenary."

A chuckle ran around the table. Keala El-Hashem was a dark-skinned, dark-haired woman who'd most recently served as the tactical officer of the cruiser *Tremendous*. She knew several of Brad's secrets and he was glad to have her in command of *Montgomery*.

"I'm not sure I'll ever be used to this, sir," she replied cheerfully. "But it definitely has its virtues!"

She toasted him with her beer as she spoke, highlighting one of said virtues.

"That it does. Unfortunately, it has its vices, too: the big one is that we actually need to make money. Our happy holiday is at an end, folks. As of twelve hundred GMT today, I have advised the Guild that we are available for contract and are looking for clients."

The Mercenary Guild was an unfortunate necessity of human civilization in the Solar System. There were distinct limits on how far and how fast the Commonwealth could project power—and even harder limits on how much *will* the Commonwealth had to project it. To keep order and peace, and to protect assets and people, the people of the system turned to mercs.

The Guild kept those mercs in line and following rules of *some* kind. They also acted as a broker for contracts.

"I'm not sure what work is going to come our way, but Platinum companies generally don't sit idle unless we choose to," he continued. "I'm also not entirely sure of the breakdown, but we're somewhere in the top three companies for spaceborne firepower—and we might make the top ten for Saburo's troops, too."

Each of his ships carried roughly thirty ground troops and even more spacers. All told, Brad was responsible for a hundred and seventy-five troops and three hundred officers and crew.

It was more intimidating than anything else.

"I'll be keeping my ears to the ground for news," he told them all. "I suggest you do the same. I have no intention of deploying partial forces right now. Too many of us are too new to this gig. I'm not letting you out of my sight with my destroyers just yet!"

That got him a chuckle, as it had been intended to.

"Any idea what kind of op we'll get?" Captain Fabia Laurent, commanding officer of *Grant*, asked.

"Well, I don't know of any wars going on, and I doubt anyone is going to look at six destroyers and think we make a great amphibious landing force, so I'm guessing station or colony security," Brad told them. "Possibly convoy escort, maybe blockade." He grimaced. "Someone would have to have some *damn* good reasons for me to accept a blockade contract, but I'm sure there's something out there I haven't thought of.

"Whatever comes up, unless it's in the Jupiter planetary system, we're days' to weeks' flight away from the mission locale. We'll have time to plan and practice.

"We got our Platinum rating by being the best. Let's make sure we live up to it."

CHAPTER TWO

"COMMODORE, this is Factor Parisi from the Io office of the Guild."

Brad gave the dark-skinned, redhaired woman on his screen a calm nod. He hadn't worked much with Bohumila Parisi, but the Io-born administrator had a solid reputation with the Mercenaries Guild.

"Greetings, Factor," he replied. "How may I assist the Guild today?"

"I saw that you put the Vikings back on available status this morning," she said. "I wanted to touch base and see what kind of contract you were looking for."

If Parisi *hadn't* seen the Vikings changing availability status, the Io office would have needed a new Factor. There were only three Platinum companies headquartered in Io local space at the moment, and the Vikings were the only ones actually "at home" right now.

"Of course," Brad replied, none of his thoughts showing on his face as he settled back in the chair in his office. He'd spent more time in the room in the last three months than he had in the previous three years, and had finally come to appreciate the *very* nice chairs that Saburo's father had acquired for them when the office was set up.

"With the expansion in our strength, I'm looking to avoid anything of the more meat-grinder variety," he said dryly. He'd yet to meet a merc who looked for those missions, but they happened. "Of course, with six destroyers in play, I'm also looking for something that's, well, worth the price my company now commands.

"Preferably a space-based contract, *definitely* a fully escrowed and approved contract."

The last probably didn't need to be said, but even Platinum companies were known to take contracts where the payment wasn't in escrow or the Guild wasn't fully comfortable with the legitimacy of the job if enough money was on the table.

"That's about what I expected, Commodore," Parisi told him with a smile. "I have a contract that has crossed my desk that might fit your needs. To be honest, it's been being bounced around the entire system as the Guild tries to find the right fit for what the client needs."

Now, *that* was intriguing. And strange. The Guild usually acted as more of a clearinghouse than a broker, and it was rare for more than the local Guild office to get involved in trying to fill a contract.

"Who is the client?" he asked carefully.

"That's confidential and I can't discuss it over a radio link," Parisi told him, which only increased his intrigue. "The client has an agent on Ganymede right now, however. I can arrange an in-person meeting tomorrow if you can grab a shuttle over to Ganymede Landing by morning."

"I can take one of my own," Brad noted, "but that's quite the expe—"

"The Guild will cover the cost of your shuttle fuel and time," Parisi said instantly. "We have a large interest in getting a company on this contract, Commodore Madrid, and the distances add a layer of complexity we don't normally deal with.

"I can't say more over the radio, as I said, but if you can make it to the Guild office in Ganymede Landing, I'll explain more in person."

"Are you on Ganymede yourself, Factor Parisi?" Brad asked.

"Not yet," the Factor replied. "But if you can make it, I'll make it."

There was no way Brad was going to miss this now. Just what was going on?

"I'll have to check which of my shuttles and pilots are free," he told the factor. "But you've definitely piqued my curiosity. I'll be at the Guild in Ganymede Landing by ten hundred hours tomorrow."

"Excellent, Commodore. I will see you there."

———

"Why Ganymede?" Michelle asked once Brad had pulled his usual command staff together. Membership on that staff had far more to do with how long someone had been a member of the Vikings than rank, with Michelle, at least, outranked by every ship Captain.

The only ship Captain present other than Brad was Brenda Andre. Saburo was there for the ground troops, and *Oath of Vengeance*'s chief engineer, Mike Randall, spoke for their technicians.

The odd one out in the meeting was Shelly Weldon, formerly the executive officer of *Heart of Vengeance* and one of the few survivors from that corvette's crew. The blonde officer was currently the woman in charge of their main base there in Io.

Among other things, she was supervising the build of two more destroyers. One would be hers, since she'd turned down command of any of the *Warriors*.

"And some days, it is blatantly obvious to me that only Saburo and I are actually from Jupiter," she noted now with a small smile. Brad was perfectly willing to be uninformed if it got a smile out of Shelly. Her husband had died on *Heart*, and she was far from over that just yet.

"Illuminate me," he asked.

"*We* may look to Io as the most important thing in the Jupiter System, but that's only because of the shipyards," Shelly told them. "Ganymede is the largest moon, the political center point everything else revolves around—and the big Fleet base."

"It's also the primary source of water for the entire planetary system," Saburo pointed out. "Hence the Fleet base. The Fleet base, of course, is why the Jovian militias keep a significant presence there, too."

Brad snorted.

"Because task groups led by destroyers are a threat to a pair of cruisers," he replied.

"One task group might not be," Michelle said. "But the Jovian militias have, what, sixteen between them?"

"And rumor has it that there are a few of the big fifteen-centimeter guns Fleet likes to mount on cruisers hidden in some of craters on Ganymede itself," Saburo said. "Moon's got no atmosphere, so they can fire from the ground."

"And good luck taking out ground installations on a moon bigger than some of the planets," Brad allowed. "I know, I know. So, what, someone's at Ganymede because they're doing something more important, huh?"

"I'd guess they're not here to talk to mercenaries," Michelle concluded. "Probably politics or water, but since they're looking for mercs, the Guild will make the meeting."

"Makes sense. And if they're a big enough deal for politics or bulk water, they can probably afford us. We'll need to make the trip."

"Fortunately, the orbits are close," his wife told him. "I can have you into Ganymede Landing by midnight if you want."

"You, my dear?"

"I'm not letting anyone *else* fly your cute butt around while my ship is sitting in drydock," she said with a grin. "You were going to bring me anyway, weren't you?"

"You, Saburo and Brenda," he confirmed with a chuckle and a gesture at the other two officers. "If you fly us, then that saves a seat on the shuttle and a hotel room at the other end.

"Any guesses as to who the mysterious client might be?" he asked.

Saburo snorted.

"Given all of the runaround? I'm guessing we're not even talking to the client. We're talking to a rep, and the client is political. Senate, maybe."

The Senate was the elected body that ran the Commonwealth, with some help from the President and the various planetary and station governors.

"Or corporate," Brad said. "There's at least a dozen corporations out there big enough for this much trouble. We'll find out in the morning. Do we have a shuttle ready to go?"

"Of course we do," Michelle replied. "Everlit, do you realize how many people you'd have to fire if we'd managed to *not* have a shuttle ready to fly?"

He snorted.

"We could always take *Oath of Vengeance*," he pointed out.

"Overkill. And Ganymede Traffic Control likes at least twenty-four-hours notice of moving warships into their space," Shelly told him. "You'll survive on a shuttle for six hours, boss."

CHAPTER THREE

GANYMEDE TRAFFIC CONTROL, thankfully, was much more lenient toward regular space shuttles. The shuttle Michelle had grabbed was armed, of course, but for some reason, the guys with half a dozen corvettes orbiting the moon weren't bothered by the shuttle's machine guns.

Ganymede Landing itself was an impressive sight. The south side of the city was an artificial lake where large chunks of the moon's surface had been blasted away to expose the water underneath. Since the planet had no atmosphere, an immense but flimsy-seeming dome of plastic had been raised over the hundreds of square kilometers of water.

"There's no logical reason to do that," Brad noted as they swept in for a landing at one of the domes on the "shore." Ten domes made up the majority of Ganymede Landing, each roughly two kilometers across. Most of the city was almost certainly underground, but the glittering crystal domes shone brightly with the reflection of Jupiter.

"Nope," Saburo agreed. "They did it because it would be pretty. The dome helps keep the uncovered water liquid and is a bit hardier than it looks. They apparently installed a 'beach' along one side of it." The mercenary Colonel chuckled. "They don't recommend swimming outside the marked areas. *Those* areas are heated and rendered nontoxic. The rest…"

"Swimming," Brad echoed. "I am…vaguely aware of that as a concept. Seriously?"

"Seriously," the other mercenary confirmed. "Remember, Ganymede was colonized directly from Earth. They wanted something to remind them of home. So…" He gestured expansively. "Beach."

"The *actual* money is in the silos to the north of the city, there," Andre noted, the ship Captain pointing toward a series of tall concrete structures. "Those are hiding some *massive* wells pumping up water and running it into purifiers. That set you see there provides, oh, sixty percent of the moon's water."

Brad blinked.

"Damn."

"Yeah. Fleet knows *damn* well there's guns in the mountains that could actually threaten the picket squadron—because Fleet helped put them there. Without Ganymede's water, a good third of Jupiter's population would probably die before a secondary source could be established."

"There's water on the other moons," Brad objected. "They've all got water sources of their own. Plus the ice in the rings."

"And that's why someone taking out Ganymede's water extraction and refining would *only* kill about two million people," Brenda said quietly.

"Depressing as this conversation became, we are coming in for a landing at Ganymede Landing's Hidden Valley Dome," Michelle told them. "I'm looking forward to a nice hotel. It can't be *worse* than our apartment on Io."

"Hey, *I* wanted to sleep on the ship," Brad replied.

"Oh, so *that's* why we rented a shoe closet instead of a suite!"

He blew his wife an affectionate kiss and shut up. Interrupting the person landing a space shuttle was *always* a bad idea.

———

Brad had never visited Ganymede's surface before. He'd also never been to Earth, and his time on Mars had mostly been spent in tunnels. He was familiar with the concept of a "car," but his experience was with the vehicles designed to move around the corridors and tunnels of space stations and underground colonies.

The vehicle waiting for them at the landing pad was something quite different. It was still more compact than the vehicles he'd seen in movies set on Earth, but it was longer and broader than any land vehicle he'd ever seen before. Most of its length was a passenger compartment large enough for six people, with the driver sitting in front, on top of what he assumed was an electric motor turning the wheels.

The driver was a young woman with a shaved head, wearing a burgundy bodysuit. The heavy collar clearly contained an emergency helmet, and he nodded approvingly at the concession to the fact that Ganymede Landing was under a dome.

The dome might allow them to pretend they were an Earthside city, other than the three-tenths gravity maintained throughout, but if it was breached, the locals would be retreating to the buildings around them *very* quickly.

"Commodore Madrid and party?" the driver asked as they exited the shuttle. "The Guild sent me to pick you up." She gestured to the shuttle, where robots and humans were already starting to swarm.

"The pad crew will take care of your shuttle; she'll be refueled and waiting for you when you return."

"Thank you. Can you recommend a hotel?" Brad said.

She smirked.

"That's why Factor Parisi sent me. The Guild has booked you rooms at the Hidden Valley Starview. Your meeting will be there in the morning, so I understand it to be convenient, and I'm relatively sure the Starview will meet your needs."

"All I really need is a bed for about six hours," he told the driver. "Though I'd definitely love a shower."

"Oh, I think the Starview will *definitely* serve," she replied.

———

The Starview turned out to be Ganymede Landing's premier luxury hotel, positioned on the edge of an artificially-constructed lake and under one of the clearer sections of the dome. Polite staff saw Brad and his people to gorgeously comfortable rooms, and collected them in the morning for their breakfast meeting.

They met Factor Parisi, the replacement for Brad's old friend Sara Kernsky, who'd moved to a bigger office on Mars, in a fifth-floor room of the ten-story building, where floor-to-ceiling windows looked out over the lake, currently reflecting the bright colors of Jupiter. The dark-skinned Guild agent looked tired, but she gestured them to seats around a good-sized dark stone table.

"I landed an hour ago," she told them by way of apology. "Coffee and food will be coming; our guest will be joining us in about half an hour."

"We're playing by their schedule, are we?" Brad asked.

"Yes," Parisi confirmed flatly. "You're meeting with the Jovian Trade Attaché of the Governing Council of New Venice. Her job is to make sure that water flows to the floating cities, at a minimum, and that trade in general moves smoothly.

"As you can imagine, Kaura Jenkins is a busy, busy woman. But the Council wants mercenaries, so she's willing to meet with us."

"New Venice," Brad repeated. "I know that's on Venus, Factor, but I'll admit that's as far as my knowledge goes. Care to fill me in?"

"I didn't expect much more," she told him, quieting for a moment as hotel staff came through with coffee and laid out platters of hot food on the side table. Once she'd grabbed her own coffee and the mercenaries were digging in, Parisi settled back down and considered.

"New Venice is the capital of Venus, the largest and wealthiest of the aerostat cities," she continued. "Something like sixty percent of Venus's population is concentrated into the cluster of aerostats that surround New Venice. They make their living by gas skimming, tourism, and mining.

"The Governor of Venus sits as the senior member of the Governing Council of New Venice. In practice, they're the closest things the planet has to rulers." Parisi shrugged. "What they *haven't* told us is what they want mercenaries for. They've given us their specifications: a significant space-based force with boarding-trained troops, but they haven't told us what for.

"They've agreed to escrow and the contract is approved in principle by the Guild, but until we have final details, that approval is preliminary. We may revoke it, depending on what the Council wants you to do."

Brad nodded. The main reason the Commonwealth not only allowed the Mercenaries Guild but encouraged its existence was that the Guild made sure that mercenaries didn't fall too far into murky waters.

Even a contract that the Guild didn't *approve* still had to meet minimum criteria to even be listed. There were ways to get unlisted contracts, but few Guild companies would take them.

No one really wanted to break strikes or blockade stations into submission, for example.

"Kaura Jenkins will fill you in on the contract details and will make at least an initial recommendation to the Governing Council on whether to hire you," Parisi told him. "I'm here to make sure Guild rules are respected, not that we have a concern about *you* breaking them, Commodore."

"I appreciate that," Brad allowed. He glanced around at his officers. They all looked as intrigued as he did. "If she'll be here that quickly, I suggest we get another round of food and coffee into us all before she arrives. This sounds like it's going to be an interesting meeting."

CHAPTER FOUR

Kaura Jenkins was an extraordinarily tiny woman who entered the room with brisk efficiency. Two much larger bodyguards accompanied her and split off to flank the inside of the door after Jenkins entered.

They loomed impressively, though Brad didn't rank their threat level particularly highly. In compliance with Ganymede weapons laws, he was only *officially* carrying a stun baton…and he figured it would take him under twenty seconds to disable both men with it.

He wouldn't even need to break out any of his other tricks—and that was assuming Saburo didn't beat him to one or both guards.

Jenkins herself was more intimidating in many ways. Her hair had been night black once but was now fading toward silver. Her skin was darker than many Brad had known, and she had a small red tattoo he was unfamiliar with between her brows.

"All right, Mr. Madrid," she said briskly. "To business."

"Commodore Madrid, if you please," he asked. "Or Brad, if you wish. The Guild is quite specific on who may use flag ranks among our number. Like any doctor, Ms. Jenkins, I earned my title."

He doubted she even realized she was being rude, hence his calm explanation. Jenkins didn't strike him as the type who had much interaction with mercenaries—or even Fleet, for that matter.

"And how many people do you have to kill to be a Commodore, then?" she asked as she sat down, and he winced.

"Quite a few, usually," he replied—mostly to make her share his wince. "The title, however, is primarily based around the size and… respectability of the company I control. I command multiple warships and am a Platinum-rated company commander, therefore I have the title."

"I see." Her voice was prim and tight. She didn't seem very happy with his explanation, but if she was going to poke him, he was going to return the favor. "In that case, *Commodore*, I suggest you call me Doctor."

"Of course, Dr. Jenkins," he allowed instantly. Mentally, he kicked himself. He hadn't had a lot of time, but he could have at least made sure he knew if the attaché was a PhD or not.

"To business, then," she repeated. Saburo delivered a cup of milky tea to her elbow, distracting her for a moment. She nodded her thanks and took a sip.

"I represent the Governing Council of New Venice, on Venus," she laid out. "While I do not necessarily approve of the Mercenary Guild, I understand the occasional need for an organization such as yours. The decision is not mine, in any case, but I have been briefed and asked to assess you and your company."

"Why don't you lay out the mission, Dr. Jenkins, and I'll tell you what my company can do to fill your needs?" Brad suggested.

"Very well." She took another sip of tea and considered. "How much do you know about Venusian deep-dive mining operations?"

"I don't know very much, but I am extremely familiar with Jupiter and Saturn gas-mining operations," he replied. "My understanding is that Venus operates similar gas-skimming operations, and I can imagine that any surface mining would require massive amounts of specialty gear. I may never have visited Venus, Doctor, but I understand the surface to be spectacularly hostile."

"It is," she allowed. "And you are correct. We have gas-skimming operations similar to that done out here, but the mining environment is entirely unique. It is, of course, that unique environment that creates the compounds and materials that we extract.

"There are, at any given moment, between three and six hundred vehicles of various sizes carrying out mining operations in the mountain ranges and plateaus of Venus. Mining the actual surface itself is... fraught. There are only a handful of vehicles capable of the process, and even they usually stick to the mountains with their less-robust brethren."

A kilometer or two of altitude wouldn't make that much difference, from what Brad had read—but on the other hand, it clearly made *enough* difference.

"Given the number of mining vehicles, gas skimmers and, indeed, aerostat cities themselves, Venus sees in excess of three thousand daily flights of various transport aircraft between worksites, warehousing facilities, refineries and residential aerostat platforms. The Venusian atmosphere is difficult to navigate and almost impossible to scan through.

"You can imagine, I suspect, what this leads to, given the violent nature of some men."

Brad got the impression that Dr. Jenkins figured he was more capable of that imagination than she was, and she might even have been right.

"What's your loss rate?" he asked quietly. "Do you know the numbers for piracy versus natural hazard?"

"We *normally* lose about fifteen to twenty craft per standard year," Jenkins replied. "We can confirm about half of those are natural hazards, and my understanding is that we believe most of the remainder are as well. The estimates I have seen previously are that we have between one and five hijackings a year. We have caught, usually, about two hijacking teams a year."

There had been some spikes in the past, Brad knew. His occasional Agency partner, Kate Falcone, had been involved in an operation against them several years earlier.

"In the last six months, Commodore, we've lost over a hundred aircraft."

Brad's wince was in sympathy this time.

"And you want us to stop that," he said calmly. "We...can probably do that, Dr. Jenkins, though I'll need more information before I can devise a strategy."

"We don't *have* more information," Jenkins admitted. "Normally, we have *something*. There are satellites covering sixty percent of Venus's surface at any moment. They can't see that deeply, but weapons fire is obvious.

"We haven't detected anything. Just aircraft that don't reach their destinations. Always cargo craft, not passenger planes. Between cargos and the aircraft themselves, we're looking at a billion dollars gone up in smoke, Commodore. So, what would *you* suggest?"

"More information on the missing planes would be a good starting point," he repeated. "But also more information on usual flight parameters, destinations, journey times, previous similar problems... I know there was a problem with wreckers a few years ago."

He glanced at his officers thoughtfully.

"Right off the bat, I'd suggest moving my ships into key positions on the shipping routes. We have more powerful sensors than your satellites, which would give us more information—and if we get lucky, I'm comfortable in my gunners' ability to pick off pirate craft without damaging the cargo planes."

"That might be valuable," she allowed. "What the Council wants is for you to bring your ships to the key aerostat cities, the ones with spaceports, and establish a customs blockade. They want you to inspect every ship leaving Venus. There's no value in piracy if they can't get the cargo off-world."

"Venus has, what, six million people?" Brad asked. "That's quite the market if they're trying to sell things without leaving."

"Perhaps, but there's only so much of an ability to market stolen ore and refined metals in the aerostats, Commodore. To make a profit, they have to move the cargos off-world."

"We can stop that," he confirmed. "Each of my destroyers carries a platoon of thirty troops and three shuttles. If we can borrow refueling facilities and barracks from your Council, we can even use the shuttles to maintain customs patrols and use three or four of the destroyers for the kind of interception I suggested earlier."

Brad paused thoughtfully. There was one part of this that bothered him.

"I hate to try and turn down work," he said, "but this is the Commonwealth's responsibility, isn't it? I know Fleet moved against the wreckers you had a problem with in the past. Why aren't you going to them?"

"I asked the same question, Commodore," Jenkins told him. "I was told that Fleet is now too understrength to spare us assistance and we have been told to find our own solutions. Since New Venice and the other aerostat cities don't maintain any space force beyond a basic search-and-rescue capability, we simply do not have the ability to deal with this ourselves.

"I have no enthusiasm for you or what you do, Commodore, and I am inclined to suggest we simply find the cheapest rent-a-thugs we can. I'm frankly unconvinced of the difference that justifies your astronomical price tag."

Brad smiled.

"Believe me, Dr. Jenkins, if you hire 'the cheapest rent-a-thugs you can,' we'll be back in this conference room in three months...and a lot more people will have died."

She glared at him silently for several long seconds, then nodded.

"I see your point, Commodore. I will pass on a recording of this meeting to the Council. You meet the requirements as well as I can see, but the final decision is theirs."

"Of course, Doctor." Brad bowed his head slightly. "Factor Parisi can provide you or the Council with our fee schedule. You might not see the difference between types of 'rent-a-thug,' Doctor, but enough people do that the fee schedule is quite inflexible."

Jenkins, thankfully, was looking at Brad instead of Parisi and missed the Factor's long blink of despair. Even the Platinum fee schedule was negotiable, especially when you were hiring six destroyers and combat platoons.

Unless, of course, you called a senior mercenary officer a rent-a-thug to his face.

Brad was going to take the contract. He was going to help the government and people of Venus and stop the pirates, to save lives as much as anything else.

But if they wanted to insult him, they would pay extra for the privilege.

CHAPTER FIVE

They'd returned to Io and were in the process of moving back aboard *Oath of Vengeance* when Parisi finally got in touch again. Brad checked his wrist-comp as it chimed, then waved one of the spacers nearby over to him.

"Sabina, can you grab this for me and drop it off at my quarters?" he asked the tech. "Hopefully, this call means we've got work!"

The Slavic woman saluted briskly and took the box of bedding that Brad was hauling.

"Will the XO need help setting up your quarters?" she asked.

"That's what we've got a steward team for," Brad replied with a chuckle. "She's got it in hand; I'm just helping with the lifting."

The tech disappeared deeper into the ship as Brad stepped out of the flow of traffic and accepted the call.

"Madrid," he answered. "Apologies for the delay; we're transferring back aboard our ships."

"No one told you if you had a contract yet, did they?" Parisi asked. "Seems a bit premature."

"Some contracts are rushes," he replied. "Even if this Venus one falls through, it's hardly valueless to have my crews back aboard. What if someone attacks Io?"

The Factor's derisive snort told him what she thought of that possibility. Brad wasn't so sure himself, but then, he knew how powerful the Cadre's "Independence Militia" front had grown. He was grimly certain that, unless Fleet had reinforced more than he knew about, the Cadre now had the force to at least take control of Jupiter's orbital space.

"Well, if that scenario takes place, we'll have to find someone else to defend us," she told him. "Like, oh, Fleet. Because *you*, Commodore, should be on your way to Venus."

"They agreed to the contract?"

"At full Platinum daily rates and combat premiums," she agreed. "I was *planning* on being at least somewhat flexible and arguing with you over it, but they didn't even blink."

"You wouldn't have had to argue hard," Brad admitted. "Even if Jenkins is an ass, there's at least a couple of million people on Venus who aren't."

"They must be more desperate then she let on," he continued with a shake of his head. "They didn't even counteroffer?"

The time delay for a roundtrip communication between Venus and Jupiter was *long*. When everything lined up perfectly, it was over an hour. The current point in Venus's year meant that it was even worse, with the planet not *quite* on the opposite side of the sun.

Even so, he'd assumed part of the delay had been the need for back-and-forth negotiations.

"I think the Council argued over our position for at least five or six hours before agreeing," Parisi told him. "I'm guessing someone there made all of our arguments for us—and yes. I think the situation is worse than they've told Jenkins. They didn't even tell *us* as much as they'd told her."

"It still makes no sense to me," Brad said. "This is a Commonwealth problem. Where's Fleet?"

"I don't know," she agreed. "It should be Fleet. That's not really our problem, though, Commodore, is it?"

"True enough." *Commodore* Madrid didn't necessarily care why Venus was hiring him instead of turning to Fleet. Brad Madrid, however, was also a sworn agent of the Commonwealth Intelligence Agency—and wearing that hat, it definitely *was* his problem.

"What's our timeline?" he asked instead, making sure he was wearing the right mental hat for this conversation.

"They want you on station in twenty-one days," Parisi told him. "They're paying travel rates for that long—but if you're late, they start deducting percentage points off the whole contract."

"We won't be late," Brad replied. "Thank you, Factor. We'll be under way in about twenty-four hours. If you can pull all the Guild files on Venus, New Venice, and the last round with the Wreckers, I'd appreciate it.

"Any intel we have on the current situation would be worth its weight in gold, but I don't think we have much."

"You know as much as I do, I think," she admitted. "I'll get you everything we've got, Commodore. The Guild's cut on this pays *my* salary for a few years."

"Yeah, but you don't have destroyers to maintain," Brad said with a chuckle. "They're a tad more expensive than apartments."

———

Even with the move back aboard ship ongoing, it took Brad less than twenty minutes to get his Captains and platoon Majors on a videoconference link from *Oath of Vengeance*'s main briefing room.

"We have a contract, people," he told them. "The Governing Council of New Venice is bringing us in to help deal with a piracy and smuggling problem. They've had a major upsurge in piracy in the last six months."

He grimaced.

"And before any of you ask the question *I* asked, we're not entirely sure why Fleet isn't intervening. The New Venetian representative we spoke to had been fed a line about Fleet being 'too busy,' but that doesn't add up."

He'd be digging into that from his other sources as soon as this briefing was over. Something was rotten in the state of Venus.

"Our task, at least initially, is a customs blockade," he told them.

"We'll move in above New Venice itself and maintain a security perimeter with the shuttles. No one is allowed to leave the planet without allowing our teams aboard to inspect their cargo.

"Once we've got that pattern established, I intend to move at least two of our destroyers out to play watchdog over the more-vulnerable shipping routes. If we get enough support from New Venice, we may be able to move most of our ships out to do that.

"Regardless, we will keep a minimum of one ship at New Venice itself to back up the boarding parties. Civilians and potential smugglers will likely be *much* more cooperative with an actual warship looming in the background."

"A blockade seems weird," Captain El-Hashem noted. "If the government of Venus is bringing us in, aren't we just backing up their customs patrols?"

"It's complicated," Brad replied. He'd wondered that himself, but the Guild files on Venus had answered his question. "While the official Governor of Venus is on the Governing Council of New Venice, the truth appears to be that his authority is nominal at best. There are six groupings of aerostat cities that each send a Senator to Earth, and, well, they're all functionally independent of each other.

"Even with the cluster around New Venice, the individual aerostat cities act as city-states. There are planetwide agencies for traffic management and such, but they're more like cooperative endeavors than true government offices."

"So, New Venice doesn't actually have the authority to impose a customs lockdown," Laurent added. "I was posted there for a while and it's a headache—the Governor is elected by the populace of the whole planet and *officially* has the authority to do everything a Governor normally can.

"In practice, he runs the intercity agencies and interacts with the Commonwealth. The cities manage their own affairs—including customs."

"So, while the Governor had the official authority to impose a customs lockdown, he doesn't have the actual power," Brad finished for her. "Traditionally, when that level of force has been needed, the Governor has called in Fleet. This time, New Venice is hiring us.

"We're covered on paper, but we're going to get pushback. Some will be legitimate. Some will be covering for people attempting to smuggle stolen goods off-world.

"Given that the theft of those goods involved the presumed deaths of over a thousand people, my patience with the legitimate gripers is limited," he concluded. "We'll do our damn job, understand me?"

Nods rippled around the table and video screens.

"Saburo, I've pulled you the Guild training files on customs inspections. I want every one of our troopers to be able to do a customs inspection blindfolded by the time we arrive at Venus."

"How long will that be?" the Colonel asked.

"We have three weeks," Brad told him. "How long it will take us depends on how much fuel I'm willing to burn—and there are both refueling facilities in New Venice and bonuses for getting into position early."

He grinned.

"We're going to push it in two weeks, a direct burn-flip-burn. My calculations say we'll make it to Venus with just over ten percent of our fuel left."

"And if someone jumps us along the way?" Andre asked.

"Then we'll get to Venus nearly dry on fuel and short some munitions," Brad said brightly. "We could use the workout. We've got good ships and good crews, but outside of *Bound by Law* and *Oath of Vengeance*, they haven't worked together.

"We'll need to fix that."

———

With his senior officers onboard and his course to Venus being double-checked and validated by the actual navigators in his crews, Brad made his way down to *Oath of Vengeance*'s engineering spaces.

Mike Randall, his chief engineer, was many things. Talented, intelligent, brave…but also obnoxious, disrespectful, arrogant…

He was currently bossing around the team of techs responsible for managing the destroyer's power core. Currently, the fusion plant was off-line and *Oath* was running on station power, but the feed-line diagram next to the main control center was lighting up to show fuel lines starting to fill.

"Should I come back later?" Brad asked as he peeked over a railing at the diagram and his chief engineer.

"Nah, we're just in feed-line mode," Randall replied. "It'll be at least twenty or thirty minutes before we even start running He-3 into the core. What can I do for you, boss?"

Oath of Vengeance was rare among destroyers in using helium-3 fusion for her main core. Most used basic hydrogen fusion—a cheaper and more readily available fuel source, but not as powerful. Fleet reserved He-3 for its bigger ships: cruisers, drone carriers and battleships.

One of the reasons for Fleet restricting operations in the outer systems right now was a Cadre attack that had destroyed their main helium-3 refueling base. They were rebuilding, but for the moment, nothing heavier than a destroyer went much past Jupiter.

Frustrating to everyone was that the Cadre had at least one cruiser and drone carrier and was fueling them somehow. Brad's information on how was unpleasant: he'd learned that they'd funded research into an entire new line of small-scale refining. There was no way Fleet could locate the Cadre's refueling bases.

"We're heading to Venus," Brad told his chief engineer. "Going to be any problems with fuel?"

"Not a chance," Randall said firmly. "We'll run the *Bound*s dry a week before *Oath* comes up short. The *Warrior*s will be in the middle."

He shook his head.

"Those birds can out-accelerate us, but they can't outlast us," he said proudly.

"Good. So, you'll have some free time on the trip, then?" Brad asked with faked innocence.

"I *know* that voice, boss," Randall replied. "What do you need?"

"We're going to Venus and we're hunting wreckers," Brad reminded him. "Most of our shuttle fleet is going to be tied up on customs duty, but I'm going to hold *Oath*'s shuttles back. I want them rigged up for atmospheric flight."

His chief engineer stared at him for several long seconds.

"You're serious."

"The birds are rated for atmospheric flight; it just almost never comes up," Brad said. "I want to be able to send *Oath*'s birds into atmosphere after pirates. There's only so deep I can take destroyers."

"If you want the birds to land on Earth and come back up, they don't even require refits," Randall told him. "The wings are retracted in normal ops, but they're there. At full load, they can drop to a one-g surface and come back up. Easier the lower the gravity, of course.

"But Venus? Boss, the surface *melts lead*."

"And our shuttles have heat-resistant ceramic coating," Brad replied. "And you have twelve hours to get anything you need from Io. It has to be doable."

"Reaching the surface is *doable*," Randall confirmed. "With custom-built, specially-designed ships. I'm not sure I can refit our shuttles to do anything remotely like it. I *might* be able to get you a temporary refit that can get you down to the mountains, with a frigging blank check."

"Done," Brad said instantly, then grinned as his chief engineer realized he'd been played. "Please, Mike, I *know* we can't get to the surface. But I don't think our pirate friends can either. Give me shuttles than can reach the mountain mining tunnels and I'll be happy—and it costs what it costs.

"So, make it happen."

CHAPTER SIX

It was apparently impossible to move a destroyer squadron through the Solar System without attracting attention. Brad's previous fleet had been a "mere" four ships, two of them corvettes, and that had attracted some scrutiny.

Six destroyers attracted a lot more, and he ended up spending two hours clarifying his course and contract to traffic control for the Jupiter System. And then about the same talking to Fleet.

The sad reality of interplanetary travel, however, was that after spending five hours explaining where he was going with a fleet of warships, his little flotilla hadn't yet left the space around Jupiter. Moons, rings, and space stations still glittered on his displays, and there was a near-infinite amount of radio chatter scattering across any wavelength and angle one cared to look at.

"We just got tagged with a tightbeam, Commodore," Xan Wong, his communications officer, told him. "They hit us, interrogated us to confirm our ID, then pulsed a compressed data packet. Entire communication took under three seconds. I could *probably* trace it…but I don't think anyone else could.

"Oh, I think we know who that was from," Brad told the Chinese woman. "Check the package for the Agency tags I gave you."

In the aftermath of their most recent clash with the Cadre, he'd used his Agency credentials to order a Commonwealth Fleet cruiser group to stand down. He'd lost a degree of secrecy doing so, but at least now his bridge crew knew about his other allegiances.

It made his life a lot easier in some ways.

"Bingo," Wong replied. "I don't have the decryption key, but it's definitely Agency. I think your other employers have something to say."

Brad snorted.

"They always do," he admitted. "I'm surprised I've gone so long without hearing from them."

Though, to be fair, he didn't usually get radio messages from the Agency. Usually, his missions turned up in the form of Agent Kate Falcone unexpectedly showing up aboard his ship.

"I'll go over it in my office," he told Wong. "Michelle has the con. Let me know if anyone *else* wants a two-hour briefing on just where I'm taking a hundred-thousand-odd tons of warships."

"Will do, boss."

———

Brad settled down into his office and checked the data package. There were three indicators in the metadata that he'd directed his com officer to look at…and seven more that told him which decryption key to use.

It took a good minute for the key to turn the packet into something useful. The video message started automatically, but all it showed was the rotating crossed sword and scroll of the Commonwealth Intelligence Agency.

"Agent, the authentication for this message is Whiskey Postal Auburn Seven Nine Five. Secondary confirm is 'Democracy dies in darkness.'

"Please validate before continuing the message."

The code went into a separate module that never touched his wrist-comp, let alone the destroyer's computer system. It popped up the confirmation message, and Brad resumed the message.

No one without that module would have been able to validate that set of codes—but their purpose was more that no one without the counterpart to his module would have been able to send them. It confirmed that the sender had the authority to issue him orders.

"You are headed to Venus," the recorded voice—a man, Brad thought—continued. "The situation there is graver than the local government may have told you. They are potentially facing a large-scale armed rebellion, but what there is of the planetary government has dismissed the evidence and rumors as posturing.

"Legitimately so, we would suspect in other times, but in the current environment, we have to wonder. There is no reason for Fleet to have refused to intervene, and yet that is exactly what they've done.

"Other Agents will investigate the Fleet connection, but we want you to look into the piracy issue the New Venetian Council has hired you for. While doing so, we want you to keep your eyes open for Cadre connections."

That was roughly what Brad had been expecting. Posturing about rebellion from fringe groups was as old as the internet if not the printing press, but it rarely came to anything. If the Cadre was funneling supplies and arms to those fringe groups, however, the concern became much more severe.

"Unlike Fleet, we have not refused to become involved," the speaker continued. "We had an Agent on the scene attempting to infiltrate the organizations, code name Mulroney. They went dark three days ago and we haven't heard anything since.

"Agent Mulroney may attempt to make contact once you're in position, as you'll be closer than any other Agency operative and possess a force capable of launching a rescue expedition or, well, even something as straightforward as orbital bombardment of rebel bases.

"Everything we've learned from Mulroney and other sources is attached to this message. Your orders are to discover everything you can about the threat to Venus and the Commonwealth and to see if you can learn what happened to Agent Mulroney.

"Extraction of Mulroney is preferable, but the retrieval of their data is an absolute priority. We are operating blind in our own backyard, Agent, and this is unacceptable. More resources will be deployed independently, and they may also contact you for fire support.

"If we are lucky, we can neutralize this before it turns into a conflagration that will see too many innocents killed. Find Agent Mulroney, Agent. Stop the pirates. Protect the people of Venus.

"You know your duty."

The message ended and Brad sighed. There was nothing in the orders from the Agency he wouldn't have done on his own, but he couldn't help feeling that an Agent going missing should be a bigger deal.

What would they do if he disappeared one day? Send in someone to quietly look for him, to make sure nothing made it to the news?

It wasn't a reassuring thought. Fortunately for this "Agent Mulroney," however, the Agency was sending him. He wasn't egotistical enough to think that no one else could do what they were asking him to.

But he was certain that very few people could do it better than his crews.

———

Something in how Brad was walking when he returned to the bridge told his wife what was going on. She took one look at him and sighed.

"Lewin." She gestured *Oath of Vengeance*'s new tactical officer, Narendra Lewin, over. The petite blonde officer didn't *look* Pakistani, though Brad's understanding was that she was only two generations out of that country on one side of her family.

"You have the watch," Michelle ordered the other woman. "From the skipper's look, I'd say I need to be briefed on that data packet."

"Not a bad assumption," Brad admitted. "My office, XO?"

"Sure."

He'd barely left the room before she shuffled him back into it and closed the door. With a concerned gaze on her face, Michelle sat on his desk and studied him.

"I take it the Agency has some wrinkles to throw into our vacation on sunny Venus."

"Just a few," he agreed. "They think the pirates are tied up in a movement that's been talking rebellion on the planet lately—and potentially being supplied by the Cadre."

His wife sighed.

"That would fit their MO—and this whole 'Independence Militia' they're using as a front."

"Agreed. The Agency had an operative on the ground, but they've gone missing. We're tasked to find them and to fulfill our contract by dealing with the pirates."

"Because anything else would be easy," Michelle replied.

"The Governing Council called for the best. The Agency, it seems, agrees with that assessment," Brad told her. "We'll have our work cut out for us, *especially* if there are Cadre-funded groups on the planet. The last thing I want is a mono-blade fight with Cadre commandos in a tunnel."

"When do we get what we want?" she asked.

"Sometimes," he said. "For example, you *did* marry me. I call that getting what I want *and* amazing luck."

She snorted and kissed him.

"That's going to be a mess, though," she admitted. "Searching for a missing person on a strange planet without telling anyone just what we're doing? While running a customs blockade, cargo escorts, and potentially a small war?"

"Our people can do it," Brad told her, his own confidence rising as he said it. "We have some of the best damn troops and crews in the system. If anyone can do this, we can.

"We've fought the Cadre everywhere from Mars on out. I guess it's time to fight the Cadre closer to the sun."

"We can keep that optimistic outlook," she agreed. "Or, of course, we could actually *realistically* assess our chances."

"We really do have some of the best," he said, his tone more serious. "I don't actually expect us to get ambushed on the way to Venus, or even to face opposition at Venus that can seriously threaten the ships.

"It's going to be the boarding teams and landing troops that are going to be at risk. We're going to be meeting these pirates and smugglers on their own ground, and they're going to be waiting for us."

He shook his head.

"I'd love to assume we'll just scare them off, but you're right: realistic is good. Our people are retraining on boarding ops and customs as we speak. We won't be ready for *everything*, you never are, but we'll be ready for a lot of problems."

"And this missing Agent?" Michelle asked.

"That, I think, will be our problem," he concluded. "We let the rest of the company get on with going through the contract, and then you and I start quietly poking around and asking questions."

"Fair enough," she allowed. "May I make a suggestion, oh great and wise husband?"

In the absence of safe things to throw, he stuck his tongue out at her.

"You always do and you're almost always right," he said. "What is it?"

"Let's bring Saburo in. There's nobody on this ship with more of a weasel brain."

"See, I told you you were brilliant," he replied. "That was *exactly* what I was thinking for our next step."

CHAPTER SEVEN

Brad Madrid was a child of merchant shippers and the asteroid belt. His life experience was almost entirely the corridors of spaceships and space stations, broken occasionally by tunnels drilled into asteroids by miners. The domes of Ceres had been the highlight of his childhood and teen years, even if he now knew them to be a poor second-rate version of Mars or Ganymede's domes.

Venus, though, was entirely outside his experience. The shuttle carrying him down from *Oath of Vengeance* cut through clouds of yellow like he'd never seen before, but it was the aerostat cities themselves that caught his eye.

New Venice was a disk almost a dozen kilometers across. An immense lightweight crystalline dome rose above the disk, containing the air that balanced the pressure of the atmosphere outside. For all of its size, Brad's experienced eye could tell that New Venice was extremely lightly built.

It was, quite literally, lighter than the air beneath it. The city hung suspended in the atmosphere of a planet politely described as a steaming mess—and impolitely as a literal hell. Careful design balanced the weight of the city against the air around it, holding the city well above the levels of the atmosphere with crushing pressure.

Venus's air was still toxic up there, but technology could handle that. The heaviest part of the floating city was probably the massive air refineries loosely attached to the west side of the city—and Brad's practiced eye picked out the gravity generators that offset that mass and allowed massive balloons to hold the refineries aloft.

"That's damned impressive," he murmured.

"New Venice is the biggest, but what's truly impressive is that there's over four *hundred* of these cities," Saburo told him. "I did some research. This isn't our backwater colonies at the ass end of beyond, boss.

"This is where people set up their fancy luxury condo cities to get away from Earth. The miners and regular people came later. That's why the government is such a mess."

"So, it's not so much city-states as overgrown condo boards," Brad suggested. There were a *lot* of condominium-style organizations aboard space stations, and he'd rarely had good experiences with them.

"Probably. With the metaphorical backstabbing possibly gone literal," his friend said. "Can I argue the point around guns again?"

"We don't break local law," Brad told the Colonel. "They ban guns, we don't carry guns. They don't even mention mono-blades, we carry mono-blades."

The cylinder hanging at his belt held roughly one hundred and twenty centimeters of coiled monofilament wire. The wire had been manufactured by nanites under the control of specialized smiths using neural interfaces and had a carefully designed lattice of crystals that would straighten when charged with electrical energy.

The resulting blade repelled other blades and could cut almost anything but could also retract into a fifteen-centimeter cylinder.

Saburo snorted.

"And how many concealed weapons are *you* carrying, boss?"

Brad counted in his head.

"Five," he admitted. "I won't ask how many you've got. You *taught* me that habit, after all."

The landing pad was next to an honest-to-goodness park, easily a hundred meters on a side and filled with trees. Carefully positioned blast shields protected the greenery, but the exit also led directly into the park.

An older man with dark blue eyeshadow and a shaved head was waiting for them. Two bodyguards, both attractive young women in low-profile body armor, hung back slightly watching him.

They, of course, had guns. The man with the eyeshadow didn't, but he did have a disarming smile and extended grip.

"Commodore Madrid, welcome to New Venice," he said brightly. "I'm Councilor James Fisk. I'll be your contact with the Governing Council here while this contract is ongoing.

"You're earlier than expected."

"It sounded like the sooner we were on the scene, well, the fewer people were going to be in danger," Brad admitted. "It's a pleasure, Councilor Fisk. Do you have an intelligence update for me? We've been watching the news and so forth while we flew over here, but I'm assuming you know more than is in the public eye."

"Unfortunately, yes," Fisk admitted. "We'll have a data update sent to your ships, but I have a few people you need to meet before we get too tied down with business."

Politics. Brad's favorite.

"Of course, Councilor," he allowed. "Perhaps you can give me the basics on the way?"

"I think we can do that," Fisk told him. "Lacy, Tracy, can you get Stacy to bring the car around?"

There was no way that list of names was an accident. Someone had…*interesting* hiring criteria.

"Yes, boss."

The second large car that Brad had seen that month rolled up to the curb a few moments later.

"Your Colonel is welcome, of course," Fisk told them. "The car is secured against most methods of spying; we should be safe to speak in private."

Brad nodded his acknowledgement and followed the Councilor

into the vehicle. With the two mercenaries, the politician, and the two bodyguards, it was a cramped but still surprisingly comfortable fit.

"The situation is shit," Fisk said bluntly as the doors closed. "The losses have accelerated since we hired you, and we're reasonably sure someone is rushing cargo off-world. My colleagues on the Governing Council don't believe the rumors and threats of rebellion we're hearing, but I have to wonder."

"Who would someone even rebel against here?" Brad asked. "My understanding was that most of the cities were independent."

"That would be…part of the problem," Fisk said slowly. "You have to understand, Commodore Madrid, that Venus's society is a very careful balancing act between the original colonists, who came here to get away from everything, and the later additions of mining and skydiving work.

"That industrial class and those industrial platforms continue to provide a large portion of the planet's wealth, but the residents don't like being reminded of it or dealing with it. They just want the money to keep flowing and the workers to know their place."

"That doesn't sound like a situation that's sustainable long-run," Saburo said calmly. "History says that balance will break."

"I agree," Fisk confirmed. "My colleagues on the Council have more…nuanced opinions. The status quo has worked for Venus for almost a century. New Venice was a playground for the wealthy when it was built, and it remains that on the backs of a working class that, while well compensated, compares themselves to the ultra-rich around them.

"Reform is a slow process—a *working* process, but there are always those in a situation like this who will not wait and will attempt to take what they are owed by the sword."

"I was not hired to put down a rebellion," Brad pointed out. "And frankly, I'm not sure you can pay me enough."

"Good. Because the Council may try and twist your contract to that," Fisk warned him. "This is New Venice, Commodore Madrid, and the word *Byzantine* doesn't do our politics justice. Trust no one."

"What about you?" Saburo asked dryly.

"Don't trust me, either," Fisk said with a chuckle. "I have my own agendas, Commodore. Fortunately for you, right now I just want you to do your job, get paid, and go home.

"I suspect that aligns quite well with your own objectives."

———

Brad might not have known his way around New Venice in the slightest, but his wrist-comp had happily downloaded a map of the city and was tracking his location. He knew they were roughly halfway to the New Venetian House of State when the vehicle suddenly pulled to a sharp halt.

"What is it, Stacy?" Fisk asked.

"Flash alert from the NVPD," the woman driving reported. "They got an alert of a planned attack on the Commodore. They're advising we change routes and rendezvous with an escort."

"I see I'm already making friends," Brad murmured. "I haven't even got to work yet."

"Give our people time; I'm sure you'll grow on them," Fisk replied. "All right, Stacy. Does the NVPD have a location on that escort?"

"We're to meet a dome cruiser at Sixty-third and Fiftieth," she told him. "They've given us a recommended route."

"We'll meet the car, but let's take an alternative route, if you'd be so kind," the Councilor ordered. "Not that I don't trust the NVPD—but I don't trust our com security."

"On it," the woman replied. "And could you *please* put on a vest, boss? This is already going off-script, and I'm *not* explaining you getting shot to your partner."

Fisk shook his head, but he pulled open a side panel of the car and extracted an armored vest. He looked over at Brad and Saburo measuringly.

"I've got spares, but I'm not sure they'll fit either of you," he admitted.

"Councilor, if I'd left my ship without wearing higher-quality body armor than that vest, Saburo would hurt me," Brad told Fisk. "And my wife would *help*."

There was nothing wrong with the ballistic vest that the Councilor was putting on; it was a quality piece of police-issue gear. The skintight bodysuit he wore under his uniform was somewhere around twenty-five times the price, custom-fitted, and rated for heavy rounds at a range of one hundred meters.

He wouldn't walk away from being shot with a sniper round even at that distance, but it wouldn't pierce the armor. The suit's main purpose was to shed the low-penetration shotgun rounds favored for fighting aboard ships, and it could do that reliably at point-blank range.

"I'm not a soldier, I guess," Fisk said.

"No, that's what you're paying us for," Brad agreed. "Saburo?"

"Pulling the map right now," his friend replied. "Linked into the shuttle's systems, I've located the dome cruiser. Cute piece of hardware, that."

"Oh?"

"Gravity wheels on the top; it moves around the dome above the city. Light armament and quick-rappel system. Nothing major, but effective for the environment."

"Thank you," Fisk said.

"Of course, I can see four ways to evade one and six to take it out in under ten seconds," Saburo continued. "And that's *without* breaking out heavy gear, because *nobody* wants to pop the dome on this place."

Fisk's bodyguards both winced in unison, and Brad finally noticed what they were doing. The sidearms they were carrying had been pulled out, and a series of parts were being extracted from panels inside the car. The light pistols had rapidly transformed into lightweight but effective-looking carbines.

"What are you thinking, Saburo?" Brad asked.

"There's only three routes between where we were and where the dome cruiser is supposed to meet us. The cops flagged one, but if I was planning this, I'd assume Fisk was paranoid enough to avoid that one —and send my goons to the other two."

Fisk and Brad shared a long look, and then the politician leaned forward.

"Stop the car, Stacy!" he barked. "I'm being played for a damn fool. *Stop the car!*"

The vehicle careened to a halt on the side of the road, just out of the traffic. Brad began to breathe a sigh of relief—only for it to be interrupted by the road they had been *about* to drive over erupting in a burst of plastic and metal as the embedded explosives went off.

"That was almost very bad," the Commodore said slowly. "I suggest we get out of the vehicle and wait for backup. I doubt this was a one-string operation."

CHAPTER EIGHT

Fɪsᴋ's three bodyguards were out of the vehicle in moments, external panels on the car folding out to provide some impromptu, presumably-bulletproof cover.

"I have contact with the NVPD," the shortest of the three—Lacy, Brad thought—reported. "The dome cruiser is redirecting towards us. Several ground and dome units are being pulled off-task and sent our way as well. They say to keep our heads down."

Brad dropped down next to the Councilor they were covering, making sure his own briefcase was with him. It was bulletproof in its own right and had other virtues as well.

"Easy enough," Fisk muttered, tucking himself into the shell of the barrier. "This was not in my daily briefing."

"We *would* tell you if we knew someone was going to assassinate you," the tallest bodyguard told him. "I think the NVPD only found out about this a few—"

The entire unfolded shelter of the car rang like a bell as a heavy bullet slammed into it. The round went clean through the barrier, missed Brad by about four centimeters, and then smashed into the ground.

"Sniper," Saburo said sardonically. "I don't suppose you're willing to reconsider the gun thing now, boss?"

"Oh, shut up," Brad snapped. His wrist-comp was running a triangulation program, but he could already tell that the shooter was well out of range of any of his concealed weapons. "That way," he noted to the bodyguards, pointing towards a nearby building. "Shooter is on the ro—"

That shot hit Brad in center mass. A perfect shot even through the barrier the bodyguards had assembled, it hit him in the chest and hammered him into the ground.

Between his own armor and the theoretically bulletproof barrier they'd folded out of Fisk's car, Brad was...alive. He didn't think he'd even broken anything, but he'd definitely had better days.

Gunfire echoed above his head, and he saw that all three bodyguards had taken his directions to heart. The sniper's second shot had let the women pick out the shooter, and they were returning fire with carefully aimed shots.

"That's not going to do much more than keep their head down," Brad half-gasped as Saburo knelt down next to him.

"That's enough," his subordinate told him. "The armor held?"

"So did my ribs. Just feel like I got kicked by a loose thruster. ETA on the cops?"

"Sixty seconds," Saburo responded. "Bets this is still a distraction?"

"Oh, at least a week of your salary," Brad croaked. "Help me up."

"*Shit*," Stacy suddenly swore. Even before the mercs could ask what was up, they heard the explosion and looked up—in time to watch the strange looking upside-down-car shape of the incoming dome cruiser detach from the roof.

Smoke was still spewing from the lower chassis where a bomb had taken out the gravity generators, and Brad swallowed hard. There was no way anyone in that vehicle was going to survive the two-hundred-meter drop.

"How many cops?" he asked softly.

"If they were loaded for tactical cover...seven," Saburo replied. "Fuck me."

"I suspect our assailants have something *much* less pleasant in mind," Brad told him. "Blades, Colonel. We're out of time."

———

There were enough people on the street to qualify as a crowd. They'd been scattering away from the moment the bodyguards had started unfolding the bulletproof barriers, but the falling dome cruiser sent part of the crowd recoiling back toward Fisk's car.

A large-enough part of the crowd to cover the approach of the next —and hopefully final—string to the assassination attempt's bow. The three figures didn't look remotely out of the ordinary in the crowd until one produced a gun and the others produced mono-blades.

All three of Fisk's bodyguards were down in moments as a spray of automatic gunfire walked across the interior of the barricade. Brad was pretty sure all three would *live*, but the attackers had clearly prioritized the women with guns.

From the perspective of the lead swordsman, that was a mistake. Saburo stepped inside the man's reach and uncoiled his mono-blade in a strike that slashed through the attacker. An elbow slammed the trooper back—but not fast enough to stop the blade nearly bisecting the intended assassin.

The second attacker moved around, balancing on her feet with enough skill to suggest that these were *very* good people. These weren't local rebels. These were either Cadre or pro assassins.

"You know, I'm always up for buying the names of the people who try to kill me," Brad suggested as conversationally as he could with the bruising on his chest. He was digging into his briefcase as he spoke, however, and wasn't expecting a positive response.

The response he got was *another* bullet. The sniper seemed to have stopped shooting, at least, but the hanger-back of the current group was a disturbingly good shot.

Not good enough to aim for the head, but even the armor he was wearing only did so much against gunfire at that range. Brad went down again, and this time he was certain he had at least one cracked rib.

The surviving bladeswoman was trying to close with Brad, but Saburo had her completely tied up. The gunner tried to shoot at Saburo, but the old battler twisted his opponent in between them. Several rounds slammed into the first attacker's back, and *her* armor wasn't as good as Brad's.

It was probably good enough to save her life, but she went down hard. Something in Saburo's free hand flashed as she collapsed, and Brad doubted she'd be getting back up until the merc decided she was getting up.

That left the gunman with a free shot at all of them, but Brad had finally managed to get into the lining of his briefcase. The black leather case fell away from his hand and the toy-sized crossbow snapped out its arms.

Toy-sized or not, the weapon was made from the same material used in his body armor and carried a small motor to wind it on activation. He had spare bolts, but he didn't expect to have time to reload.

He didn't need to. Saburo had trained him well and the range was short enough there was no drop. The monomolecular wire-edged bolt took the gunman in the throat in a spray of blood, and Brad lay back down.

"So, Saburo," he said slowly. "I'm just going to…lay here for a few minutes. Can you make sure our friends and our prisoner live?"

"I can do that," his subordinate replied. "I take it the gun rules don't apply to you?"

"This?" Brad waved the crossbow weakly. "This isn't a gun. No explosives; would plug any hole it pierced in the dome with its own shaft. Completely harmless."

The dead gunman was a mute counterargument that Saburo didn't even need to make.

CHAPTER NINE

"WELL, Commodore, it seems you make an impression on arrival."

Brad looked up from the emergency room bed on New Venice and snorted at Councilor Fisk.

"I really would prefer to arrive with a very different type of fanfare, if I can't arrive quietly."

"So would we all." Fisk pulled up a chair, trading a nod with Saburo. "Thank you, Commodore, Colonel. I may not have been the target, but I doubt they planned on leaving me alive, either."

"Your guards?" Brad asked.

"The Aces are still with me," Fisk said with a smile. "All three are in urgent care, but the prognoses are good. Like me, though…I don't think they'd have survived a successful attack."

"Our attackers were good," Saburo replied. "Cadre-good."

"Or professionals in general," Brad allowed. "Lots of hardware, lots of prep. I'm guessing there was a similar team on the other road?"

"The NVPD are looking now. You were only out for a couple of hours while they worked on your ribs," the Councilor assured him. "We're still sorting out the details. It was surprisingly low-resourced for how well it was put together."

"That's usually how it goes," Brad said grimly. "Resources let you be crude. Sophistication comes when you can't just walk over the enemy. How bad, Councilor?"

Fisk didn't even pretend he didn't understand.

"Nine police officers dead. My bodyguards wounded. Two civilians dead, crushed under the falling cruiser. Another dozen wounded from debris and stray fire."

"Damn." Brad shook his head. "And we were supposed to *stop* the violence."

"That was why they moved, at a guess," a new voice interjected. A tall and broad-shouldered man entered the room. His head, like Fisk's, was shaved clean. His eyeshadow, however, was dark green.

New Venetian styles were *not* what Brad was used to.

"There are people who want to see this endeavor fail. Some of them sit on the Council with us," the new speaker continued. "The best are activists in the working classes who don't want any violence at all but would prefer we made concessions to end this. The worst, well, are active opponents of New Venice and the Commonwealth.

"Is this going to delay your operations, Commodore?"

Brad glanced at the stranger, then at Fisk.

"Commodore Madrid, meet Governor Karl Ngu," Fisk said with a small, almost helpless hand gesture.

"Governor," Brad said. "My contract said that we were to commence operations immediately upon arrival. If I'm reading the clock on my wrist-comp correctly, the first customs inspections launched four hours ago. My crews don't need me to babysit them."

"I see. It seems you may be worth your princely price tag after all," Ngu said genially. "You saved one of my Councilors, Commodore, so I am indebted to you beyond the contract. Is there any assistance that we can provide you?"

Fisk's body language suggested that he and Ngu might not get along very well...but also that he didn't think the big man had ordered the attack. That was reassuring.

"There were a number of requests we forwarded the Council while we were on our way," Brad replied carefully. "I was told those would need to be debated by the Governing Council."

Ngu made a large, expansive throwaway gesture.

"I don't recall the exact list," he freely admitted. "What would you say your priorities are, Commodore?"

"I need to refuel my ships and set up a resupply depot for my shuttles, preferably on New Venice, though I'm not picky. While I want to keep at least some of my ships above New Venice, the destroyers will be more useful playing watchdog over the cargo routes than orbiting your capital."

"Fisk will make sure the crews of High Venice know your needs immediately," Ngu replied. "We'll get your ships fueled. I'll have to speak to some others about the depot, but I see no major obstacle. Anything else?"

Brad smiled grimly.

"I need access to the full, unredacted police reports on the missing aircraft, any pirate or wrecker attacks in the last three years, all meteorological reports for the same time period, and all of your missing-person reports."

The big Governor blinked.

"That seems…excessive, Commodore. Missing-person reports?"

He needed those to track down Agent Mulroney, though he was planning on getting multiple uses out of every piece of data he got his hands on.

"Just because someone wasn't officially on one of the missing transports doesn't mean they weren't aboard," Brad pointed out. "Those discrepancies, those people who are missing and we don't know why, can easily point us at clues to the operations in play."

"You were hired for customs duty, Commodore," Ngu said calmly.

"That's not what my contract says, Governor," Brad replied. "It calls for me to operate a customs blockade and to prevent any further attacks if at all possible. With that data, Governor, I believe that stopping the attacks may well *be* possible."

Ngu grunted, studying him with flat eyes.

"And yet you aren't competent enough to avoid getting shot on your first day here?" he asked. His tone was still genial, still brightly cheerful.

"Security inside the city is far from my responsibility," Brad replied, his voice carrying a forced equal level of cheer. "That falls on the NVPD, who I believe report to…you?"

The Governor chuckled.

"I'll pass your requests on to the Commissioner," he conceded. "You can talk to her. She'll understand your needs better than I, one presumes."

———

"Please, Commodore Madrid, we may have stitched the fractures back together, but you were just *shot*," the doctor told Brad as he carefully redressed in his armor and uniform. "There could be half a dozen different types of damage our first examination wouldn't reveal!"

"Then my ship's doctor will find them," Brad said firmly. "I appreciate your care, Doctor, but I have work to do. I have a job to do—and it doesn't normally involve being shot, I promise."

The ER doctor shook his head and glanced at Saburo.

"Is he always this bad?" he asked the ground trooper plaintively.

Saburo paused thoughtfully, then passed Brad his briefcase. The crossbow was back in its concealed compartment, the Commodore noted. Probably reloaded, too. Saburo was *very* thorough.

"Nah, he used to be worse," the mercenary finally responded to the doctor. "He's mellowed in his old age."

The doctor probably had thirty years of age on Brad and visibly paled at that idea.

"I'll be *fine*, Doctor," Brad assured him. "And past history suggests that keeping me in a hospital bed isn't healthy for anyone else in the clinic. Forward your scan results to *Oath of Vengeance* and I promise to check in with Dr. Terzić when I get back aboard.

"For now, however, the NVPD Commissioner has generously managed to find a time slot in her schedule today. I have no intention of missing that appointment."

Unmentioned was the marked police cruiser parked outside the hospital waiting for him—or the armed cop having a stare-off with Corporal Jimenez outside the room they were arguing in.

"And if something goes wrong along the way, Angelica Jimenez is a fully trained combat medic," Brad continued. "People have already been injured and killed in an attack on me, Doctor. I *won't* put your hospital at risk for longer than I have to."

That, it seemed, was enough. The ER doctor threw his hands up and gestured for Brad to leave.

"Very well, Commodore. I'll be in touch with Dr. Terzić shortly. You're an expensive investment for New Venice; I'd prefer to make sure you live!"

Brad chuckled.

"If you think I'm expensive for New Venice, you should consider that I'm Dr. Terzić's *employer*. He'll make sure I don't die, I promise."

And if the worst came to pass, well, Brad now had reason to be comfortable with the competence and integrity of New Venice's hospital staff. That was nothing to sneer at.

Though he'd prefer to not have been *shot* to get that reason.

———

There was no question which side of the stare-off Brad was coming down on, so his emergence got them to the NVPD headquarters in surprisingly brisk time.

To his surprise, Commissioner Emeka Lagos was waiting for him at the front entrance. The tone of the email notifying him she had an appointment available had prepared him for less-courteous treatment.

Lagos was a tall black woman, heavily muscled, with a shoulder-length dark braid and bright pink eye shadow. Meeting him might have been encouraging, but her shoulders were set and her face was grim.

"Commodore Madrid. You'll understand if I don't say this is a pleasure," she said crisply.

"Commissioner Lagos, my condolences on the loss of your officers," Brad replied quietly. "I didn't have the chance to meet them, but no one needed to get caught in that ambush. I'm sorry it came to that."

"Wasn't you," she said flatly, but her tone had softened a little. "Condolences don't mean much to their families. We'll do what we can."

She gestured for him to walk with her, and he obediently fell into step beside her. His own gesture sent Saburo and Jimenez to the waiting area. If he wasn't safe there, he had far larger problems than a few cracked ribs coming.

"I would hope there is some pension for the families," Brad murmured as they walked. "I would assume so, in fact."

"There is," Lagos confirmed. "And despite my best efforts, it sucks. I can sell the Governing Council on a *lot* of things when it comes to living officers to maintain their precious order, but the purse strings get real tight when they aren't looking at immediate return."

The mercenary's sympathy for the rebellion was minimal—they *had* tried to kill him—but he was beginning to understand where they were coming from.

"If I wanted to make sure some money made it to the families of those officers, would you be able to assist me?" he asked.

Lagos stopped in the middle of the hallway and turned to study him.

"You're serious."

"Those officers died in an attempt on my life," Brad replied. "From what you are saying, their families may be in trouble from that— trouble no family needs on top of the loss of a loved one. I would ease that burden, if I can."

"I see." Lagos continued to study him, then nodded. "I'll provide your staff the names of the officers involved and a reliable lawyer to set up trusts for their family. I would recommend against doing anything through more official channels, Commodore. A quiet trust is better for everyone, especially the families."

"I can do that," Brad said.

Lagos shook her head in disbelief, then took off down the corridor to her office. The door automatically unlocked at her approach, and she flung it open without breaking her stride. She gestured Brad to a seat and dropped behind her desk.

"If you think paying out the families is going to make me more inclined to approve your frankly ridiculous requests, however, you're wrong," she told him bluntly. "Data related to the pirates and the missing transport is already packaged up; we'll have it to your ship by nightfall. Meteorological records are publicly accessible; I'm sure you can manage them yourself.

"Historical cases and missing-person reports? Those are confidential information, Commodore. I could barely justify releasing redacted versions, let alone the unredacted ones you've requested."

Brad nodded slowly, leaning back in the chair to study the woman. It was fascinating, really. She wasn't using particularly aggressive body language or any of the usual tricks to project power, just a firm tone and a decisive attitude.

She was good at her job.

"Whose side do you think I'm on, Commissioner?" he asked.

"Yours, Commodore. Potentially your bank account's. Not New Venice's."

"You haven't looked at my record, have you?" Brad said with a chuckle. "About the only thing I've consistently been over the years is on the opposite side from the Cadre. The opposite side from the pirates.

"This isn't my planet. This isn't my city. These aren't my people—but I'm being paid to help and protect them, which makes that my job. And I do my job, Commissioner, to the highest and best standard.

"*Especially* when innocent lives are at stake."

She even seemed to believe him, which was nice. There were always people who'd doubt mercenaries on principle.

"I'm not asking you for data I don't need, Commissioner," he told her. "I can probably make do with redacted reports, but *any* piece of data might be critical to finding our answers. The sooner I find those answers, the sooner I find the assholes killing people."

Lagos sighed.

"You're asking a lot, Commodore. And I don't see the relevance, to be honest."

"I need the past to judge the present. I have some information on the Wreckers, but I know I don't have it all. These people aren't following the same paths, but I'm betting they know a lot of the same tricks.

"And I need to know who is missing because that will tell me two things: who was on those ships who wasn't supposed to be, and our potential list of people who've disappeared to join a revolution."

The Commissioner looked down at her hands.

"You're not the first person to use that argument on me, Commodore," she said very quietly. "And I'm suddenly wondering just what type of mercenary you are."

"The type that is on your side right now," Brad replied. It seemed Agent Mulroney had made contact with the Commissioner as well. That was…interesting in and of itself.

"All right. You'll get your data," she promised. "And if I find even one scrap of evidence that it leaked, you will get *zero* support from the New Venice Police for your damn contract; am I clear?"

"As vacuum, Commissioner. Thank you."

CHAPTER TEN

"I'VE HAD BETTER WEEKS," Saburo said dryly as he dropped into the extra chair in Brad's office. Michelle was already sitting in front of the desk, and Brad was leaning on his hands as he studied the reports on the screen.

Twelve days. Twelve days of absolute quiet and of Brad wondering if he'd been misinformed about the severity of the threat to Venus.

It was also twelve days of getting yelled at by angry transport pilots, starship captains, and merchant brokers. While the Commonwealth might regard Governor Ngu as having the full authority of every other planetary Governor, including the right to impose customs searches, the people of Venus were less convinced.

"Are they yelling less yet?" Brad asked.

"If we'd actually found something, some of them might be quieter," Saburo admitted. "As it is, they're yelling *more*, if anything."

"Wonderful."

Michelle shook her head as she looked at her wrist-comp.

"Report in from *Grant*," she told the two men. "Captain Laurent finished her patrol. All cargos delivered successfully, no interruptions. She's returning to High Venice for refuelling."

Except for the three Brad had kept aboard *Oath of Vengeance*, newly retrofitted for Venus's atmosphere by Mike Randall, all of their shuttle-craft were either based in the aerostat cities themselves or aboard High Venice.

High Venice was in a not-quite-geostationary orbit that kept it above the not-quite-stationary New Venice at all times, allowing it to act as the main channel to the rest of the system. A channel that Brad's people now thoroughly controlled.

Nothing was making it in or out of High Venice or New Venice without their inspection. Some cargos were almost certainly sneaking out through direct flights from the aerostat cities themselves, but those were going to be expensive.

"No new attacks. No evidence that they're getting cargos off-world." Brad shook his head. "Well, we seem to be achieving the main goal of our contract just by sitting here. To my surprise, that's actually the Governing Council's opinion of the matter."

"We're burning their money just sitting here," Michelle said. "But given the losses they were taking and the boost to their authority just having us up here gives them…yeah, I can see why they think it's worth it."

"I didn't come here to play guard dog," Brad told his people. "We came here to *fix* a problem, not band-aid it. If we were only in this for the money, well, I wouldn't have six destroyers."

"Well, we have a pattern now," his wife replied. "We've got two destroyers at High Venice, four pulling low-orbit sweeps to guard the main cargo routes. Everlit, when *Horatio* pulled those transports out of a storm two days ago, everyone stopped complaining about *that* part."

"What about our dig into the data Lagos provided?" Brad asked.

"I've had our people rip it apart and put it back together six different ways," Michelle told him. "I've got a list of about fifteen people who were *probably* aboard transports they weren't supposed to and are likely dead—and about twice that who are likely rebel recruits."

"I can't even blame the rebels," Saburo pointed out. "This whole planet is a powder keg, and the Council and various city leaderships are only doing so much."

"Something is going to explode," Brad agreed. "And they're trying to fix that, and power to them. But the problem right now is the pirates, and I wish we knew more. Any sign of Agent Mulroney in that data?"

"It would help if the Agency had given us more than a code name," Michelle complained. "I've got a few potentials flagged, but…" She shook her head.

"What?" Brad asked.

"One of the reasons I've flagged them as potentials is that they were all visitors that went down to visit mining operations—and haven't come back."

———

From *Oath of Vengeance*'s bridge, Brad had eyes on over half of Venus's upper atmosphere at any given moment now. Six ships moving around the planet and a link into the satellite network gave him a lot of information.

None of it was giving him any *answers*, but he definitely had a lot of *information*.

"Not even an unscheduled flight," Lewin complained as she swept over the sensor data again. "Seriously, what kind of planet goes twelve days without someone taking an unscheduled aircraft between cities?"

"The kind that's about two steps short of a police state for half of its citizens," Brad said. "And I get the impression it used to be worse."

"Such wonderful people we're working for," Michelle snarked. "I guess it is getting better."

"Humans aren't perfect. Getting better is the best we can hope for." Brad shrugged. "Plus, well, Venus isn't our fight. We don't know enough about what's going on here to get involved beyond dealing with the actual criminals on either side."

"So long as we stick to the criminals," his wife muttered.

"Right now, I'm sticking to active pirates and the Cadre," he said. "I'm not being paid to get involved in this brewing revolt, and I'm not comfortable enough with the sides for getting me involved to be affordable for anyone."

"Commodore, can I borrow you?" Xan Wong suddenly asked from across the bridge. "I've got an odd blip I want to run by you."

Brad gave his wife a smile and crossed over to the coms officer.

"What is it, Wong?"

"We just got a compressed-pulse transmission. It went out omnidirectional, so it's really weak, and I haven't pulled much useful from it, but what does this fragment look like to you?"

She tapped her finger at a segment on the screen, a partially scrambled list of numbers and letters.

"Code," Brad replied. "Give me a second."

He pulled up his wrist-comp and ran the scanner over the code. His system hummed for half a second and then popped up a partial translation. The translation was garbage, but it told him what he needed to know.

"Agency code," he concluded. "I can't read it; we don't have enough here. How many of the ships and satellites would have received this?"

"Everything on this side of Venus. Probably four of our ships, at least a dozen satellites."

"Pull it all," Brad ordered. "Every scrap, every fragment—triangulate the source and get me as much of the transmission as you can."

"That's somehow less than I was expecting," Michelle said a few minutes later as they looked over the datastream.

"It's still incomplete," Wong warned them. "But yeah, it's not very long. Pulse was under two seconds and was interrupted."

"Interrupted?" Brad asked.

"Hard to say, but I'd guess jammed at the tail end," the coms officer told him. "Can you decrypt what we've got?"

He was already transferring the stream to his wrist-comp and running it through the Agency program. It was a pure text message.

ALERT. ALERT. EMERGENCY ALERT. REQUEST FOR IMMEDIATE RESCUE. DETAIL TO FOL—

"It's an emergency alert, but all we got was the wrapper," Brad told his people quietly. "Details would have told us who was sending it and any other information they tried to attach, but it got interrupted as you said."

He looked at the message. There was no way it was anyone except Agent Mulroney—but why hadn't the Agent made contact earlier?

"Can you triangulate it?" he asked.

"We've got scraps from three of our ships and eight satellites," Wong confirmed. "I can tell you the origin to within twenty meters, even in Venus's atmosphere."

"Do it."

Wong was already working, and Brad brought up a map of the planet as a series of lines rippled across it.

"Here." A latitude and longitude marker intersected on the screen Brad was watching. An altitude measure was added a moment later.

"Transmission was from the Sagan Plateau," Wong confirmed. "Not quite dead center. Roughly eighteen hundred meters above the surface."

"Not much down there," Lewin noted. "That's above crush depth for the aircraft they send down, but not by much. Chunks of the plateau can only be reached by specialty planes from what I'm pulling up."

"What's there?" Brad asked.

"Nothing anymore," his tactical officer replied. "Records say there was a mining facility built there twenty years ago, but maintenance costs exceeded any practical value of the extraction about three years ago.

"There's something in here about a recurring plan to use the tunnels to set up a logistics base for the deep-dive ships, but nothing seems to have come from it."

"And now I'm guessing we know why," Brad said grimly. "Pre-dug tunnels, an existing landing site. For the same reason they'd want to repurpose for the deep-dive ships, you could easily retrofit it into a base for higher-altitude boarding craft."

He shook his head, studying the map.

"Have Saburo meet me in the shuttle bay with first squad," he ordered. "We'll need to make a scouting pass before we drop a platoon or six on the place. If nothing else, only three of our shuttles can make it that deep."

His wife and XO was silent for now, but from her look, he knew he wasn't getting off the ship without a *discussion*.

———

Michelle caught up to him in the corridor halfway between the bridge and the shuttle bay. Brad stopped as he heard her behind him and turned to look at her with a smile.

"Yes, love?" he said. "You're going to ask why *I* have to go."

"Yes," she agreed. "Not just as your wife who'd rather you didn't get shot, stabbed, burnt, or lose any more limbs, too."

He unconsciously flexed his right hand. The entire limb from just about the elbow had been regrown after it had been chopped off in one of his duels with the Terror, the previous leader of the Cadre. Even now, he didn't have full sensation back in that bit of limb.

Full *control*, yes, and he was an even deadlier duelist than he'd been then, but not sensation. Everything from his right forearm was slightly muted.

"As your executive officer, I also need to remind you that you are responsible for this contract and over six hundred lives," Michelle continued. "If something goes wrong and you and Saburo are both taken out, who takes command?"

Brad snorted.

"You inherit my shares, Saburo's father inherits his. You become majority shareholder and company commander, and Hiroshi becomes your silent partner. You were there when we set that up."

Michelle glared at him.

"And do you think that for one damn instant I can hold this collection of overcompetent mercenaries and ex-Fleet together without you?"

"Yes," Brad told her simply. "Because you're already doing half of that work as my executive officer."

He held up a hand.

"But you're right, for all that. It *is* irresponsible of me to risk myself on this scouting mission. On the other hand, we have no choice. I'm the only one with the Agency recognition codes and countersigns, and they're locked to my wrist-comp."

He'd tried, once, to copy the Agency sequences to Michelle's machine. His Agency control had ended up giving him a new wrist-comp and a *very* pointed lecture about information security.

"We're responding to Agent Mulroney's assistance request, which means we need some way to be sure the Agent knows we're legit. That means it has to be me. No one else can do it."

He shook his head.

"You're *right*," he repeated. "But those concerns are secondary to completing the mission."

"We need to have a long chat with the Agency about that," his wife said after several long seconds of thought. "They don't want you to turn up dead either."

Brad reached for her and she folded herself into his arms.

"I don't like it," she murmured into his ear. "But, dammit, you're not wrong. Be careful."

"I'm always careful," he told her.

"I know. That's what terrifies me."

CHAPTER ELEVEN

BRAD HAD RIDDEN shuttles into the atmosphere of Mars and into the upper reaches of Jupiter and Saturn. He should have expected the trip down to Venus to be closer to the latter, but the size of the planet had left him expecting something closer to the former.

After the second time he was nearly thrown from his seat in the cockpit, he tightened his seat belt and settled in grimly. Pale yellow air surrounded them, and thicker clouds of a sick yellow color swept over the spacecraft as it dropped.

"We're going to be coming back here, aren't we?" his pilot asked, almost conversationally. Bakarne Pitts was a young Spanish woman and also the best pilot *Oath of Vengeance* had. Like most of Brad's crew, she traced her ancestry to specific points on Earth—and had never actually set foot on the homeworld.

"This is a scouting expedition," Brad confirmed. "We need to learn what's down here. Then, once we know what we're getting into, we're coming back with at least the full platoon from *Oath*."

"Oh, good." She sighed. "I was hoping to never have to fly this mess again."

As she spoke, the entire twenty-meter-long spacecraft *bucked* underneath them as a cloud came up from below and almost physically picked up the shuttle.

"We're basically swimming now," Pitts continued conversationally. "What did the Chief even *do* to make this work?"

"Duplicated some plans from the locals, as I understand," Brad told her. "Are we going to be okay?"

"I'm not sure I trust my altimeter and we're heading for a location that's barely a hundred meters above what Chief Randall said was our minimum distance from the surface," she pointed out. "So, I *think* we're going to be okay, but this is going to *suck*."

"Is our radar still holding up?" Saburo asked from behind them.

"Barely," Pitts replied. "I'm focusing on keeping us in the air, but we should be close enough for at least distant sweeps."

"I'll run it," Brad told his subordinate. "You make sure the squad is ready if something goes wrong."

"Feeling paranoid?"

"*Always.*"

"There's only so much we can do," Saburo admitted. "We upgraded our gear at New Venice, but our suits won't last ten minutes out there. If something goes wrong, I hope you can deal with it with the shuttle's guns."

Pitts snorted.

"Didn't anyone tell you, Colonel?" she asked. "We took the guns off to free up the mass for the atmospheric seal."

Brad didn't even need to see his Colonel to realize that no, no one had told Saburo that. *He'd* left that to Randall and the pilots. Apparently, they'd thought he would do it.

"No guns?" Saburo asked slowly.

"No guns," Brad confirmed as he brought up the radar array. "Sorry, I think everyone thought someone else was telling you."

"So, *this* is what reply-all is for," the Colonel said grimly. "All right. Let's try not to die."

"Easy for *you* to say," Pitts muttered, twisting the shuttle through another buffeting storm. "I don't know how much closer I can get, Commodore."

"Let's see what the radar gets us," Brad replied. Pulses swept out from the emitters, but it was a far slower process than he was used to. "All right. I've got a dome, looks like local stone. That's probably the cover for the old mine and our likely target.

"I've also got...towers?" he looked at the readings in concern. "Tubes connecting them to the dome, they're self-contained, but what would they need to mount twenty meters above the base?"

"Threat warning!" Pitts suddenly half-screamed as half a dozen lights lit off on their panel. "I've got missiles inbound!"

"Anti-radiation, kill the radar," Saburo snapped.

Brad was already on it. The towers were SAM sites, and they were automated to shoot at anyone who tagged them with radar.

"They're designed for this muck. We're not," Pitts said grimly as she brought the engines to full. Fire encased the shuttle as she maneuvered. "I can't dodge them."

"Put us on the ground," Brad ordered. "If we can't dodge, we've got to hide!"

She made it most of the way down. They were roughly ten meters above the ground when the missile slammed home into their engine assembly. The trip through Venus's atmosphere had apparently wrecked the detonator and the warhead didn't go off...but it was enough.

They were still going almost thirty kilometers an hour when they hammered into the top of the plateau.

———

It took Brad at least a full minute to regain something resembling composure and balance after the impact. Finally, he slowly detached the safety belt and rose to his feet. It was immediately obvious, first, that the shuttle was at an angle and, second, that the shuttle's gravity plates were off-line.

He almost fell forward into the cockpit window before regaining his balance.

"Pitts, you okay?"

"Yeah," the pilot replied, her voice muffled. He looked over to see that she'd closed her helmet and had streams of data flickering over the inside of it. "Cockpit screens are gone, but the computer's still online. I'm checking our status."

"Keep at it," he ordered. "I'll check on the troops."

He carefully balanced his way up the chairs to the cargo compartment. Saburo was about halfway along the spacecraft, where he'd managed to catch himself on some of the seating. Brad couldn't see the Colonel's expression, but he'd known Saburo a long time.

"Seatbelts, Colonel?" he asked carefully.

"You are *not* as funny as you think you are," his subordinate snapped.

"Is everyone okay?" Brad replied, ignoring the complaint.

"Yeah. Stiller's unconscious, but he'll be awake in a minute or two. Assuming we've *got* a minute or two. Boss?"

"Air in the shuttle is clean, so I don't think we broke the atmosphere seal," he told Saburo. "More than that, well…"

"That's what I'm pulling from the computers," Pitts announced as she climbed up into the cargo compartment.

Two of the troopers were helping Stiller upright from where he'd hit his head on the side of the spacecraft. Brad took a moment to check the man's vitals himself, but Saburo had summed it up: he'd been briefly knocked out, but he looked like he'd be fine.

Well, minor concussion, but that barely ranked on their problems right now.

"Good news," Pitts told him. "We didn't break the atmosphere seal, and if I were them, I'd assume we were dead."

"And the bad news is that they have good reason to think so?" Brad asked.

"Bingo," the pilot replied. "Our engines are wrecked; this shuttle will never fly again. Atmospheric seal is holding, but it's only rated for about an hour at this depth, and we've been down here for fifteen minutes already."

"So, we have forty-five minutes to come up with a miracle," Saburo concluded. "Commodore?"

"Well, *my* bad news is that I disagree with your assessment of how long our suits will last out there," Brad said dryly as he linked his wrist-comp into the shuttle's systems to locate where they'd "landed". "I make it about six minutes. Maybe five."

"I said they wouldn't last ten minutes, not that they *would* last ten minutes," his subordinate replied. "Any miracles on your mind, boss?"

"I don't know about miracles, but I can point out some luck," Brad replied with a chuckle as he used his wrist-comp to project a map of the Sagan Plateau on the shuttle wall.

"This is the plateau and I'm overlaying what we detected on the way in," he continued. The dome was added as a green wireframe. Six towers, each twenty meters high, went in around it, as did the half-buried surface tubes connecting them to the dome.

Several other items appeared, green marks on the map of the plateau.

"What are those?" Saburo asked.

"Tunnel caps," Brad replied. "At one point, they'd have been secondary docks for mining ships, quick connections to deploy drills or miners before getting back under cover. Some might have always just been blockers where they broke the surface when mining.

"All of them would have personnel accesses, for safety's sake, and they're all interconnected. I'm not sure I'd trust them to have survived —but the *dome* wouldn't be safe if any of those tunnels were breached."

One last icon appeared on the plateau map.

"And we're here," Brad concluded. "The closest tunnel entrance is twenty-two meters away. We're basically swimming in the air out there, but I think we can move twenty-two meters in under five minutes."

"Cross twenty-two meters, override a five-to-twenty-year-old airlock—while hoping the damn thing still works at *all* and hasn't had its security updated—then get everyone in. In under five minutes." Saburo shook his head as he spoke.

"You have a high opinion of us, boss."

"Yes," Brad confirmed. "I also know we don't have a damn choice. Either we get into those tunnels and take that base, or we all die down here. I know which one *I'm* choosing.

"How about you, Colonel?"

CHAPTER TWELVE

The AIRLOCK DOOR slid open and the atmosphere of Venus rushed in. Until that moment, Brad has not truly understood what "air pressure equivalent to underwater" had meant.

What was filling the airlock around him was technically a gas. Very technically. From the perspective of the man trying to walk into it, however, it was functionally a liquid. He could have swum upward in it if he wanted but instead let the planet's gravity hold him down.

He was heavier on Venus than he was on most planets, and the tons upon tons of gas pressing down on him didn't help. Warning lights started lighting up in his helmet, and he inspected each of them grimly.

Warning one: pressure was too high. His combat vac-suit was designed, as the name suggested, for vacuum, but it had optional modules and upgrades to also allow it to function in high-pressure environments. It could survive the current environment for about thirty minutes.

Warning two: temperature was too high. His suit was designed for absolute zero, but it ran primarily off insulation, so controlling heat was a key part of the design. It could protect him in this heat—for about thirty minutes.

Warning three: the suit was literally being eaten by the atmosphere around it. A significant portion of Venus's atmosphere was sulfuric acid, and the cloud covering the Sagan Plateau right now was even more acidic than usual.

His suit could survive the acid for an unknown period of time, almost certainly under ten minutes, and the damage to the suit would undermine the temperature and pressure protections. The temperature and pressure would make his body irretrievable, but it was the acid that was going to kill him.

For some reason, he hadn't thought it necessary to get combat vac-suits that could survive immersion into a condensed and superheated vat of sulfuric acid.

"Come on, Commodore," Pitts told him. "I'm not liking these suit warnings and we're the last ones out."

The faceless shape of the pilot's helmet turned back toward the shuttle as they slowly pushed out against the miasma holding them.

"Damn. Poor girl didn't deserve this. Without serious protection, she won't last two weeks. There'll be nothing left of her."

"She did her job, Pitts," Brad replied. He managed to keep any audible strain from his motion across the plateau out of his voice. Given how much effort even the tiniest motion was demanding, that was hard.

"She got us down safely. Now we have to get ourselves back up. And the way home is thataway." He gestured toward the waypoint on his helmet while taking another laborious step.

"Twenty-two meters. We can make it."

The pilot fell in behind them as they struggled forward. Brad, at least, did most of his combat training in a full-gravity environment, but *nobody* could afford to maintain a full gee of artificial gravity all the time.

Most stations, colonies, and starships set their gravity at thirty percent of Earth's and called it a day. Pitts, it seemed, was rarely out of those environments. She was lagging and they were running out of time.

"Come on," he told her, opening a panel on the side of his suit. The rope inside *hissed* when exposed to the "air," acid eating into its polymers almost instantly. "The rope won't hold long, but it'll help me pull you."

She didn't argue. She took the other end and hooked it into her suit as Brad pressed forward.

"Saburo, we're coming in, but I'm basically carrying Pitts," Brad radioed forward on a private channel. Adding the pilot had barely slowed him down. The advantage, he supposed, to the environment was that she could basically just float and let him pull her.

"Please tell me you've got the door open."

"It isn't secure, but it's in terrible shape," his subordinate reported. "We're only going to get it open once, so we're holding for everyone." Saburo paused. "It's going to be a tight squeeze, but I am *not* leaving anyone behind."

"No, we're not." Brad stumbled, barely managing to catch himself before he hit the ground. If he tore his suit…

"You okay, boss?"

"Next time, can someone suggest orbital bombardment as an alternative plan to landing on Venus?" he asked.

"I believe this was a rescue op," Saburo pointed out. "Otherwise, I'm totally on board with that plan. We see you. Five meters, Commodore. We're standing by with the outer door open."

With a sharp inhalation—one now tinged with a hint of fear as more lights began to flash red on his suit—Brad lunged forward with Pitts. Reaching the door, he basically tossed the pilot in.

The rope snapped at the last moment, but one of the troopers was there. Pitts didn't even have enough time to panic before armored arms grabbed her out of the air and pulled her down.

"You're okay," the woman told Pitts. "We've got you. You're okay."

Saburo gestured them inside. Brad didn't move fast enough for his subordinate, however, who grabbed him by an arm and *yanked* him into the airlock.

"Go!" the Colonel barked.

A heavy door slammed shut behind them, a massive metal shutter pitted even on this side.

"Locked down," a trooper reported. "Seal is clean, somehow."

They were pressed together, suit against suit, and Brad had to suspect that the acid on each of their suits was rubbing against each other.

"Air system?" Saburo asked.

"Negative," the same trooper replied. "Refusing to activate. We're feeding it power, but the motor is toast. It can't move enough of this crap to stabilize the airlock. Inner door won't open at this pressure either."

"I am *not* dying in here." Brad wasn't sure whose panicked voice that was, but he couldn't let it carry on.

"Belay that Everdarkshit," he snapped. "Are we talking a hardware block or a software one on the door?"

"Little bit of both," the tech told him. "Any software is long dead, though. Manual sensor and pressure readers."

"This is a spaceship lock with an extra heavy door added outside," Brad pointed out. "Can you relay me a picture of the sensor?"

The tech obeyed and Brad studied the familiar workings. Once, long ago, he'd been an engineer, and he still remembered some of it.

"All right, it's old enough that I know the unit," he told the tech with a chuckle. "Any familiarity yourself?"

"I know the *software* override to force this damn door open. There's too much pressure on the sensor for me to manipulate it any way I know of."

"You never worked on a freighter with a shoestring budget, I see," Brad replied. "You see that gap at the far side of the panel?"

"Yeah, it's less than a centimeter deep; it's the input for the sensor reader."

"Exactly. Stick something in and lever it off."

A blade appeared in the video feed as the tech obeyed, tearing the sensor panel open. There wasn't much visible behind it, just the inner workings of a device that was determined to keep the door open.

"All right. Upper left corner, see that panel?" Brad kept his voice very level and calm, hopefully keeping his people from panicking even as he struggled with a moment of claustrophobia.

They had a dozen people in an airlock designed for five. This wasn't going to end well if they didn't get the door open.

"Yeah…electrical cover, right?" the tech asked.

"It's an add-on for this unit to protect against the corrosive muck this place calls air. Get it off, force a connection between the contacts before they corrode. It'll trigger an override sequence that doesn't even check to see if the outer door is closed."

He heard the tech swallow.

"I didn't think you could make an airlock do that," he pointed out.

"That's why it isn't easy and isn't advertised much," Brad said. "But sometimes, you've got to break it to fix it cheaply. Make it happen, soldier."

The people who'd assembled the tunnel cap had known what they were doing. There was probably a factory in one of the aerostat cities that turned regular airlocks into these special-purpose units, and the *last* thing they wanted was this override activated at the wrong time.

In fact, from the perspective of the designers, what they were doing was a bug, not a feature. They wouldn't have wanted someone to release an airlock full of Venus's atmosphere into the tunnels.

There was a limit to how thoroughly you could attach a single panel, though, and that limit failed against the monomolecular cutter in an electronics technician's emergency kit. You couldn't have *much* of a monomolecular blade without a secure end-point, but if you only needed a five-millimeter blade, well…

The panel popped clear and the tech shoved a wad of conductive putty into the gap. There was no attempt at precision; he just filled the electrical box with the conductor.

If they'd been planning on ever using this airlock again, it would have been a *terrible* idea. As it was, the door unlatched and swung open…and sparks blasted clear of the box as the few remaining intact systems burnt out.

"We're in," the tech reported with a long exhalation. "We're in."

———

Brad and his people stumbled out of the airlock into a completely unlit tunnel. The twenty or so cubic meters of Venus's pressurized air they brought with them exploded along with them, spreading out into the massive tunnel complex with an almost-eager will.

"Dump the suits," Brad ordered grimly as he checked over everyone's status reports. "We're not going to get enough of the acid out of them to stop them degrading, and we might be better off without them."

About half of the suits' modules could be retrieved and used separately, and he started on the effort of extracting them from his own suit with a will. An inner armor layer from the helmet became an unsealed combat helmet, with a coms system and projected HUD. Key pieces of armor linked into a harness and went over his body, and a voice-controlled light from his helmet went on his shoulder as he retrieved his weapons from their panels.

"Long arms didn't survive the trip," Saburo reported. "Blades, pistols, a few grenades, and special tricks. That's what we've got."

"Then that's what we'll use," Brad replied. "I don't suppose we've got a map of this warren?" he asked, looking at the tunnel that stretched off in the dim light of their relocated helmet lights.

"There might have been one in the door computer once," their tech reported. "But...long gone. Looks like all the new owners did was occasionally come by and spray some reinforcement on the outer shutter."

"I'm surprised the damn thing opened," Brad admitted. He could do that now that they were safe. "I only gave it fifty-fifty odds."

"And what in Everdark were we going to do if it didn't?" Saburo asked after few long seconds of silence.

"Blow the cap off and hope that being underground minimized the environmental effects enough for us to make to a working interior airlock," Brad said instantly. "Our odds of survival would go way down, but they'd still be above zero.

"And staying in the shuttle had survival odds of zero. We had to take the chance."

"Right." Saburo's voice was dry, but he didn't argue the point. "So, now what, boss?"

Brad's helmet was linked into his wrist-comp, but it was still easier to work with the computer itself instead of trying to use voice commands. He brought up the holographic screen and studied it.

"Okay," he said aloud. "Whatever we paid for the multi-system navigation program we're running? We didn't pay enough. Linked into satellites as long as it could, piggy-backing on the shuttle the whole way, then inertial-reckoned us down.

"I know where we are," he concluded. "And I know where the dome is and I know where the signal we're here to rescue is." He smiled grimly. "And fortunately for my peace of mind, they're in roughly the same place and they're both that way."

He pointed along the one tunnel they could see.

"Somewhere through these tunnels is a Cadre base where they captured and interrogated an Agency operative. Fortunately for *us*, they will have shuttles that can reach orbit. Unfortunately for *them*, they almost certainly think we're dead—and while I won't expect the Cadre to be incompetent enough to *not* lock their shuttlecraft, I am confident that we can break the locks they've got.

"So, folks, our way home is through the Cadre. Who's with me?"

CHAPTER THIRTEEN

BRAD LED the way into the warren of tunnels, pausing at every junction with another tunnel so that Saburo and his troopers could make sure they weren't about to run into an ambush. The airlock they'd forced had obviously not been connected to a warning system, or someone would have already been there checking for a breach.

That wasn't to say that the burst of Venus's atmosphere that they'd brought in wouldn't trigger some kind of environmental monitor and make someone wonder if they had unexpected guests. If so, they'd be ready.

Based on the condition of the tunnels and airlocks they'd passed, someone came down occasionally to make certain the inner airlock doors weren't leaking by spraying reinforcement on them. They didn't bother changing any of the lights that had failed, however, and there were massive pools of inky darkness punctuated with dim lights where fixtures were still operating.

"I'm guessing they don't get down here much," he said over his private link to Saburo.

"Hard to argue that," his ground commander agreed with a brief chuckle. "They've obviously had more pressing matters on their minds than base maintenance. Do you think this is the main base of Cadre operations?"

"I suppose they could have more," Brad allowed, "but it seems unlikely that they'd bring a captured Agent to a secondary base. No, I'm betting this is where the Cadre leadership is operating out of. That gives us a chance to rescue the Agent, capture some prisoners, and maybe get our hands on their computers."

Saburo shook his head. "Sorry to pour cold water on your enthusiasm, but now that they've shot our shuttle down, odds are damned good they're packing up shop. They have to suspect someone followed up on that transmission and have to expect it's us. They know more shuttles will be heading this way once the ships in orbit notice we've failed to return.

"We have a very brief window to interrupt those plans before they're gone. Odds are they think they've killed us, but they'll still be on high alert. With our relative lack of weapons, we're at a big disadvantage."

Brad grinned coldly. "Then we'll just have to even the odds. The first group of pirates won't really be expecting us. We need to take them out before they can sound the alarm. We'll add their weapons to ours."

Following the twisting path to where the navigation program in his wrist-comp said the dome was took another five minutes. They found the access to the dome about where he'd expected it to be, protected by an airlock in much better condition than the one they'd had to force.

The tech checked it while they waited impatiently. After a minute, he straightened.

"There was a monitor, but I think I have it bypassed," he said. "It wasn't very sophisticated. I guess they didn't expect anyone to break and enter."

Brad laughed. "I'd imagine not. The exterior security measures are better than anyone else in the system can manage. Open it up."

The airlock passed them through into a wide chamber in much better repair than the tunnels. It held a freight elevator and a wide set of stairs. The lights there were much brighter and all were lit.

"Bypass the elevator," Brad ordered. "Someone might hear it."

Saburo sent his men to the stairs and they started up into the base. The next few minutes would decide their fate one way or the other.

———

Brad found out that fate hated him as soon as they opened the door leading to the main dome level. Standing not fifteen feet away was a single pirate, and he was staring at them in shock. Shock that didn't prevent him from screaming a warning into his com and scrabbling for his sidearm.

Saburo coolly shot the man down, but a low, hooting alarm was already sounding. They'd failed to get the advantage they'd needed. Now they'd have to do this the hard way.

"The transmission came from somewhere ahead of us," Brad snapped. "We have to get there before the Cadre closes in on us."

One of the troopers paused long enough to strip the dead pirate of his weapon, handing the captured pistol and its magazines to Pitts. Like all Brad's people, she knew how to use a gun, but she wasn't a trooper. If it came down to her needing the weapon, she was probably screwed.

The corridors were eerily empty as they raced deeper into the abandoned settlement that was now a pirate base. Where were the defenders?

He learned the hard way not to question their good fortune. Three men in unmarked uniforms of dark gray came out of a side corridor, firing military-grade rifles at Brad's people.

Stiller, likely still suffering from the mild concussion, failed to throw himself down as quickly as his comrades and took the brunt of the attack, falling dead under the merciless barrage of bullets.

Brad rolled against the wall and returned fire, striking the leftmost pirate in the chest even as his comrades sought cover. It must not have been fatal, because the man was able to join his comrades behind the nearest corner.

While the wall made for excellent cover for the pirates, they still had to expose themselves to shoot. That gave Saburo and his troopers a chance to return fire effectively. Someone hit a pirate in the head, sending blood and brains across the wall behind the man and dropping him to the floor.

That added a layer of caution to the pirates' fighting. The next man stuck his rifle around the corner and fired blind. He hit a trooper in the arm, but it only caused the man to curse. Several rounds struck the wall just above Brad, making him try to flatten himself even more.

"We can't let them keep us pinned down," Brad told Saburo as he discovered the limits on how far he could compress himself. "We need to dislodge them and get moving."

"On it."

Saburo crawled forward, keeping himself low and close to the wall nearest the pirates. Time flowed like old Earth molasses and the stalemate held until the Colonel reached the corner, stuck his pistol around it, and emptied his magazine into the shooter.

The pirate's rifle clattered to the floor and the troopers were on their feet, rushing the remaining pirate. It turned out to be unnecessary. Brad had killed the man, but it had taken him a few moments to die. He lay sprawled on the floor just past the rest of the dead.

"Collect the weapons," Brad ordered. "There'll be more."

"What do we do with Stiller?" Saburo asked quietly as his men carried out Brad's order.

"I hate to do this, but we'll leave him for now. We'll either be coming back for him or none of us will be getting out at all. These three were holding us in place. We need to get clear of the area before the force they were holding us for puts in an appearance."

———

That plan also ran afoul of the enemy. Even more of the Cadre's elite troops showed up behind them, obviously having just missed trapping them in a pincer. His men, now armed with captured rifles, set up an ambush of their own while Brad and the rest made their best speed to find a defensible position.

The Cadre troops proved their elite status by overwhelming his men before he'd found anything that would provide them any cover at all. It infuriated Brad that his men had had to trade their lives for getting the rest of the team clear of the ambush, but he knew they probably hadn't had a choice. None of them did.

Examined dispassionately, the odds of them making it out alive were slim. Unless he changed the calculation.

"Break contact," he ordered. "Get as far into the dome as we can."

The settlement inside the dome was still almost completely unused. Signs of disrepair were all around them as they ran: doors agape, nonfunctional fixtures, and trash scattered about. Whatever the pirates were using the place for, they didn't need all the space.

Brad checked his navigation system and found that they were almost at the area the transmission had come from. If the Agent was still there, this would be the time they could rescue them. If they could manage that, they might just learn what the pirates were up to.

"We're about a hundred feet from where the transmission came from," he said over the general channel. "Keep an eye out for any place they could be holding the Agent and watch out for guards."

They slowed their headlong rush and moved forward as cautiously as they could. They didn't find any guards, which suggested that the pirates had moved their prisoner or that they no longer needed to worry about them being rescued.

A call from one of the scouting troopers confirmed the grim latter guess. "We found a body, sir. It's bad."

Brad left the defense of the area to Saburo and made his way forward to see what the man meant. He immediately saw that it was ugly. Very ugly.

A redheaded woman sat bound to a chair, dead. Someone had used snippers to cut off her fingers, bit by bit. The abandoned torture implements lay on the floor beside the dead Agent.

"Dammit," he muttered as he knelt to examine her face. She was young and had been pretty before someone had used a knife to slice her face. Her unfocused green eyes stared into infinity.

"She held," Saburo said. "They wouldn't have cut off all her fingers if she'd talked. They'd have just shot her."

"And she couldn't have sent that signal without them," Brad

agreed. "They probably tried to get her to unlock her wrist-comp and she triggered the signal. There's no other reason she'd have had access to it."

He touched her bloody arm and felt fading heat. She'd have died about the time they crashed, he suspected. While killing pirates was always a worthwhile endeavor, he hated that their primary mission had failed. That he had failed to save her.

"Find the com unit she used," he said heavily. "Or a terminal to their computer system. They'd have had her nearby, I suspect."

"Found it, sir," Pitt said almost as soon as he'd finished speaking. "The computer terminal, that is."

He followed the sound of her voice to the next room over. It looked like this was where the Agent's guards had been living. And where they'd died.

Four bodies lay sprawled across the floor, all riddled with bullet wounds. Someone hadn't been pleased that they'd allowed the Agent to get a signal out.

"Search them," he ordered as he sat at the computer terminal.

It wasn't locked, but it also wasn't very helpful. The system was in the process of erasing itself. Most of the data and control interfaces were already gone. Only one remained: a self-destruct countdown.

"Well, isn't that just peachy," he muttered, attempting to interrupt the counter, which showed less than fifteen minutes remaining.

Only, it wouldn't let him. It kept prompting for a code that he didn't have. He didn't have even the most basic interface to try and hack it, either. No, this base was doomed and so were they, if they couldn't get clear in time.

"Found what looks like the Agent's wrist-comp in a Faraday cage," Saburo said, holding out a wrist-comp. "It seems intact but it's locked."

"We'll have to check it more closely later, if any of my Agency codes will work on it," he said, gesturing at the timer. "We have to get to the shuttle pad and hope we can steal a ride."

Saburo took one look that the countdown and started ordering his troopers into motion.

They were down to eight people, if they counted Pitt, so Brad sincerely hoped they didn't run into more elite Cadre fighters. One good firefight might end them.

Of course, most of the enemy were getting the hell out of there, too, so the chances of that shrank with every second. So did their chances of getting off Venus alive.

While he didn't have a map of the settlement, all domes were laid out in a roughly similar pattern. The shuttle pad would be on the outer edge of the dome so that the small craft could take off and land with a minimum of fuss. The challenge would be figuring out where that might be in time.

That's when he spotted a set of bloody boot prints leading away from the makeshift prison. Admittedly, the person that had made them might have been going somewhere other than the shuttle pad, but it was a chance they'd have to take.

"Follow the boot prints," he ordered.

His crew fell in and they rushed forward, slowing only when they came to an airlock. They had no way of seeing what was on the other side. It might open to the surface, which would be a rude and painful mistake to make.

"Look there," Pitt said. "That's probably a control booth for the shuttle pad."

She pointed at a hatch a dozen feet down the corridor. "We can take a quick peek in there and see what's going on before we attack."

"Will it be occupied?" Saburo asked, motioning a pair of the troopers forward.

"Does it matter?" the pilot asked with a shrug. "Time is wasting."

"Can't argue with that," the Colonel said. "Go in hot, boys."

The troopers opened the hatch and raced up a short set of stairs, with Brad and Saburo right behind them.

As Pitt had guessed, this was indeed a control booth for the shuttle pad. There was no one inside and none of the interior lights were on, but the wide glass had a good view of the lit pad below. A single shuttle remained, pirates hastily loading boxes aboard it.

"This looks like our ride," Brad said, looking for and spotting four pirates with rifles watching the airlock from behind cover. "If we can figure how to take it without being shot to pieces."

According to the timer on his wrist-comp, they had less than ten minutes to take the shuttle and escape. It looked as if the pirates would be done loading in less than two. This was literally the time to do or die.

CHAPTER FOURTEEN

"You know what I don't see in there?" Pitt asked. "Atmosphere suits."

Saburo grunted slightly. "Not much need when you have a protected shuttle pad like this one. They can work in shirtsleeves and be perfectly safe. I'm not sure how that helps us."

The pilot smiled coldly. "Commodore, do you remember how you knew that trick with the airlock in the tunnels? Big airlocks like this have something similar buried in the fire-suppression protocols in space, and I'll bet no one bothered to remove that from the basic controls. I think I can convince the system to open both outer doors at the same time."

Brad felt his eyes narrowing as he considered her words. Such a thing made sense in space. It would be really helpful to dump the atmosphere in a landing bay to extinguish a fire instantly. Down here on Venus, of course, the results would be very different.

The outside air pressure would force the sulfuric acid–laced soup into the shuttle pad like an ocean would flood a holed ship with water. The men below had no protection against something like that.

"Okay, I get how that would be bad for them," Brad said. "But how is it good for us? We don't have suits either."

"I can close the airlock and use the pumps to pull the tainted air back out. The part I'm not sure about is how long it will take to clear the atmosphere on the pad. We need to hit them while they're still screwed up."

Brad nodded sharply. This could work, and it wasn't as if they had a lot of time to come up with a different plan. They had to execute an attack now if they hoped to survive the self-destruct charge. He even thought he had a plan to deal with Venus's atmosphere.

"Do it," he ordered. "Saburo, get the men into the airlock. I'll be down as soon as it's safe to go in."

Pitt leaned over a console and started paging through system screens. "Here it is. Fire suppression. Dammit, the command to open both doors is locked out."

"Maybe it needs to detect a fire," he suggested. "Or at least be told one is present. Systems on a ship have decision trees like that."

With that, he leaned forward beside her and pressed the fire alarm on the panel they were looking at. Red lights began swirling over the shuttle pad, and he could hear a high-pitched siren sounding. The pirates looked up with expressions of alarm and confusion.

"That did it," Pitt said, pressing another button that had switched from gray to red.

The large airlock doors above slid rapidly open and a wave of toxic yellow poison flooded the compartment in seconds. Its pressure was more than sufficient to push the regular air out of its way with ease.

Brad lost sight of the pirates in the haze but could imagine how they were reacting to that crap in their eyes and lungs. Even the pirates aboard the shuttle would be in the same pickle, unless they were already suited. And even if they were, what were the odds they'd donned their helmets?

"Start pulling the bad air out of there," he said. "Call out the moment the pad has a breathable atmosphere and we'll rush them. I'll leave the outer door locked open so that the air inside the base will come in with us. That means you can follow as quickly as you're able."

"Will do, sir. Good luck."

Brad ran down the stairs and joined his troopers in the lock. He manually tied the first door open with a cable provided for that purpose. It was used during maintenance when someone wanted to be sure a hatch didn't close behind them.

He gestured to the tech. "Open that panel up and be ready to force the hatch open. Don't trigger it until Pitts gives us the green light, or we'll all regret it."

Thirty seconds passed before Pitt transmitted. "You're good."

"Blow the hatch," Brad ordered. "Hang on, everyone."

The tech bridged the connection and the hatch in front of them slid open. Air from inside the base rushed past them, tugging strongly at their arms and legs. Ten seconds passed before the pressure equalized.

"Go!" Brad yelled, rushing into the shuttle pad.

The Venusian atmosphere had had a profound impact on the men out in the open. The four guards and two pirates loading boxes were all down. None were moving.

He suspected that meant they were dead, but he had no time to make sure. They had to secure the shuttle before someone inside decided to seal it up. Though, if they hadn't done so by now, he suspected they might not be able to.

Brad led the charge into the shuttle and found two more men on the floor of the main compartment. They weren't moving, so he ran for the cockpit. That compartment held the first man they'd seen in a suit. He had his helmet on and was seated at the controls.

"Hands up," Brad shouted, aiming his pistol at the back of the man's helmet.

The man didn't move. In fact, his arms hung limply at his sides.

Brad turned the pilot and looked into his helmet. All he saw were dead eyes floating in a haze of yellow. The man had sealed the poison in with him and his suit had failed to scrub it.

"Shuttle's clear," Brad said over the general channel. "Let's go!"

He strapped into the copilot's seat and started checking the readouts. Some of the systems were showing yellow, probably from exposure to the acidic air, but they'd just have to hope the shuttle held together.

Pitt raced in and threw herself into the pilot's chair. "Shuttle sealed. Opening main airlock doors."

The massive doors ahead of them opened, revealing a chamber

large enough for the shuttle. Once they were inside, the inner doors would close and the outer ones would open.

"Here we go," Pitt said as she hit the engine controls.

Nothing happened.

———

"Oh, for fuck's sake!" Pitt howled as she started running her eyes across the controls. "Seriously?"

Brad checked his timer. "We only have seven minutes until this base goes boom. What's wrong?"

"The engines are locked out. There has to be an override here somewhere."

She searched franticly, cursing all the while. Then she unstrapped and levered herself out of her seat, bending over the dead man in the vacuum suit.

"There's a manual key," Pitt said. "He has to have it on him."

Moments later, she triumphantly held up a key on a bright red ribbon. "Got it!"

She threw herself into her couch, inserted the key into a slot he hadn't noticed, and twisted it. Several lights on the console changed from yellow to green.

Pitt manipulated the controls. "Engines coming up. Everyone strap in. This could get rough."

"I have the controls," Brad said. "Strap yourself in."

He wasn't the best pilot in the system, but he could move a small craft around when it suited him. He slowly brought the shuttle into the lock and hovered as Pitt finished strapping back in and resumed control of the shuttle.

"Cycling the lock," she said.

He couldn't see the hatch behind them close, but he saw the one in front of them start to open. Once again, the yellow atmosphere of Venus poured in. Then the shuttle was moving out over the plateau and up into the deadly sky.

"Can we get coms with *Oath* or any of our other ships?" he asked.

"Probably not," she said. "I can't imagine how that wrist-comp punched a signal all the way through. A regular shuttle com can't."

"Maybe this one isn't normal. The pirates have been working down here for a while. It would be useful to be able to talk with their friends."

He activated the communications systems and switched to the frequencies his ships used. "*Oath of Vengeance* or any Vikings ship, this is Commodore Madrid. We're on our way up in an enemy shuttle. Please respond."

Nothing but static met his call.

"No joy," he said with a grumble. "We'll just have to hope the shuttle makes it all the way up."

She ran her eyes across the controls. "Things seem to be in decent shape, so I think we'll make it. They've obviously been using this shuttle to get up and down for a while. I'm more worried about what kind of self-destruct charge they're using. The Venusian atmosphere is thick and will transmit shock really, really well."

He hadn't considered that. If the charges were standard explosives, they'd be clear by the time they went off. If they were nuclear, that would be chancier. Under normal circumstances, he wouldn't have been as concerned, but a small tear in the hull would flood the compartment with poison gas.

Brad opened the private channel to Saburo. "You might want to look for emergency oxygen bottles. If we have a hull breach, you don't want to be breathing that stuff."

"Don't teach your grandmother how to suck eggs. We've got enough to go around, and I was just about to bring some up for you two."

"Touché," Brad said with a grin. "Thanks."

The door behind them slid open and Saburo handed him two emergency masks. They looked like old-style gas masks, with clear faceplates and straps to hold the masks securely in place. Short hoses ran to small cylinders made to clip to one's belt.

"This won't be good for long," Saburo warned. "Looks like about twenty minutes. They're designed to allow someone in a breach to get to somewhere with air. They won't protect your exposed skin if we have a breach, either."

"Then let's hope we don't have any problems like that," Brad said. "I don't want to have to sit here while Venus eats my skin off. Strap in tight and get the masks ready. Leave the hatch open and I'll shout out when it's time to get them on."

The time left paradoxically seemed to rush ahead and simultaneously drag. When the timer was down to twenty seconds, Brad turned his head toward the open hatch.

"Masks on and hold on tight." He got his mask in place and opened the oxygen feed.

Nothing seemed to happen when the timer reached zero, but he knew that it took some small amount of time for a blast wave to propagate. Since he had no way of calculating how long a blast wave took to travel through this atmosphere, he'd just have to wait and see what happened.

"The clouds are getting brighter," Pitt said, her voice tight. "I doubt that comes from normal explosives, so we'd best brace for a nuclear shock wave."

As soon as the words left her mouth, something seemed to smash into the shuttle. Not in the figurative sense, either. An alarm began screaming in the cockpit and the air began turning yellow in front of his eyes.

"Hull breach," Pitt said coolly. "We're losing atmospheric pressure and taking on that crap."

Brad felt the skin on his exposed arms start to itch.

———

Thankfully, the sensation on his exposed flesh didn't get much stronger. They'd risen high enough that the overall pressure was falling rapidly. Higher than the floating cities, in fact. In front of them, the sky was transitioning to the black of space. It seemed he wouldn't be melting today.

Of course, that meant they had less than twenty minutes to get another source of air or they'd all die. As the atmosphere slowly bled away, taking the tainted atmosphere with it, he again tried signaling any of his ships. With the low pressure, he wasn't sure if they heard him, and he couldn't tell if he'd gotten a response. Sound was useless without air to transmit it.

Brad unstrapped and floated back to the open hatch. One glance told him his people had made it through without further injury.

He also saw the breach: a hole about the size of his hand in the ramp that allowed him to see the planet behind them. The blast had actually sent a piece of debris after them with enough force to penetrate the hull. He supposed they were lucky that it was something small. It could've been a boulder.

Saburo touched his faceplate to Brad's, almost making him step back because the man was in his personal space so deeply. The Colonel's voice, when he spoke, sounded odd in his ears, being transmitted by vibration through the masks.

"That was crazy. We heard it hit the shuttle and then something was bouncing around inside here like a bullet. It's a bloody miracle that it didn't hit anyone."

"That might not end up being such good luck. We're in space now. If someone doesn't come find us in short order, we're going to suffocate—assuming the vacuum doesn't *freeze* us to death."

Saburo grinned. "Even in shirtsleeves, freezing before we suffocate isn't going to be a problem. Someone will come for us, just you wait and see. Hell, this is the kind of thing we've been watching for. A shuttle racing away from the planet? We've got to look like smugglers for sure."

Brad laughed. "I hope they don't take our silence as a reason to open fire, then. Without air or a helmet, I can't interface with the radio."

"Go forward and keep watch," Saburo said with a smile. "If I'm wrong, well, I guess you'll get to brag about finally beating me at a bet in the afterlife."

"You're incorrigible."

Brad made his way back to his couch in the cockpit and gave Pitt a thumbs-up. Then they waited.

Five minutes before the air supply ran out, he saw a shuttle racing in from in front of them. He started flashing his shuttle's running lights to tell them who they were and that they only had a few minutes of air remaining.

The other shuttle immediately passed directly overhead toward the rear of his shuttle.

Brad gestured for Pitt to follow him out. Once in the main compartment, he opened the ramp and saw that the Vikings' shuttle was suspended directly behind them. Its ramp lowered as he watched, and someone in a vacuum suit gestured for them to jump across.

All of them managed the jump without issue and the crewman closed the shuttle's ramp as Brad's air started getting foul. He'd run out of oxygen.

He controlled his breathing and waited with what patience he could as the crewman opened the valves and started flooding the compartment with breathable air. Once the crewman started undoing his helmet, Brad pulled off his mask and took a deep breath of sweet air.

They'd made it. Now they just had to hope they'd gotten enough information to follow the pirates to their new hideout.

CHAPTER FIFTEEN

As soon as they docked with *Oath*, Kirabo Terzić had them in his sickbay, checking them over while a worried Michelle hovered over his shoulder. The doctor gave his wife a repressive glance. "We don't exactly have room for more people in here. Can't this wait?"

"No," Michelle said. "I'm Commander Hunt right now, not his wife. I need information to guide the company."

The man looked at her for a moment and then nodded. "Stand over against the wall, then. My people need the center of the compartment to do their jobs."

Brad turned to face Michelle as she moved and filled her in on what they'd found as quickly as he could. It didn't take long to let her know that almost all the pirates had escaped before using a nuke to destroy their base.

And that Brad had lost four troopers in the fighting due to what he considered lack of foresight on his part. If he'd just have made sure they had the right gear and sealed their heavier weapons in something that could keep the Venusian atmosphere out, this might have turned out differently.

"Stop that," Michelle scolded him. "Who was it that taught me that I can't prepare for every single potential outcome or I'd never accomplish anything? You had no reason to suspect that they had heavy anti-air weapons on the surface.

"I'm sorry that we lost people and we'll learn from that, but we need to focus on figuring out where the Cadre went so we can cause them an even worse day."

Brad sighed as Terzić started spreading some lotion on the reddened skin of his arm. The burn he'd been feeling immediately started to fade. Thankfully, he hadn't had his eyes or lungs exposed to the acid or vacuum.

"We found the Agent, too," he said. "She was dead. We also found her wrist-comp in a Faraday cage. My guess is that they tortured her to open it and she used a code on the lock screen to send a call for help. They rushed it back to the cage and then finished her off as painfully as possible.

"Someone wasn't satisfied with their efforts, though. Riddled them with bullets and left the corpses behind when they ran."

Michelle grimaced. "I was afraid of something like that after the Cadre captured me. I blew up some of their ships, so needless to say, they were less than pleased with me."

Brad well remembered that time with rage and agonized terror. First, he'd thought she'd died in the fight. Then he'd learned that the Terror had her and was holding her hostage until Brad found him. Torture had been a distinct possibility.

"Just one more reason we need to kill these bastards," he said. "To keep them from doing this to anyone else. Did our ships pick up any unusual shuttle activity from the area where they had their base?"

Michelle shook her head. "No activity at all. They must've moved quite a distance away while staying at low altitude. Or they have another base on the surface."

"They're like cockroaches," he muttered. "Turn on the lights and they scatter. Then you can never find them all."

"Cockroaches with nukes," his wife said with a grim scowl. "Even for them, that's way out there. Even if it is Venus, that's a planetary surface. A big raise in the stakes. Why? What's changed?"

She shook her head. "I can't help worrying that this means their plans are further advanced than we'd like, and we still don't know what they intend. Were you able to use your codes to access the Agent's wrist-comp?"

"I was a little busy with armageddon coming. Saburo, toss me the wrist-comp."

The Colonel, who was being treated on the other side of the compartment, dug the wrist-comp out of his suit and tossed it to Brad.

It looked like a standard unit, but it couldn't be. It had a transmitter capable of punching a signal to the aerostat cities above the base from the surface of Venus. That was impressive and something he'd love to have his people study for a bit. It might come in very useful at some point.

He used his own wrist-comp to attempt every code he had without success. The unit remained locked and unresponsive. He sighed. That was only to be expected, he supposed.

"No joy," he told Michelle. "We'll have to ship it back to the Agency. They can pry out its secrets and then give us any relevant data. I do have one concern, though. Something feels off."

Michelle frowned. "I don't follow."

"Agent Mulroney was a prisoner before we even got orders to Venus. She wasn't signaling us for help, but she used Agency codes in her transmission. Who exactly did she expect was going to come to save her?"

Michelle opened her mouth for a moment and then closed it again, obviously thinking before she answered.

"There's another player," she finally said. "Someone was *already* on Venus that she could call on. Someone from the Agency."

"The possibility was mentioned," he said. "We're going to need to find them and ask a few pointed questions. Like why they didn't contact us."

Michelle shrugged. "It's not as if anyone outside the company knows who you are. Like you said, Mulroney disappeared before we were ordered here. The remaining assets had no way to know, did they?"

"The Agency contacted us," he said. "They also knew that Mulroney had been missing three days when they ordered us to Venus. They've had plenty of time to let the asset know and send them to meet us. Either they haven't chosen to do so or the asset just hasn't done it. We need to know which.

"As soon as the good doctor is done with me, I'll send an update off to Earth and see what information I can shake loose. Hopefully, we'll get the contact information for the remaining asset and they'll know something useful."

"If the Cadre doesn't have them, too," Michelle muttered darkly.

"Let's hope not. We really do need a lead if we want to exterminate the bastards."

———

He was still waiting for a response from Earth when a shuttle with Governor Ngu aboard rendezvoused with *Oath*. Brad could only imagine what the man was going to say. Someone had set off a nuke on the planet he was responsible for.

Odds were good the governor would blame Brad. First an assassination attempt, and now this. He'd have to be wondering what the next escalation would bring.

The large man extended his hand as soon as he boarded. "Commodore Madrid. I'm pleased to see you whole and hale. I understand you lost people on the surface, and I'm very sorry to hear that."

Brad shook the man's hand. "I appreciate that, Governor. I doubt a man as busy as yourself came all the way out here just to extend his condolences, however. If you'll accompany me to my office, we can talk more privately."

He led the man to his office and closed the hatch behind them. "Would you care for something to drink?"

Ngu shook his head and sat in one of the chairs. "I'll have to decline. As you said, I have a lot of things on my plate today. Our business won't take long, but it's not something I'd trust to even an encrypted channel, and you deserve to hear this from me in person.

"Succinctly put, I've come to thank you for your work and declare your contract completed. I'm declaring you've met all the stipulations and adding in a hefty bonus for going well above and beyond in your efforts. Venus thanks you for your service."

Brad felt his eyebrows rise as he sat. "I have to say that I don't understand, Governor. We haven't captured the people responsible for the hijackings. Even though we cost the pirates their base, we killed less than a dozen of them. They're still here and they will keep attacking your people."

"As much as it saddens me, I'm only the first among equals here, if you know what I mean," Ngu said, spreading his hands wide. "A governor without real teeth. The Governing Council makes all the decisions here, and they have voted to mark your contract as completed over my objections."

Leaning back in his seat, Brad considered the governor for a moment. "Curious. If they were going to be convinced to let us go without actually stopping the marauders, why did they vote to hire the Vikings to manage the customs duty in the first place?"

Ngu smiled slightly. "A well-thought-out question, Commodore. The vote to hire you was close, turning on a single vote. One that now seems eager to send you packing, even in the face of strong evidence that the hijackings will likely pick back up as soon as you're gone."

"Blackmail or threats of force," Brad said. "Otherwise, this person wouldn't have voted to hire us. Someone got to them."

"That matches my assessment," Ngu agreed. "Yet it still leaves us with the situation we find ourselves in, whether we suspect foul play or not. Your mandate to operate in Venusian space is unfortunately rescinded."

Brad nodded slowly. "I hope the loss of the base impacts the pirates' ability to operate, but I'm very much afraid it won't." He rose to his feet when the governor stood, extending his hand. "Thank you for taking the time from your busy schedule to tell me in person. I appreciate it."

The governor's handshake was extra firm this time. "You risked your lives and almost died carrying out your duty. That demands respect, Commodore. You can rest assured that the most glowing recommendation my staff can write will be winging its way to the Mercenary Guild shortly. Safe journeys and may your next contract be less…confrontational."

Brad laughed as he led the governor to the hatch. "I'm a mercenary,

Governor Ngu. Every contract is built on confrontation. I'll just hope that there are no nukes next time.

"Speaking of which, I'd be expecting a Fleet element to come investigating that if I were you. Trust me when I say that the use of one is a red line that they won't tolerate anyone crossing."

"I've sent them a report," Ngu said dryly. "They'll get back to me, I'm told. Frankly, I couldn't believe it. No one uses nukes on a planet. Something odd is happening with Fleet, Commodore, and I'm worried. They're not behaving as I'd have expected, and that bodes ill for the Commonwealth."

———

"Are you kidding me?" Michelle demanded when he told her they'd been paid off. "That's insane."

"It's certainly not going to solve their problem," he agreed. "Yet what can we do? One thing I've discovered in life is that you can rarely save people from themselves. They've made the choice, or were driven into it, and they'll have to sleep in the bed they've made.

"We'll take on fuel and supplies before leaving. That was part of the contract, and it might leave enough time for the Agency contact to get instructions to meet with us before we depart. Drag it out as long as you can without making us look completely incompetent."

His wife nodded. "I can have the other Captains take their sweet time. With our full fleet here, that'll eat up three or four hours even without slowing the process down. Do you think we should expect another visitor or a com contact this time?"

"Damned if I know," he admitted. "Have everyone be on the lookout for a direct contact, and we'll just have to see if anyone steps forward. To give them as much time as possible, let's have *Oath* serviced last."

Michelle managed to drag out the servicing to almost six hours by the time his flagship was taking on supplies. She'd managed that by having everything inspected before it was brought on board. When the Venusians complained, she made a mushroom cloud gesture with both hands. That seemed to do the trick.

Xan Wong turned away from the communications console as they were wrapping up taking on fuel and supplies. "We have an incoming signal, sir. It's using Agency encryption."

"Well, it certainly took the Agency long enough to get back with us," Brad said.

"Actually, sir, it's not from Earth. This is a live call from New Venice."

He sat up a little straighter. "Without a signal from Earth? We're close enough to New Venice to have picked up at least the edges of an Agency signal, unless it was completely disguised and using non-Agency protocols."

"That's right, sir. No signal from the Agency on Earth that we could detect."

"I'll take it in my office," Brad said, rising to his feet.

Once he was seated at his desk, he used his codes to authenticate the sender. The screen in front of him cleared and he found himself looking at a familiar face.

"Stacy, right?" he asked. "Councilor Fisk's driver slash bodyguard. Not who I was expecting."

The bald woman smiled thinly at him. "That's part of the job. It took me a while to confirm who the Agent in the Vikings was. The brass wasn't being forthcoming. I just got a private message—fully encrypted with a cypher not connected with the Agency—confirming your status. I'd have to say you've got an excellent cover, Commodore. Much more mobile than me."

He nodded. "It does have its moments. So, you were working with Agent Mulroney?"

"Not exactly. The two of us were working on different things, but we'd partnered in the past. My mission here is to keep an eye on Venusian politics. Hers was to trace criminal activity by the Cadre. When she vanished, I notified the Agency immediately."

"Can you provide any information on the Cadre operations here?" he asked.

"Sadly, no. We knew and trusted one another, but you know how the Agency is about sharing data like that. Need to know. Can you tell me what happened to her?"

Brad could see the pain in the woman's eyes. There had been a real friendship between the two women. Perhaps more.

"You received the signal from her?"

Stacy nodded. "That's how I knew someone in your organization had to be Agency. I would've gone after her if you hadn't reacted so quickly."

"Agent Mulroney never had a chance," he said. "The pirates killed her right after she sent the message. It was quick and she didn't suffer too much."

A lie and a damned lie, but one he didn't hesitate uttering. There was no need for the woman to be haunted by something she couldn't have changed.

"You should take up poker," Stacy said, a tear running down her face. "I sometimes wish I wasn't so good at spotting falsehood. Thank you for trying."

Well, dammit.

"I'm being serious when I say you couldn't have done anything," he said after a few seconds. "Once she called for help, she was dead before anyone could have gotten to her. That's the truth."

"Get them," Stacy said fiercely. "Make them pay for killing my friend."

"You have my word on that."

CHAPTER SIXTEEN

"I NEVER IMAGINED ANYTHING LIKE THIS," Michelle said softly from the pilot's console, her voice filled with awe as she stared at the main screen.

Brad had to agree. He'd thought the Jovian Cluster was busy, but it didn't hold a candle to Earth orbit. There were more ships and stations here than he could count. Big ones, too.

"Welcome to Earth," he said. "Home to humanity and still the largest population by a few orders of magnitude. Narendra, can you tell how many ships and stations we're looking at?"

His tactical officer shrugged and shook her head. "Not with the restrictions placed on us, no sir. Fleet was pretty emphatic that we stick with passive sensors. Hundreds of stations, though. Mostly small, but some bigger than the Io shipyards. Thousands of ships, if you count the runabouts."

The runabouts she was speaking about were like shuttles, only smaller and made to go point to point in Earth orbit. They swarmed around the stations like insects. He hated to think of how frazzled traffic control got with them.

The Fleet restrictions she'd mentioned were that only one of his ships could get any nearer than the leading or trailing Lagrange points.

That made sense, considering the firepower a ship could bring to bear and the fact that the Cadre had been killing people in job lots recently.

They'd allowed *Oath* in, though with significant restrictions. No active sensors and a pair of escorting destroyers sitting right behind him. If his ship showed any signs of powering weapons or maneuvering in a way they didn't like, those two ships could gut him and his command in an instant.

Frankly, he doubted they'd have let him in at all if the Agency hadn't insisted. Fleet had argued that Brad could take a shuttle in from where his ships were waiting. The discussion over the three-way com had gotten…spirited.

"Where do they have us going?" he asked Michelle as they all drank in the magnificent globe of the home world.

"A Fleet station about eighty degrees around the planet from where we are now. It'll keep us under its guns, I'm sure. That'll free the destroyers to return to their patrol area. An Agency contact is going to meet us there."

Brad grunted and nodded. He wondered if it would be Falcone. She'd been awfully quiet lately. He hoped it was her. The way things had been going for them lately, he dreaded any more surprises.

———

Brad exited the shuttle to find someone other than Kate Falcone waiting for him.

"Commodore Madrid," the short woman with green hair said, her voice light and high. "Welcome to Earth. I'm supposed to pick up something from you."

No name. He guessed that wasn't so surprising. Why lie when you can say nothing at all?

"You can have it," he agreed, "if you have the right code."

Her smile widened and she gave him the code he'd been expecting. With a shrug, he pulled Mulroney's wrist-comp from his jacket and handed it over.

"I don't suppose you can confirm that you'll pass along any information that will help us catch the Cadre, once you've accessed it."

"Actually, I can. Our lords and masters instructed me to tell you that they'll send you a burst transmission with anything they deem useful as soon as they can do so."

That surprised him more than a bit. He might as well push his luck.

"Since they're in such a giving mood, see if they'll send along some of the coms built into that unit. We're out on the pointy end and could use them."

"No promises," she said as she put the wrist-comp away. "They're stingy that way. If you hang around for a day or so, it's still possible, though. Good luck, Commodore. Give those bastards hell."

The woman stepped away and two men materialized out of the side passages to escort her away.

Before he could turn back toward his shuttle, a third man stepped out and cleared his throat. "I don't suppose you'd care to have dinner with an old man, would you, Commodore Madrid?"

Brad blinked in surprise at the unexpected sight of the man representing the Jovian Cluster in the Commonwealth Senate.

He smiled and extended his hand to Senator Barnes. "I'm surprised to see you, Senator, but I can always make time for a friend."

———

Senator Barnes hadn't been alone, of course. He'd had his own security detail and transport. Those worthies saw them to a different shuttle and off to another station in orbit. One that proved to be significantly larger than the Fleet station and also much more opulent.

At least, the section where they'd docked was. Lush white carpet covered the floors and what certainly appeared to be genuine pieces of art—originals—were spaced along the corridor and set in dedicated niches. Nothing he recognized, but undoubtedly something worth a significant chunk of his salary.

The Senator led him to a private lift that took them directly into a suite of rooms. "Welcome to my home away from home. We can relax for a bit while Javier gets dinner finalized. He's already started the preparation, you understand, but I didn't want to assume you'd be free to see me on such short notice. Would you care for a drink?"

Brad nodded. "I don't have much experience with particular brands of note, but I'll take a scotch, neat. Do you have many people turn you down, Senator? I can't imagine you get refused often."

The man laughed as he headed for a bar set into the wall beside a wide viewport showing the curve of Earth below the station. "You'd be shocked, I'm sure. That's a big part of my job, turning noes into yeses. Beautiful, isn't it?"

"I've never been to Earth before," Brad admitted as he took the tumbler from the Senator. "It's a bit overwhelming."

"That it is. I heard about your run-in with the Cadre at Venus. Nasty business, that. The use of a nuke on a planetary surface—even one as inhospitable as Venus—raises the stakes significantly. The Cadre is moving into the Inner System and that disturbs me."

Brad sipped the scotch and found it smooth and mellow. Better than he'd ever had, truth be told.

"My wife and I agree with you," he told Barnes. "Whatever they're planning, it's closer to fruition than any of us would care to admit. I don't suppose you have any insight on that? The Agency is somewhat tight-lipped."

Barnes frowned slightly. "I have my sources, obviously, but I'm still in the dark. With their actions to date, it seems certain that it revolves around challenging Fleet, but the details remain elusive.

"That's not helping me bring the Senate together either, I'm afraid. We're still split into factions, each one thinking they have a clearer idea of what is going on and what the Cadre's motives are than the rest. And then there's that so-called Independence Militia. That's really knocked everyone for a loop."

The Senator took a sip of his own drink. "That has some pushing to declare a number of colonies in the Outer System to be in rebellion and send Fleet in to crush them. In my view, that would be a disaster of the first order, but the notion is gaining in popularity the more outrageous the attacks become. That nuke will make the hawks scream even louder.

"My allies and I have had to resort to using the purse strings to reducing Fleet strength to pull the hawks' teeth. If they gain the upper hand, we'll have a full-blown civil war and we'll never manage to put the Commonwealth back together."

Brad felt his eyes narrowing. How could such a smart man be so blind? Yes, he was right about stopping a civil war, but how could he be gutting Fleet when the Cadre was growing in strength by leaps and bounds?

"Is that wise?" he asked softly. "We need Fleet strong because the Cadre isn't getting any weaker. Fleet didn't even bother sending a ship to Venus. 'Spread too thin,' they said. Gelding our only defense against the pirates might be worse in the long run."

Barnes shook his head. "You're wrong there, but I get your point. Recent events have forced my allies and me to exactly that realization. We're going to have to open the spigots more and stop Fleet from fading away until the Cadre is dealt with.

"One thing I just don't understand is how the hawks are sticking so closely together. They don't seem to have a clear-cut leader, but their policy suggestions and goals all seem to be aligned very closely together. It's almost as much a mystery as where the Cadre is getting all those damned warships."

Brad froze, his drink partway to his lips. "Excuse me?"

It was the Senator's turn to look surprised. "The warships the Cadre keeps throwing around. It mystifies me why we can't locate the damned shipyard building them or discover what means they have of stealing them."

Feeling his hand tremble just the slightest bit, Brad tossed back the last of his scotch and set the glass on a handy table. "Senator, I discovered who was building the Cadre ships almost two months ago. Agent Falcone headed to Earth to personally deliver that information."

The Senator blinked in shock. "No one has said a word. I mean, I'd heard she was scheduled to report something to the Senate, but her presentation was cancelled at the last moment."

"Oh, hell," Brad said grimly. "Something has gone terribly wrong."

———

Barnes listened with a furious expression as Brad recounted all the details they'd learned about Transplanetary Macro Fabrication building extra Fleet vessels for direct delivery to the Cadre. The man looked as if he wanted to pull his hair out. Brad completely understood and felt exactly the same way.

Not only had someone managed to bury the information they'd fought so hard to get—possibly burying Kate Falcone along with it—they'd kept it so quiet that Brad hadn't heard a peep. Not only that, they'd have kept delivering warships to the pirates in the meantime.

Someone there on Earth had gotten wind of what they'd discovered before Falcone had managed to tell anyone. She hadn't even told her superiors the details so that no one could leak it. Her plan had been to level the charges directly to the Senate so that no one could spin things.

He damned himself for assuming that she'd taken care of that without following up. Granted, the woman had a habit of vanishing for months at a time, but this had been critical. As many times as he'd told junior officers that they had to positively verify the important things, he'd screwed up badly this time.

The Senator rubbed his face when Brad was done. "I can see that you blame yourself, but I'm just as guilty. I assumed the Agency had shunted her off on a critical mission and never thought twice about it."

The two of them had adjourned to the dining room to eat, but Brad could barely taste the food. "We have to figure out where she was when they took her. I'm very much afraid that we may never see her again. The Cadre doesn't like leaving live enemies behind them. We also need to get the word about the shipyard to the Agency. Someone we can be sure we can trust."

"I'll handle that," Barnes said heavily. "I'll handle all of that personally and keep you updated every few days just to be sure nothing happens to me in the middle of doing so without you knowing."

"How can I help?" Brad asked. "We're here and I have to be able to contribute in some way."

Barnes shook his head. "I wish you could, but one of the things the Agency wanted me to go over with you tonight was a new mission. One that might be more important than either of us realize after Venus.

Or a bust. I wish I knew for sure, but honestly, I'm the better choice to work here. This is my second home."

That didn't sit well with Brad, but it wasn't as if he had a lot of choice. "What do they need?"

"There have been a rash of potential Cadre sightings at Ceres. Mostly ships that the Agency suspects are working for the pirates. That's not unusual, but there have been a lot of them stopping by the biggest asteroid in the Belt. That has the Agency very worried that the Cadre intends something like the nuke they detonated on Venus.

"Of course, it might be nothing, but Ceres has the largest population in the Belt. An attack like that could kill hundreds of thousands of people. Perhaps more than a million. That's not something they prefer to leave uninvestigated."

Brad rubbed the bridge of his nose. "The Agency has me running all over the place recently. Don't they have resources on Ceres?"

Barnes nodded. "This is going to sound awfully familiar, but the Agent there went silent two days ago. It's shaping up to bear an uncomfortable similarity to the situation you just came from. I'm hoping you can engineer a somewhat less explosive outcome this time."

"I hate this," Brad told Barnes. "Absolutely and completely hate it. I'm tired of chopping off the damned Cadre's tentacles only to see more pop up."

"They couldn't have pulled any of this off without access at the highest levels," Barnes said quietly. "For my part, that means I only have a small pool of suspects to sift through here. If we can capture the Cadre leader on Earth, we might be able to roll them up. Or at least figure out what their ultimate goal is."

"I'm tired of these bastards getting away with literal murder," Brad said coldly. "While you do your thing, I'll go make the Belt safe for decent people and maybe kill a few pirates while I'm at it."

CHAPTER SEVENTEEN

ALMOST SURPRISINGLY, the journey to Ceres went without incident. Unlike in the vids, the asteroid belt was almost as empty as the rest of the Solar System. One didn't see swarms of rocks zipping around.

That wasn't to say that traveling through it was without risk. Asteroids of any real size were known and their courses theoretically available. There was a Commonwealth agency based on Ceres responsible for keeping track of all those dangerous rocks on their orbits around the sun.

The problem was that their orbits changed whenever they interacted with nearby objects, like other asteroids and even distant planets. The charts needed constant updating and intense calculating to forecast an asteroid's future location.

Then there were the uncounted smaller bits of debris that had no name or number racing through the Belt, too small to bother with or occasionally even detect unless they hit a ship. They were like grains of sand shot out of a mass driver. Those were usually too small to fret about, but sometimes, even sand could wreck an instrument.

Most Belt objects traveled in the same direction of flow around the sun, like a great river of stone and ice, but there were sometimes unexpected exceptions. Those kept pilots busy around the clock while in the

Belt. Even in orbit around a large body like Ceres, since it wasn't massive enough to clear its own orbit.

Ceres was something of an outsider in the Belt. Neither fish nor fowl, as they said. Bigger than any other asteroid, it was designated as a dwarf planet. That meant it was in hydrostatic equilibrium, where it had enough mass to form a globe. It was the smallest such body in the system, the next largest being Saturn's moon Rhea.

Other than being spherical, it looked like any other asteroid they'd ever seen, only a lot bigger. Like a moon without the accompanying planet. He'd been there before but hadn't had much of an opportunity to see it like this. It had been in the aftermath of the destruction of his uncle's ship. His memory had been pretty badly messed up—and, well, once it had come back, Brad Madrid had been born and Brad Mantruso had stayed officially dead.

"Not much to look at," his wife said, echoing his thoughts as she brought *Oath* into orbit. "I'm a little at a loss as to why there's so much activity around it. Do they mine something valuable here?"

Brad smiled, having had to look that up for himself just a few hours earlier. "You might say that: water. Because it's easy to extract, they ship it all over the Inner System. Even places like Venus and Mercury. Because of Earth's gravity, it's a lot more expensive to get water there, so Ceres became the provider."

She spared him a glance that told him she thought he was pulling her leg. "Seriously? Unlike Ganymede, this place seems a little dry."

He held up his hands. "I'm being serious. The planet—which is technically the correct word for Ceres—has a rocky core with an ice mantle. The crust is material like you see on any other asteroid, but it's really thin. The ice, on the other hand, is a hundred kilometers thick.

"We're talking 200 million cubic kilometers of water in a relatively accessible form. One can process raw material from many asteroids to get water, but it's a lot cheaper to harvest it here and ship it out in exchange for other goods."

"That is a lot of water." Michelle admitted.

"More than all the fresh water on Earth," he said. "We should top off while we're here, as a matter of fact. It'll be cheaper than doing it later."

He turned his attention to the communications console. "What's the word from Ceres traffic control, Xan? Have they decided where to park us yet?"

The woman grinned. "I just got the word. We're to park near the Fleet station. Sounds a lot like when we went to Earth. They'll trust us with all our firepower in orbit, but only if Fleet is watching us."

Brad nodded, not really surprised. "Get us into place, then. I want to get down to either Ceres City or Piazzi and talk to some people. Not that I expect they're going to be all that helpful. What is the Fleet presence here, Michelle?"

Michelle consulted her console. "They have the station, a destroyer flotilla with a cruiser in command." She turned her head back toward him with a grin. "The cruiser CO is your old friend Mark Fields aboard *Freedom*. The information I have says he's gotten a promotion to Commodore and is in command of the mobile forces here."

Brad sat back and rubbed his chin. That was very interesting and potentially quite helpful. Fields had proven to be a good ally in the fight against the Cadre. It might be a better idea to drop in on him first. If anyone would help him sort out what was going on near Ceres, it was the man in command of the Fleet elements.

He'd also know who could be trusted down on Ceres and who was shady. Or if he didn't know, someone on his staff would.

In any case, it would be good to see an old friend.

––––––––

He'd planned on surprising Fields, but the man was obviously keeping track of who was in the area. The Commodore called *Oath* as Brad was just starting for his shuttle. After a brief conversation, the two agreed to meet aboard *Freedom*.

The cruiser looked much the same as the last several times Brad had come aboard, the personnel bustling around the boat bay on tasks major and minor, all somewhat obscure to those unfamiliar with warships.

Brad had a better appreciation of that now that he commanded warships of his own. He'd once thought about joining Fleet, but the Terror and the Cadre had changed his life forever.

Mark Fields was waiting for him and smiled as he extended his hand. "Welcome aboard, Commodore. It's good to see you again. Congratulations on the promotion."

Brad grinned as he shook the man's hand warmly. "Thank you, Commodore. I am proud of what my people and I have built. You haven't done so badly yourself."

The other man's smile turned a bit sour. "That's a complicated story. Shall we adjourn to my office? We have a lot to talk about, I think."

It wasn't the first time Brad had been in the man's office. Not much had changed. The furniture was still on the spartan side and there were few pictures or knickknacks.

Field's closed the hatch and gestured to one of the seats in front of the desk. "Drink?"

Brad shook his head. "Not now, thanks. I suspect I'll be headed down to the surface once I'm done here, and want to be as sharp as possible."

The Fleet officer took his seat and studied Brad. "That sounds serious. Of course, you showed up with six destroyers, so whatever is going on had to be serious. Venus?"

Brad nodded at his guess. "That leads into this. You're well informed."

"One pays attention to nuclear detonations," Fields said dryly. "And as for myself, while it might have been totally unfair of me, I immediately wondered if you'd been involved."

That made Brad laugh. "A guy uses nukes once and he's marked for life."

Several years before, Brad had been forced to use nuclear weapons captured from the Cadre—which they'd stolen from Fleet—to destroy a number of pirate weapons platforms, small stations, and ships while taking down the Terror's base.

That had gotten him into a lot of trouble and forced him to work for the Agency just to avoid going to prison forever. It didn't bother him much, since that aligned with his goals of taking the Cadre down, anyway.

Of course, he'd also been involved in *another* set of nuclear explosions recently, but he hadn't set those off himself. He'd just been there when an ally had done so.

He shook his head one last time and sighed. "Yes, I was involved. Though to be clear, I didn't set off the bomb. The Cadre blew up a hidden surface base when we tried to rescue an Agency operative they were holding. We failed, sadly. The Agency thinks they're active around Ceres too, so they sent me to do some discreet investigating."

Fields raised an eyebrow. "With six destroyers? That's as many as I have screening my cruiser. That's not precisely subtle."

Brad shrugged. "We're coming back from a job as a unit. We traveled to Earth together and now we're at Ceres. The Cadre has to expect that we're going to be heading for the Jovian Cluster as a group soon enough. If they're worried enough to stop whatever they're doing for a while, so much the better."

"I can't say that I've seen any signs of activity," Fields said. "Not that I doubt that they're here, but what kind of presence does the Agency suspect? If it all goes into the toilet, I'm the one responsible for fending them off, and forgive me for saying so, but your presence makes it much more likely that they'll do something hasty."

"I do tend to get them all excited," Brad agreed, "but that's more likely to generate an assassination attempt rather than a mass attack on Ceres. Just me and my ships being here shouldn't overly complicate your job."

Fields grinned. "You have more of an effect than you realize, Brad. I raised my ships to an elevated readiness level the moment I found out you were here, just on general principles."

Brad had no idea if Fields was joking or not. In the end, it changed nothing. He was here to do a job, and if the Cadre came at him, he'd deal with them.

"The Agency believes a number of merchant ships associated with the Cadre have been calling here in greater numbers than they'd have expected. Individually, that's not much to go on, but it looks suspicious.

"I'm here to figure out if this is part of a larger operation targeting Ceres. With Fleet strength down, the Agency is worried."

Fields nodded grimly. "They should be worried. The Cadre is a lot stronger than any of us thought, and now Fleet is barely able to protect the Inner System. The Belt isn't really part of that coverage and I've been worried that they'd pull me out of here any day. How can I help?"

"I need the names of people down in Piazzi that might get me a lead on what the Cadre-associated merchants were doing. If there's a pattern, I need to find it fast."

Fields frowned a little. "Not Ceres City? Or are you worried that someone there will remember your last visit?"

Brad shook his head with a smile. "I was only ever a missing person to them. The Agency saw that record purged, so unless I run into the social worker that I ditched, I'm fine.

"I picked Piazzi because the Agent stationed there vanished a few days before I arrived at Earth, probably after asking the same kinds of questions I'm about to ask. Unlike Venus, I want to find them alive this time. And if she got the Cadre's attention, that sounds like Piazzi might be their chosen base of operations this time."

The Fleet officer nodded. "I know some people there. One doesn't hold a position like mine without developing some familiarity with the people trading in the area. It sounds a lot like you're going to make yourself into a lightning rod. Be careful."

Brad smiled coldly. "This time, I'm ready. If lightning strikes, it won't be me getting shocked."

Armed with a name—Lily Khan, the woman in charge of one of the larger import/export companies on Ceres—Brad headed for Piazzi. In her line of work, the woman would either know about the unusual visitors or be able to refer him to someone that did.

Since they were dealing with the Cadre, Brad had Saburo and a team of troopers along. As they didn't want to stand out too much, everyone wore low-key armor under their clothes. Brad wore one of his expensive skinsuits.

As for weapons, rifles were frowned upon in Piazzi though technically not illegal, even for bonded mercenaries. In Ceres City, he'd had to argue long and hard just to retain his pistol and blade, even though the law had clearly been on his side.

With as many times as they'd run into the issue regarding weapons, Saburo had come up with a solution. It was too bad that he hadn't been able to use it on New Venice due to the legal restrictions there.

The troopers openly carried sidearms, but they also had discreet shoulder bags that wouldn't have been out of place on Earth. Inside each was a compact submachine gun and spare ammunition. On top of that, the bag was armored and could be used as a makeshift shield.

All perfectly legal for a mercenary company on Ceres, but best hidden from sight so as not to panic the locals or give too much warning to any ambushers.

Bakarne Pitts was piloting for him again while he rode down in the copilot's seat. "I hope this landing goes better than the last one," she said with a little smirk.

"Doesn't Venus count as a good landing?" he asked with a sly smile. "We did walk away from it, after all."

She laughed. "Worst good landing ever. At least our odds of being fired on here are lower. Ever been to Ceres, boss?"

"A long time ago," he said with a nod. "You could truthfully say it was a different me back then."

Brad kept his eye on the domes they were approaching. They were all clustered close together, some small but most really large. There was one in particular that sat low to the surface but covered a lot of ground. It was a different color from the rest, too. Less gray and more white.

"Which one is the spaceport?" he asked.

"The one just short of that bright one. In case you were wondering, that's not Piazzi. It's the rink."

He frowned. "The what?"

"The rink. The locals peeled back the crust and polished the surface of the ice so they could use it for recreation. People skate near the edges while the more daring residents take iceriggers out into the middle."

"You're yanking my chain."

The pilot held up a hand solemnly. "Serious as a heart attack."

Before he could answer, the communications system came to life. "Shuttle Viking One, this is Piazzi Control. You are cleared to land in pit 749. Come around the city on the heading I'm sending now."

"Viking One acknowledges, Piazzi Control," Pitt said.

That course took them right over the rink dome and Pitt rolled the shuttle enough that they could stare down through its transparent material. Sure enough, there was polished ice in there. He even saw several small craft zipping across the surface near the center.

"Unbelievable," he mumbled to himself. "I suppose it takes all kinds."

Pitt laughed. "True enough. Here we go."

The shuttle dropped down to just above the surface and slowed to a crawl, entering the spaceport dome and finally landing in the assigned pit. She shut everything down while he unstrapped.

"Stay here and keep the hatch locked," he ordered. "If things really go badly, we might be coming at a run."

"Are you expecting that level of trouble, Commodore?"

"No, but be ready in case I'm wrong."

Brad walked into the back and nodded at Saburo. "Let's go."

The Colonel dropped the ramp and started down with two of his men at his heels. Brad and the other four troopers followed.

The interior of the spaceport dome was just as busy as one might imagine. Cargo and passenger shuttles filled the pits. People in official-looking coveralls or in sometimes-garish civilian clothes moved in an ebb and flow toward unknowable destinations on unguessable tasks.

Brad noticed that most of the men favored mustaches, both large and elaborate as well as occasionally small and plain. Perhaps that was a local custom.

He shrugged and they made their way to the exit as a group, avoiding people where they could and getting clear as quickly as possible when they had to.

The corridors around the port were just as busy, but the people were focused into tight streams outbound or inbound. That let his people close up around him much more readily.

"We've got the address," Brad said. "It's close to the port, as one might expect of an import/export factor, so we can be there in just a few minutes."

Saburo was about to respond when something chimed in Brad's jacket pocket.

Without thinking, Brad reached into his pocket and pulled out a com. One that hadn't been there when he'd dressed that morning. As he stared at it, the screen lit up with an incoming call from an unlabeled number.

"Give me that," Saburo said, snatching it out of Brad's hand. "It could be a bomb."

"If it was a bomb, it wouldn't have rung," Brad said, taking it back. "It would've exploded. Someone wants to talk to me pretty bad, and now I'm curious to hear what they have to say."

CHAPTER EIGHTEEN

Brad accepted the incoming call. "Yes?"

"Zebra, Charlie, Alaska, Pluto, Sandwich, Sunshine," a male voice recited an Agency recognition code.

"Mountain, Flower, Pudding, Massage, Arrow, Candle," Brad automatically responded. "You've got my attention."

"Set the com to vibrate and keep walking. When it signals, turn right and keep going until I meet you."

Brad would've asked what he looked like, but the unknown man had already disconnected. He put the com back into his pocket and started walking.

"The missing Agent is a woman, but someone with her codes wants to meet," he told the Colonel. "We'll go forward until he signals me to turn right. He'll meet us some point after that."

"How do we know this isn't a trap?" Saburo asked softly. "The Cadre could've tortured the codes out of her."

"It's possible," Brad admitted. "All we can do is keep our eyes open."

They went farther down the corridor than he expected before the com vibrated once as they were coming up on a cross corridor.

"Turn right," Brad said.

The change in direction led them to a market where a number of small shops hawked their wares to a seemingly-jaded crowd. Still, they must do well enough to make ends meet.

As they were almost through the market, a shopkeeper with an outrageously waxed mustache called out to them. That wasn't unusual. Every shop they'd passed seemed to have someone championing the wares within.

But this man was different. He led with an Agency recognition word.

"Armstrong wouldn't be able to match the quality of my suits, sirs! Come in and get fitted for the finest garments on Ceres!"

Brad turned and walked into the shop while gesturing for most of the troopers to wait outside. The interior was larger than he expected. It had to go into the wall bordering the market. There were no customers.

The man moved a sign to indicate the shop was now closed. "Come with me."

"Not until you explain who you are and how you're connected with Ella Watson," Brad said. "And how you know those codes."

"Ella is my friend. My very, very close friend, if you know what I mean. She's ill and I'm taking you to her. She gave me those codes."

"How did she know that I was coming?" Brad asked, unmoving. "Why hasn't she contacted the Agency?"

"I'd prefer to have her explain that," the man responded. "It's complicated and I don't know the full story. She shouldn't have even have shared the codes with me, but she needed my help in making contact with you. Please."

Brad considered and shrugged. The man could've just blown them up. "Take me to her. Saburo, you're with me." He motioned for the two troopers that had followed them into the shop to remain where they were.

The man led him into the back of the shop and stopped next to a shelf holding bolts of cloth. He reached down near the floor and manipulated a catch. The entire shelf pivoted inward and revealed a narrow secret room.

It was obviously a safe room of some kind, but it had been converted to a sick room. A cot in the middle of the open area supported a frail-looking brunette woman with vaguely Asian features.

"I'll return to my shop," the man said. "If you don't mind, could you bring your two men back here and have your other soldiers move away from the area in front of my shop? I don't want to draw undue attention if anyone comes by."

Saburo nodded and started talking on his com as Brad walked to the cot and squatted beside it. The woman was Ella Watson. He'd seen her image before they'd left Earth orbit.

"Agent Watson?" he asked softly.

Her eyes slowly opened. Her gaze was unfocused and her eyelids twitched erratically as she focused on him. "Madrid?"

"That's right. What's going on?"

"We've been betrayed," she said, her voice weak. "You're in great danger."

———

"Can you tell me what happened to you?" Brad asked gently as he slid a chair closer to the cot. "Who betrayed us?"

"Poison," she rasped. "I trusted the wrong person. I'm starting to think I might survive, but I wasn't sure for the longest time."

That would explain why she looked like death warmed over. He'd have to get her back to *Oath* so that Kirabo Terzić could examine her. He might be able to speed her recovery and perhaps mitigate some of the lingering effects of the poison.

"Why didn't you contact the Agency for help?" he asked. "They must've told you or someone that I was coming to look for you. That's how you knew my name, right?"

She chuckled dryly and that started a coughing fit.

Brad found some water and held the glass so that she could sip through a straw.

Once she was able to breathe again, she shook her head slightly. "I had no idea you were coming, but I had a list of ships connected with the Agency. Your name was in the file with it, along with a summary of how you're connected with the Agency.

"If you'd been a direct Agency operative, I probably wouldn't have had Fraser make contact. Someone in the home office betrayed me. Ordered me to make contact with someone that tried to kill me. Only, I was suspicious and got local backup. They got me out before the contact could finish the job."

"Why are you so sure the home office betrayed you?" he asked. "They might not have known the contact was working for the Cadre."

The woman smiled sadly. "I called for extraction when I was clear. That was before the poison really screwed me up. I got a hit squad instead.

"Fraser was there with me and made sure I got out a hidden back way before the Cadre commandos could find me. There was no way anyone could have known I was there. It had to have been someone in the home office. Added to the bad contact, it looks as if they wanted me out of the way.

"Remember, just because you're paranoid doesn't mean that someone really isn't out to get you."

That was certainly true.

"Why trust me? I'm an Agent too. They sent me here."

"You killed the Terror and blew up his base. I feel pretty sure you're not in the Cadre's pocket. I'm out of options and you're the best shot I have of living. Of making the Cadre pay for what they did to me."

Brad leaned back a little and considered the situation. Senator Barnes wasn't a traitor; he'd stake his life on that. The very highest people in the Agency couldn't be all bad either. They might have leaks in their staffs, but they weren't traitors themselves. A good Cadre mole would never have sent him to look for Agent Watson at all. Not with his reputation.

He might still be in danger from poking his nose where it didn't belong, but that was a risk he'd willingly take.

"Who was the contact that betrayed you?" he asked.

"Lily Khan with Crystal Clear Importing. She was supposed to be an expert on who does business here. I'm sure she is, but she also poisoned me at the meeting in her office.

"I managed to call for help and my people came rushing in the back, but she is definitely dirty. It makes me mad that she got away."

Well, that was awkward, since she was the woman he was supposed to meet.

"Did you find out what the Cadre was up to before Khan poisoned you?"

"Not specifically," she said. "We were still in the initial stages of getting to know one another when she made her move. I found out later that she'd sent her staff off on various errands so that they wouldn't be there during the meeting. No doubt some Cadre bastards were supposed to take possession of me before her people got back."

It would've been helpful if the evil mastermind had shared her plan before Watson escaped, but Brad supposed that was a little melodramatic. He'd have to figure it out for himself after he got Watson safely to *Oath of Vengeance*.

He turned to Saburo. "Any sign of interest in the shop? We need to get her back to the shuttle and on the way to *Oath*."

"Not that the troopers have seen, but that hardly means much. Everyone will see us taking her out. Even if they don't, they'll wonder why we were in here. If, of course, someone was tailing us."

"If Fraser brought you here, he made sure no one was following you," Watson said. "Not successfully, in any case. Let's just say he's had a colorful career involving shady deals before he met me. He was the one that contacted the local muscle. He'd have done the same to get you here unseen."

That was interesting. Brad made a mental note to talk with the man before he made his move on Khan. Having a few trusted men that no one was aware of might come in handy when confronting a Cadre mole. And with what the woman had done to Watson, it wouldn't surprise Brad if the man wanted a little payback of his own.

"Does this shop have a secret exit?" he asked. "Since it has a secret room, that doesn't seem that much of a stretch."

She nodded tiredly. "It's not very big, but it comes out into a business he owns in the next section of the city. It was once used to fence… ah, creatively acquired goods. The underworld probably knows about it and could link it to him, but it's been closed since he retired. There's no reason that anyone would be watching it closely."

"I'll talk with him about getting you back to my shuttle without too many prying eyes," Brad said. "Once we make that happen, we'll get you to my ship so that you can get treatment."

He smiled coldly. "Then I'll go see Ms. Khan and see what she has to say for herself."

<hr>

It took Malcom Fraser an hour to make arrangements to get Agent Watson out of his shop unseen, but the process was fascinating for Brad. The man hardly looked like a criminal, but he was adept at getting the different parts of their little charade in place. It was particularly amusing that Watson would be hidden inside a box marked "carpet."

More interesting to Brad was how the man used different people for different tasks, and in such a way that no one other than him knew exactly what was going on: the people getting Agent Watson ready for transport had no idea where she was going, the people moving her up didn't know where she was coming from, and the people making sure that anyone watching the shuttle was dealt with at the appropriate time had no idea why they were doing it.

Once all the parts were coordinated, and Watson was ready to move, the man motioned for Brad to accompany him to the front of the shop. Once they were in relative privacy, he dropped another surprise on Brad.

"I think it best if you not accompany her," Fraser said.

Brad raised an eyebrow. "Why not?"

"The Cadre knows you're here somewhere. I had some old friends block the people tailing you before you got to the market, but they *were* following you. They're looking for you as we speak, though safely far away. If they see you headed for your shuttle again, they'll probably try to kill you. That puts Ella in danger.

"It's far better if you and your men leave here undetected and go to meet Khan. Someone will see you and the attention on the shuttle will relax. I even think the odds are good that the people watching it will relocate to bracket you, allowing Ella to board with no one the wiser."

That plan wasn't the straightforward kind of action Brad usually went for, but sneaky had its place. "I'll need to let my pilot know to expect her. If the Cadre team is any good at all, they'll intercept my call and know something is up."

Fraser smiled. "I have an associate about the same size and build as your Colonel Saburo. He's even of Japanese extraction. If they swap clothes, no one will likely be the wiser and your man can tell the pilot what is going on."

That certainly wouldn't make Saburo very happy, but if it worked, they'd get Agent Watson safely back to the ship. He could then gather a strike team and start bringing them down to the surface.

Or perhaps there was a better way.

"I'm given to understand that you have some familiarity with moving goods without the authorities becoming aware of them," Brad said. "Does that include conducting things from orbit to the surface?"

"You mean to ask if I was an excellent smuggler and fence before I met Ella?" Fraser asked with a smile, his jaunty mustache bristling with amusement. "Indeed, and I still have many friends in convenient places. What do you have in mind?"

"I'd like to get some troopers down without anyone knowing they've left my ships. Enough to give the Cadre an unhealthy surprise when they try to ambush me. Which they will."

The man considered that for a moment and nodded. "It will be a challenge to get the assets into place quickly, but I believe it can be done. I'll have another of my associates go up with your shuttle to coordinate the operation. I wouldn't count on them being down to help you in less than two hours, though.

"Until they are ready, I can arrange for some people with talents in that arena to assist you. Ones that won't know precisely who they're protecting, of course."

If he timed this right, he could have his troopers inside Piazzi to hit the Cadre forces while he made a run for the spaceport. Lure them into a trap for a change. That would be satisfying, if they could work the timing out.

"You certainly have interesting friends," Brad said at last, extending his hand. "Let's do this."

CHAPTER NINETEEN

FRASER SNUCK Brad and his troopers out the same way Watson had left, only five minutes later. The little passage between the two businesses dropped into the crust of the dwarf planet below the dome to make the connection. There was no ice in view, but Brad's breath puffed in the frozen air as they walked the short distance.

The shop they came out in looked like a pawn shop stripped of all its goods. For all he knew, that was exactly what it had been. The fact that it wasn't in use at the moment certainly helped in making sure no one was watching them as they departed.

The man dressed in Saburo's armor didn't really look like Brad's friend, but to someone who didn't know either of them, he was close enough. All they really needed to do was to fool those casually watching. After all, they knew who Brad was, and he was who they wanted.

"This way," the man said as they exited the dark shop. "We're about twenty minutes away from your destination."

"Lead the way," Brad ordered. "Everyone else keep an eye out for trouble."

"You won't see them, but we have scouts ahead of us and watchers behind," the man said as he set off down the corridor. It was less populated and somewhat dingier than the one where the market had been. It looked just the slightest bit seedy.

"They'll let me know if they spot anything unusual," the man continued. "There are people also watching your original tails as well as our destination."

Brad felt his eyebrows rise. "Just how well connected is your boss?"

The fake officer grinned at him. "Higher in the local hierarchy than you'd imagined, it seems. Let's just say that he wasn't the biggest fish in our little pond, but he wasn't the smallest by far. Those in charge are grateful for his skills and advice."

"If you don't mind me asking, how is it that the Cadre isn't in control here?"

The man's expression darkened. "It may not seem so from outside, but most of us do support the Commonwealth and despise the Cadre. Those people are fanatical monsters. Even the ones with a veneer of civility will slit your throat when it suits them.

"There's a sort of balance in most places. For whatever reason, the Riggio family boss didn't sign on with the Cadre the way most of that family did. The Cadre is too powerful to keep out of places like Piazzi, but there's almost a truce between the boss's boss and them. Only if they try to muscle in do they get their throats slit."

The man pressed an earbud tighter in his ear, listening to something. "They've gotten word of us, it seems. The original team just started heading our way in a hurry. We'll get to the destination before them, though."

"What about the people taking Watson to the shuttle?"

"No change there but…scratch that. They've just moved out, too. Our watchers will make certain they've all left before they proceed, but it looks as if the boss's woman will get out cleanly."

Brad smiled. It was nice when a plan actually worked the way they'd envisioned it. That seemed to be the exception rather than the rule these days.

"We'll press forward to the office," Brad decided. "What about our support team?"

"Already forming up near the destination. No one knows what's going on, and only the woman in charge—a trusted associate of ours—has a com. If we need help, they're only a minute away."

A minute could be an eternity, but that was all part of the game.

"Good enough," Brad said, lengthening his stride. "Let's go talk to a traitor."

———

They arrived at Crystal Clear Importing just ahead of their reported tails. That had to be infuriating for them.

The business looked prosperous enough. The lobby was very well appointed and seeded with comfortable chairs. The receptionist, a young man with an improbably large mustache, welcomed them with a wide smile. "How can I assist you today?"

"I'd like to speak with Lily Khan, please. My name is Brad Madrid."

The man checked his computer terminal and his smile dimmed. "Is she expecting you? I don't show an appointment for you, Mr. Madrid."

"Commodore Madrid, actually. She didn't know I was coming. Commodore Fields on *Freedom* referred me, and the matter is both urgent and confidential."

The receptionist blinked. "I'll check to see if she can make time for you. If you'd care to have a seat?"

"I'm good here, thanks."

Nonplussed, the young man half-turned and whispered into a boom microphone attached to his headset. A moment later, he nodded.

"She can see you. Will…ah, your entire party be going in?"

Brad shook his head. "I'll leave my men in the lobby. I assure you they'll stay out of the way. Colonel Saburo will accompany me."

The receptionist gave him a small shrug and buzzed a nearby door open. "If you'll step through, I'll escort you back."

Brad let the fake Saburo hold the door open and went through. The office behind the desk was a busy one. With half a dozen people in sight just from here, he couldn't imagine how Khan had gotten the place empty for the Cadre to take Watson. It certainly wouldn't be possible now that Brad had surprised her.

Whether that would stop the inevitable attack or not really depended on how important the woman was to the pirates. If she was important enough, the strike teams would have to attack after Brad finished here. If not, they might come in at any time.

He'd just have to count on his new associate to tell him if the pirates started moving.

The receptionist walked them to the rear of the building and to an office adjacent to a warehouse that had a lot more people moving cargo containers around. No way had that been cleared last time. The Cadre must've planned to come right through the front door.

The young man rapped on a door that looked like real wood. "Ms. Khan? Commodore Madrid to see you."

"Send him in, Wally," a husky tenor called out.

The young man opened the door and gestured for Brad to enter. This was it. Things might just get very exciting in the next few minutes. If Brad played his hand right, he could find out exactly what the Cadre was up to. If not, he might end up dead.

———

Lily Kahn turned out to be an attractive older woman with a swarthy complexion. She stepped up to Brad as he came into the office with her hand extended. "I'm not sure how I can help you, Commodore, but I'm always ready to assist Fleet."

He noted she had a firm grip. Not hesitant at all.

"I'm not with Fleet, but Commodore Fields is an old friend. He told me that if anyone could help me clear up a mystery, it was you."

"Well," she said with a smile as she closed the door. "That certainly sounds enigmatic. If you and your associate will have a seat, I'll make us some tea."

Brad sat and shook his head. "I just had something, so I'll pass on any refreshment. Thank you."

The man pretending to be Saburo also declined, so Khan took a seat behind her desk, probably disappointed that she couldn't poison them.

"I've got a busy schedule, but I can spare you a few minutes. What mystery are you trying to solve, Commodore?"

"The Cadre is active around Ceres, or so several sources inform me," Brad said as he crossed his legs. "I have a deep interest in the doings of pirates, and I'm told you might offer unique insight on their activities."

He thought he saw a shadow of a twitch before the woman shook her head slightly. "I'm not sure how I'd know that. Could you perhaps be more specific?"

Brad smiled a bit at her well-concealed discomfiture. "Certainly. I've got the names of several merchant ships known to work with the Cadre. They've been here a number of times in the last few months, and I'd like your professional assessment of what they might have been doing.

"Of course, you wouldn't know what they were doing behind the scenes, but they had to have cover cargos. I'd like to know what they claimed to have been delivering and taking back out of Ceres, as well as where they claimed to be going. Commodore Fields said to tell you he'd credit you with a favor for your help."

Without waiting for her to actually agree, he placed a data chip onto the desk and slid it over to her. He wanted to keep her off balance.

"I'll see what I can find," she said after a beat. "As one of the major import-export dealers, I have privileged access to the records other than our own, but not into the specific cargos delivered. That would be a violation of my competitors' proprietary business practices.

"That said, there are usually general cargo manifests listed. Basic categories of goods being brought in. The exports are a lot easier. It won't be anything other than water or something based on water."

She focused—or pretended to focus anyway—on her screen after she slid the chip into her computer. "These ships have fairly generic cargos listed. None of them used Crystal Clear, so all I can tell you is that there doesn't seem to be a pattern in what they brought in.

"I see everything from basic foodstuffs to luxury items listed here. The destinations they listed with traffic control when they departed are all over the map. I'm sorry, but it seems that I haven't been all that helpful."

The woman gave him a slightly sad look and slid the data chip back to him. "If that's all, I really must be getting back to my work. I can give you the name of someone that might possibly be able to give you more information, if that would help."

"That would be very kind," he said, already knowing that she likely planned to have him ambushed on the way to a dead end. It made life so much simpler when one knew someone else was a snake.

She jotted the name and address of another business down on a card and handed it to him as she stood. "I wish I'd been able to help you more. Good luck in tracking them down. Pirates are disgusting and make life so much more difficult for honest people in my line of work."

He couldn't agree more.

Brad slid the card into his pocket and extended his hand. "You've helped me more than you realize, and you still might be able to clear up one little thing up for me."

The woman frowned slightly as she shook with him. "How so?"

"Perhaps you could explain why you poisoned Ella Watson and what exactly you do for the Cadre."

CHAPTER TWENTY

KHAN TRIED TO JERK BACK, but Brad kept a firm grip on her hand. As he'd noted earlier, she was surprisingly strong. She reacted with a credible punch for his face, which he deflected with his free hand.

"Don't make me shoot you, Ms. Khan," he said calmly. "And don't scream. I'd hate to see you shot in the middle of a scrum with the Cadre hit team you have outside the building."

"You're making a terrible mistake, Commodore," she said, her eyes hard. "I can't imagine who told you this fairy tale, but they're wrong."

He allowed a chill smile to cross his lips. "Ms. Watson told me. This may come as a disappointment to you, but you didn't give her enough poison to kill her. She survived and pointed the finger right at you just before I smuggled her back to my ship. I'd imagine she's docking right about now."

Brad was pleased to see a hint of fear in the woman's eyes. She might be a good actress, but she wasn't *that* good. She knew he had her and that she'd pay the ultimate price.

Of course, that wasn't conducive to getting her cooperation. Falcone had taught him that lesson when they'd first met. Pirates might warrant spacing, but if you gave them another choice, they could occasionally be convinced to spill their guts, to turn on their fellows like a pack of wild dogs.

"I see it in your eyes now," he said softly. "You know what's coming. Payback for all the evil you've helped commit. It doesn't really matter what form it takes. I could take you to my flagship and space you. Or I could simply shoot you here and now."

As a mercenary commander, that was outside his jurisdiction. He'd have had to catch her in space, committing piracy or transporting slaves. As an Agent of the Commonwealth, though, he could do what he needed to do and explain himself later. As they said, it was occasionally easier to beg forgiveness than to ask permission.

The woman's eyes narrowed. "I hear a *but* in there. I can change my fate, but only if I help you. What are you offering?"

"I've already told you what I want. I'll also need a full and unredacted copy of all your data, as well as your complete and enthusiastic cooperation in telling me everything you know about the Cadre and what it's doing both here and elsewhere in the system."

She raised her chin. "And what do I get in exchange?"

"Life in prison with no possibility for parole," he said coldly. "A far better fate than you deserve."

"I don't want to go to the mines on Mercury," she insisted. "If you want my willing cooperation, you'll have to promise me something on Earth or Mars."

Brad sighed. He really hated smart pirates. "Agreed. We'll talk while my associate looks at your computer. I'd like to see if you lied to us a few minutes ago. It makes no sense for the Cadre-affiliated merchants to use a different import/export house when they have you."

The fake Saburo—Brad really should've gotten the man's name—moved to the desk and started tapping on the keyboard.

"Of course they went through me," Khan said with a sneer. "Would you just let go of my hand? Put me in a chair or stand me in a corner, whatever makes you feel safe, mister brave mercenary."

"Drag the chair in front of your desk out into the open space," he said. "Don't try anything or I'll shoot you and be done with it."

"So gentlemanly," she said in a sweet tone that didn't mask the nastiness underneath. "It must be horrible, being afraid of a little woman like me. How do you manage to fight real pirates without soiling yourself?"

Brad didn't rise to her bait, so she dragged the guest chair out into the open and sat primly on it.

"It looks like her company did the work for the pirates," the man at her desk said. "They brought in ore, though. No listed points of origin. They also didn't take water or any of its potential derivatives. It says here that they bought refined tungsten.

"There are some refineries that supply that kind of thing here. They use ore from all the surrounding asteroids to make it and a host of other materials."

That was odd, Brad had to admit. "What did they need that for?" he asked Khan.

She shrugged elaborately. "I was instructed to get them, not told what they were for. It cost a pretty penny, though. Came right out of my budget."

"How much are we talking about?"

"The ingots weighed a few tons each. All told, I moved about a gross. That's a dozen dozen for the uninformed. One hundred and forty-four."

What in blazes could they be using the expensive material for? They wouldn't have made that kind of investment without an ultimate plan for it, but he couldn't see much in the way of potential nefarious schemes at the moment.

The com on the desk buzzed and a stud on the built-in console blinked blue.

Khan raised an eyebrow at him. "That's Wally. If I don't answer, the sweet boy will get worried and come back to check on me."

"Answer it," Brad decided. "Be brief and don't get clever."

The woman rose to her feet, reached over the desk, and touched the stud. "Yes?"

"Just reminding you that Mr. Lloyd will be here for his appointment in twenty minutes, ma'am," the receptionist said.

"Hold on a second, Wally," she said, pressing the button and setting the stud to blinking again while the call was on hold. "Shall I tell him to cancel it?"

"Yes," Brad said. "You really don't want someone rushing me right now."

She pressed the stud again. "My meeting with Commodore Madrid is going to run long. Please call Mr. Lloyd and see if he can reschedule. Give him my apologies and tell him that I'll make it up to him."

"Will do," the young man said. The lighted stud went dark.

"That will clear the next hour and a half from my schedule," Khan said as she straightened. "I can cancel the rest of my afternoon meetings before they come due."

Brad nodded. "That should give us enough time to settle our business." He gestured for her to resume her seat.

Khan sat with a languid grace, keeping to the edge of her seat and leaning forward toward him. "I've heard a lot about you from people in my organization, Commodore. They say you're a dangerous foe. I wonder if your reputation is overblown."

"I caught you, didn't I?"

Out of the corner of his eye, Brad saw the door open and Wally step in, a shotgun raised and a grim expression on his face as he swung it to bear.

With his well-honed reflexes, Brad dropped down to the floor even as he drew his pistol. The blast of pellets missed him for the most part. A few struck his armored skinsuit, but it easily deflected the impacts.

Wally got off another shot just as Brad put a trio of slugs into his chest, sending the receptionist stumbling back out the door to fall against the wall in a bloody heap.

Khan hadn't wasted a single second and was already pulling a slender handgun from the bookshelf she'd thrown herself toward while Brad was busy. Her expression mirrored that of her henchmen, coldly furious as she brought the handgun around and started squeezing the trigger.

Brad rolled and returned her fire. Once again, his armor took the hits, and she failed to tag him on exposed flesh. Her dress was spectacularly less effective against his bullets. One of them struck her in the face, ending the confrontation abruptly and costing him his hard-won source of information.

The fight hadn't been a quiet one, and now Brad could hear people in the office screaming and running. Wise move on their parts. He could also hear the rapid approach of booted feet. He hoped that was his people rather than the Cadre hit squad.

Moments after he took cover behind the desk, his troopers raced in, their submachine guns up and tracking for threats. They relaxed marginally when Brad rose.

"The Cadre will be here in a minute," Brad said. "We need to get the hell out of here and call for backup." The last was said toward the man pretending to be Saburo.

When he didn't get a response, Brad turned and found that the man was sprawled behind the desk with half of his head missing. He obviously hadn't managed to duck that second shot as quickly as he'd needed to.

Brad knelt beside the corpse and retrieved his com. The earbud was gone, likely disintegrated, but he could probably make the call for help from the screen.

Or he would've been able to if the damned thing hadn't been locked.

"We won't have timely backup," Brad said as he rose to his feet, pocketing the com. "We need to get the hell out of here. Secure a way out through the warehouse. Don't shoot anyone that doesn't shoot at you first."

While most of his men moved out, Brad plugged his chip into the computer and started it copying the records that the dead man had been accessing. They all seemed to relate to the pirate ships that had been calling on Ceres, so perhaps there was a clue buried in there that would tell him what their game was.

As the computer copied the data, he stripped the dead man of Saburo's weapons and bag. It would give him better firepower than his pistol. He wished he could take the man with him, but they'd have more than enough trouble escaping the Cadre as it was. Besides, hauling a dead body around would certainly draw a lot of negative attention.

The computer chimed, done with the operation. Brad pocketed the chip, headed out the door, and moved into the warehouse as he extracted his submachine gun. Unlike earlier, the place was abandoned, the workers fled. His scouts had already secured an exit normally used for large cargo haulers.

If any of his people had had skill with the massive transports, he'd have considered stealing one. As it was, they'd have to secure something else.

He triggered his com as he moved out of the building and into an industrial section of Piazzi. "*Oath*, this is Madrid. Come in."

"*Oath* here, Commodore," Xan said. "Go ahead."

"We're blown and I've lost communication with our backup. Get the man Fraser sent up to call them and give them my contact code. And send Saburo down openly. We'll be coming into the spaceport hot, I suspect."

"Copy that. He just docked a few minutes ago. He says he'll be there in thirty minutes and to keep your heads down until then."

That worked, so long as they could keep dodging the Cadre killers on their trail. "Keep me in the loop. Madrid out."

He'd have been tempted to call the local police if he hadn't seen what that cost back on New Venice. The safest thing for everyone was for him to get off Ceres or deal with the Cadre himself.

"We need transport," Brad told the senior trooper. "Preferably two vehicles. We don't have long to get them, either."

To punctuate his point, he could hear sirens in the distance as Piazzi security responded to the gunfire. If he let them pin him and his people, the Cadre could kill everyone with impunity. They had to vanish into the population and pop up only once they got to the spaceport.

Sadly, the only vehicle in sight was a mobile food truck that served the workers in the area. He'd heard them called "roach coaches" before because of the supposed quality of the dining, though he had no personal opinion. The vehicle had speakers on the roof, playing some kind of instrumental music that sounded Latin to his ears.

"Beggars can't be choosers," Brad said with a sigh. "Secure that vehicle and get the civilian out of here, Corporal."

The man running the counter behind a sliding window in the side of the truck saw them coming and tried to get back to the front of his vehicle, but the troopers beat him to it.

They pulled him out of the truck and sent him running as Brad and the rest piled into the back of the truck. A trooper then got behind the wheel and started it forward at the best speed the vehicle could manage.

"Keep it down to something reasonable," Brad ordered. "With any luck, we'll be able to drive away without anyone knowing we're even in here."

That, of course, was when someone opened fire behind them with an automatic weapon. Slugs began puncturing the rear wall and door, sending pots, pans, and troopers flying. The Cadre had found them.

CHAPTER TWENTY-ONE

BRAD LEANED out the still-open window and returned fire. On the move like they were, with his driver swerving to throw off the attacker's aim and using a short-barreled weapon like a submachine gun, his chances of hitting anything were low indeed, but perhaps the fire would get the enemy to duck.

He missed, as expected, but saw three men in dark clothes scrambling for cover. They'd just come from the warehouse, so they wouldn't be able to pursue on foot. They also weren't the entirety of the hit squad, he was sure. Not with teams covering him and the spaceport combined.

That would be at least a dozen attackers. Probably more. They'd be either securing their own rides or, more likely, getting to the vehicles they already had on standby. Brad was sure they had some vehicles waiting, but he had no access to them.

His com sounded as they roared around the corner on two wheels, losing the immediate pursuit. He didn't recognize the number but assumed it had to be their local support.

"Madrid."

"Goodness, but you do love to put on a show," a woman said. "I take it Tanaka didn't make it."

Tanaka must be the man who'd been masquerading as Saburo. "I'm afraid not. We're in a food truck making a run to the…south, it looks like. We ditched three shooters at the back of the warehouse and we're angling for the spaceport."

"Bad call," the woman said. "Security is coming from that direction, I'd wager. That's where the rapid response teams are staged. You need to go east at least half the dome before you cut over.

"That'll also give you a chance at evading the bad guys. They're swarming out of the import/export building, so I can't be sure what direction they'll end up going. Any space between you and them is a good thing, though."

"Go east," Brad ordered the driver before returning his attention to the com. "We don't have them in sight at the moment, so it's possible we'll lose them. Can you meet us?"

"We're loading into vehicles right now. You have my number now. Call me if they find you before we do."

He put his com away when she disconnected and leaned out the window far enough to see if anyone was behind them. The road looked clear.

"Is everyone okay?" he asked.

"Only one hit, sir," a trooper said. "A pot fell on Ricky, but his head is too hard for it to have hurt much."

"You're an ass," the targeted trooper said when his comrades laughed. "I'm fine, sir."

Well, better a little horsing around than someone dead on the floor.

"Be ready," Brad said, chuckling. "If the bad guys find us, they'll come in hard and fast."

Just as soon as he said that, two security cars with lights on and sirens howling raced past from ahead of them. They didn't even slow at the sight of the food truck, as far as Brad could tell.

That was a good sign. The big vehicle wasn't what they associated with gunmen, so they didn't see it as a threat. He had little hope those cars would run into the Cadre and stop them, though. The pirates were very skilled at getting in and out of places they shouldn't have been without raising any eyebrows.

His pessimism was rewarded a few minutes later when a low-slung vehicle with an open top skidded around the corner behind them, swerving to follow the food truck closely. The man in the rear of the car rose, shouldering a rocket launcher of some kind.

Brad put a burst of submachine gun fire into him and then emptied his magazine into the driver. At this closer range, his shots were devastatingly effective, and the vehicle instantly lost speed and veered into a parked car.

The crash was spectacular, and the only thing that made it past the pileup was the rocket launcher bouncing down the pavement of the corridor.

"That's torn it," he said. "We'll have company shortly. Driver, look for a good place to turn off this corridor."

He called their backup and told her where they were, ending with the fact that the pirates knew where they were.

"We'll hit the larger set of attackers before they get close to you," the woman assured him. "I think the group originally at the spaceport is in front of you, though. You'll need to dodge them. Turn left on the next major cross corridor. That'll get you somewhere they won't be looking for you. If they do, there's a handy escape route."

"Copy that. Madrid out." He gestured for one of the troopers to cover the window in his place, stepped up to the driver's cab, and dropped into the passenger seat.

"Turn left up here," Brad ordered the driver. "It's supposed to lead someplace they won't expect us to run to."

The man did as ordered, and Brad almost immediately saw why the pirates wouldn't expect him to run there. The corridor ended in a parking area just ahead of them that serviced the largest surface of polished ice Brad had ever seen.

Their guide had directed them to the rink, and he couldn't see any way his people could run. He was about to order the driver to turn around when a trooper in the back called out that they had company.

They were trapped.

———

Brad scanned the parking lot ahead of them with dismay. This was a freaking tourist destination and it was packed with innocent people. If they confronted the Cadre there, it would end in a bloodbath. What the hell had that woman been thinking?

He frantically looked at their options and finally saw a way to get clear. At the end of the parking lot was a pier. At the end of that was a dock filled with iceriggers, most with jaunty, brightly colored sails that couldn't possibly be for anything other than show inside the dome. If they could get one of those, they could get out onto the ice and away from these people.

"Go right up to the pier," he ordered the driver. "Everyone be ready to hustle. Weapons back in your bags. The less we stand out and the faster we move, the less likely we are to cause a panic."

Brad slid his weapon back into Saburo's bag and clenched the door's armrest as people dodged out of the way of the speeding food truck, shouting and shaking their fists. As soon as they reached the pier, Brad jumped out and looked back the way they'd come.

An open-topped vehicle like the one he'd shot up was just pulling into the parking lot. The two men in it were standing up and watching him, grins spread across their faces.

The passenger was jabbering into his com, so Brad knew the rest of the pirates would be there soon enough. Time to move along.

"Down the pier," he ordered when the pirates seemed disinclined to get any closer. "They probably haven't realized we have a way out yet. Let's try to be gone before they figure out how wrong they are."

As a group, they set out down the crowded pier. It was packed with families. If the pirates had followed him, he'd have been inclined to surrender without firing a shot just to spare the kids around him.

Thankfully, he didn't have to make that decision just yet.

He and his men drew some odd looks as they abandoned the food truck and headed down the pier, but no one tried to stop them. The closest sections of the pier seemed to be filled with overpriced food stands and booths with games of chance that were probably heavily rigged in favor of the operators.

The iceriggers were farther out over the ice, situated on smaller arms that came out from the main pier. Many of them looked like private vehicles, but there were some for rent. A bargain at any price, he was sure.

His com sounded, so Brad answered after seeing it was the contact. "Did you really have to send us directly into all these people?"

"We took out the main group already," she objected. "No way they'd attack in public like that."

"You don't know how much the Cadre hates me. We're out on the pier and we're about to get an icerigger from someone. Possibly at gunpoint."

"No need," she said. "Look for a rental place near the end of the pier called Roscoe's and you'll see a big guy with a shaved head. That's the man himself. He'll get you into one with a driver, since I'd imagine you're a little lacking in ice skating skills."

"You could say that," Brad admitted. "Then what? We ride around until what's left of the Cadre hit squad comes after us?"

"You'll only have to deal with the folks that originally came from the spaceport. They can't have too many heavy weapons. The driver will get you to another exit from the rink that's close to the spaceport. At that point, you're in the hands of your people. Good luck."

The woman disconnected and Brad put the com away. He strode forward until he saw the icerigger rental she'd told him about. A large man matching her description was standing there. He waved cheerily at Brad.

"Some more vehicles just pulled up," one of the troopers said. "They're coming onto the pier."

"And we're leaving," Brad said. "Come on."

Now the race was on to see if they could lose the Cadre out on the ice and get to the spaceport before the pirates cut off their only means of escape.

———

The big man motioned for Brad and his people to climb into the nearest icerigger. "I'm Roscoe. Better if I don't hear any names from you, I think."

In seconds, they were all in the icerigger, and Roscoe had tossed two lines off and brought the controls to life. He adroitly applied power and sent the vehicle out onto the ice at a speed high enough to get some distance from the pier but slow enough not to capture anyone else's attention.

The sound of the large metal blades cutting into the ice was like the one time Brad remembered going ice skating, only a million times more intense. The temperature out over the ice plummeted and he dearly wished he had a thick jacket and gloves like Roscoe.

The remains of the Cadre hit team arrived at the icerigger rental a minute later, but Brad's fleeing craft was out of weapons range by then. Their armed presence had caused a panic and people were screaming and running. Some fell out onto the ice, but no one seemed seriously injured.

"Put on some speed," Brad told Roscoe. "They're getting into your other icerigger."

That convinced the man to speed the craft up smoothly until it was racing over the smooth surface. The cold was even more biting with the increased speed.

Behind them, the pirates had decided they knew enough to give chase without coopting a bystander to drive for them. That was a blessing. Brad wouldn't have to worry about killing some poor bastard when the fight came.

"I was told you knew of a different way to get to the spaceport," Brad said. "Is that true?"

The man nodded. "Sure. They have to have a way to pump the water to the cargo shuttles at the port. It comes from a heated zone way down under the rink. I can get you to the tunnel serving those pipes."

"Can you beat the pirates there?"

"You mean the buggers chasing us? Certainly, supposing they don't just flip the rigger and kill themselves first."

Brad had to admit the pirates weren't performing all that well.

"The sail is for show, right? How does this thing move?"

"It uses the same kind of gravity control they use in flyers back on Earth. Rather than lifting us, they propel us forward with speed. The ice doesn't have much friction, so it doesn't take much."

Brad checked his wrist-comp. Saburo wouldn't get there in time to provide any covering fire. They were going to have to keep the pirates occupied for a bit before they made a run for the spaceport tunnel.

"Is it just me or are they speeding up?" one of the troopers asked.

The enemy icerigger was getting closer, Brad had to admit. He took a moment to scan the area around them and was pleased to see that only a couple of other iceriggers were anywhere close. If this came to a fight, he wouldn't be risking a lot of people.

"How maneuverable is this thing?" Brad asked the driver.

"See those straps? They're there to keep people from being thrown off the rigger during risky maneuvers. And inexperienced fellows have been known to flip a rigger when they did something particularly perilous. Why?"

Brad grinned. "Have you ever heard of a game called chicken?"

CHAPTER TWENTY-TWO

ROSCOE STARED at Brad in alarm. "Of course I know what chicken is. Have you lost your mind? We can get away from them!"

"And we probably will," Brad said levelly, "but they're not showing any signs of losing control. Someone over there has figured things out, but if we make them do something like dodging, what happens to them?"

"They'll probably overcorrect," the man said immediately. "Everyone without experience does the first few times. That's why it's critical to have someone seasoned at your elbow when learning the ice."

The man seemed to consider that for a few seconds. "That'll be ugly. The steering blade will tip them over for sure, and that'll be fatal at this speed. But why not just try to beat them to the tunnel?"

Brad hugged himself in the cold. "Because they have antivehicle weapons and we don't. Imagine what happens if they get close enough to hit us with a rocket."

"If we turn around, they'll sure as hell be in range!"

"They almost certainly don't have experience with vehicular fighting. We'll close the range before they understand how fast that'll happen. Those kinds of weapons have to go a certain distance before they arm.

"If we come around and charge them, we cut that distance fast. Even if they fire it at us, it won't go off. If we keep running, they'll get a comfortable range and start shooting explosive munitions at us. If we run out of space and try to get off the ice, they'll blow us to pieces."

Roscoe cursed. "Tell your people to hang on. A close hit might make me lose control."

The man sent their icerigger into a wide turn as Brad warned his people and then held on himself, watching the pirates behind them. The enemy vessel corrected course to keep coming directly at the fleeing vessel, but they didn't seem to grasp that this was a significant course change yet.

While this was different from a space battle, Brad could see the maneuver playing out in his head. The range was closing slowly now, though a bit faster than before, but that would change quickly.

"You'll need to vary your speed in an unpredictable manner," Brad told Roscoe. "And don't stay on a constant course that they can predict."

"I better get combat pay for this," the man grumbled. "Security is going to grill me, I'll end up losing one or both iceriggers, and I could die!"

"We can fix everything except you dying, so I suggest you focus on that part."

Brad turned to his troopers. "Get your weapons out, men. Wait for my order and then open fire when I say. It'll be at the closest pass, so it'll happen fast."

He checked his weapon and satchel. He'd emptied the magazine he'd fired earlier, but there were five more in the satchel.

Brad swapped out the spent magazine for a full one and waited. Roscoe was jigging course and varying their speed, but there was only so much he could do. A miss was still likely to be a close one.

Worse, since his enemies were unskilled at this kind of thing, bad luck could convert what would've been a near miss into a hit. Or a miss forward of the icerigger might wreck the ice and cause them to flip.

If he'd been in the pirates' shoes, that's what he'd have done: tried to put a crater in front of the target vessel. Hopefully, these people weren't that smart.

Of course, they might not even have a rocket launcher. Sometimes, the Everlit smiled on them.

"I see a rocket launcher on the bow," one of the troopers called out.

So much for positive thinking.

Brad saw the man setting up for his shot, lying down on the deck to get the most stable shot. It looked as if he might have some skill in firing the weapon, curse the luck.

"Punch the speed as high as you can," Brad ordered their driver. "Hang on, everyone!"

The icerigger bucked a little as it jumped forward, gaining maybe ten percent more speed moments before the rocket launcher fired.

The bright missile raced across toward them, falling behind the icerigger after that last burst of speed. It passed maybe twenty meters back and hit the ice off to their left rear. It didn't explode, though. The rocket simply bounced off the ice at a flat angle and went clattering across the surface.

"Looks like it was set for impact detonation, sir," one of the men said. "There wasn't enough of a hit to trigger it. Someone is going to have a fun time defusing that."

Their icerigger was now arcing in toward the enemy. The next shot was going to be easier for the rocketeer.

"Roscoe, when I give you the word, I want you to go as hard to the right as you safely can, then straighten out when you're going right at them. Men, half on each side. Be ready to fire when they dodge off our course."

"What do I do if they don't?" the man demanded.

"Brace for impact. I wouldn't worry about it too much. If they don't break first, we won't have time to do more than twitch, anyway."

He focused his attention on the enemy gunner and positioned himself on the driver's left. When he thought the man was about ready to fire, Brad tapped Roscoe on the shoulder. "Now!"

The second rocket flared toward them just after Roscoe turned them. The projectile had a small arc this time and hit the ice where they would've been if they'd maintained course and speed.

The rocket detonated, blowing ice in every direction in a hail of deadly fragments. Brad ducked his head but otherwise used his body to shield Roscoe. A couple of pieces of ice slammed into him hard, making him grunt, but they didn't penetrate his armored skinsuit.

Now their icerigger was on a direct course for the enemy and the range spooled down at an insane rate. The rocketeer might get one more shot off, but it wouldn't have the travel time to arm.

"Fire on my command," Brad said, aiming at the rapidly approaching icerigger. "Three… two…"

The rocket launcher fired, sending the munition right at them. For a moment, Brad thought the rocket would hit the icerigger's hull, but it cleared the front by the narrowest of margins, flashing to Brad's left close enough to singe him with burning propellant.

A muffled impact and a yell told him that it had hit something, but since he was still breathing, he knew that it hadn't exploded.

Brad saw the woman piloting the other icerigger. Her eyes were wide with sudden fear and she yanked her controls to her right—his left—hard.

"On the left, fire," he ordered.

Roscoe was more adept than Brad had given him credit for, managing to jink to the right when he saw how things were playing out. The other icerigger passed only a few meters away and was already flipping as it went by.

Brad emptied his magazine into the enemy icerigger as it raced past, but he suspected that he'd only hit the hull. He pivoted and watched the other vessel tumble and come apart, scattering wreckage and bodies across the ice.

With a grin, he turned and clapped a hand on Roscoe's shoulder. "Well done! Let that be a lesson to you about the value of keeping your nerve. If we ever form an icerigger combat team, you're on it."

"To the Everdark with that!" the man averred. "You people are crazy!"

"Commodore, we lost one of the men," a trooper said. "The rocket hit him and he went over the side."

"Take us around," Brad ordered. "We'll pick up our man and then we'll see if any pirates survived the crash."

Roscoe killed much of their speed and brought them back around.

Even before they'd made it to the fallen trooper, Brad could see that the man was alive and on his feet, sort of. He was trying to stand on the ice and kept falling.

"Come alongside and we'll pull him up," Brad told Roscoe.

The icerigger slowed and came to a stop next to the trooper. Some of his fellows pulled him aboard. His armored helmet had a burned dent on the side, telling of a glancing blow from the rocket. The man was lucky the hit or the fall hadn't broken his neck.

"It's Ricky!" one of the men shouted. "That hard head saved him again!"

Everyone laughed, including Brad. "Get him on the deck. He probably has a concussion. Now let's go see if we can find a live pirate."

———

The crash of the other icerigger had torn it completely apart and scattered its remains along a wide swath of ice. Without appropriate footgear, it took a short while to locate all the pirates. None were still breathing.

He called Saburo while they searched. "We took out the Cadre team without losing anyone, but we're not going to be able to get to the spaceport before security catches up with us. Even if we did, they'd never let us take off. We'll wait here for them."

"I'm glad to hear that you're alive," Saburo said. "Not that it's going to save you from some ribbing when we finally spring you. If we do."

"Call Commodore Fields and see if he can bring some pressure to bear. Also have Michelle contact Senator Barnes. Either he or the Agency might be able to influence the situation, too."

"Good luck," the Colonel said. "I'll be in touch as soon as I can."

They'd just finished their search when Piazzi Security arrived in an icerigger of their own. All four of them.

Brad knew more would be coming, so he had his people put their weapons down and surrender. Somehow, he didn't think the fact they'd been defending themselves was going to carry a lot of weight.

And he was right. The security officers secured them with binders and searched them closely, finding a surprising array of weapons his men had "forgotten" to put down.

When one of the security officers demanded to know what had happened, Brad declined to elaborate. "This isn't a simple story. I think it's best if I wait until I'm back at your station and talking to whoever is going to end up investigating this fiasco."

"You *think*?" the uniformed woman demanded. "There are dead people scattered all over Piazzi and you *think* you'll just hold off on explaining yourself?"

Brad smiled blandly. "That's what I just said."

The woman tried to stomp off but slid on the ice and fell. Rising, she cursed the ice and probably him, too, before waving over an approaching icerigger filled with more security officers.

"Take this trash back to the station. He's not talking other than telling me he's a mercenary. As if that's going to save his ass."

————

An hour later, Brad was handcuffed to a table in an interrogation room with a nice big one-way mirror in front of him. No doubt there would be a number of interested parties on the other side watching as he was grilled.

The door opened and a tall woman in a rumpled suit came in with a thick folder of papers in her hand. She said nothing as she sat across from him and set the folder between them. She just stared at his face, her expression neutral.

They sat like that for over a minute, with him allowing the silence to drag on. Falcone had told him that people she was questioning often couldn't stand the quiet, needing to fill the void with something. In some cases, even the most amazing admissions.

He wasn't going to let the woman spook him in the opening rounds. This wasn't going to be a pleasant conversation, but he'd do as much of it as he could on his terms.

"Goodness, but you sure know how to throw a party," the woman said at last. "A total of twenty-three people dead, a number of vehicles and other property destroyed—including an import/export business with attached warehouse—and all within a few hours of your arrival here in Piazzi.

"What would you manage with a few days to work up a good head of steam, Commodore Madrid? If you can earn rocket launchers in a few hours, do you get nukes if you wait a few days?"

Brad allowed her a small smile, more than a bit uncomfortable with how close that assessment had been to reality recently. "To be fair, they came looking for me. I just did what I had to do to get my people safely clear, Detective…"

"Lieutenant Pearson," she said. "That might not sound like much compared to your own lofty rank, but I'm big enough around here. Are you going to tell me what you think happened, or are you going to stall me like you did Patrolwoman Leeds?"

"I'll tell you everything," he assured her. "Starting with the fact that I didn't come looking for trouble. Someone else decided to bring heavy hardware to the party. We just tried to stay alive while we ran."

She gave him a sardonic look and leaned back in her chair. "Did it perhaps occur to you that you should call security? That we should've come in to stop these people?"

Before he could answer, she opened the folder and started spreading pictures of death and destruction. The Crystal Clear Importing building, now burned to the ground, the wrecked vehicle that had attempted to intercept the food truck, another several vehicles —all wrecked and burned—that he'd never seen before but assumed were what was left of the main strike force after his allies had dealt with them, and then the wrecked icerigger.

"Twenty-three dead strangers, all armed," she said slowly. "We recovered rocket launchers and other heavy weapons, too. They blew a hole in the ice trying to take you out after you waltzed through a crowd of people to hijack your own icerigger."

So, that was how Roscoe was playing it. Not that he blamed the man for throwing him under the bus.

"We didn't exactly know we were going to run into the rink," he said truthfully. "If I'd known, I'd have found another path. These are Cadre pirates and this isn't the first time they've attacked me recently. On New Venice, they blew up a police van and killed seven heavily armed officers. I wasn't about to let more innocent people walk into that kind of thing."

Without mentioning Agent Watson or her underworld lover, Brad recited the short version of events that had brought him into conflict with the Cadre on Ceres. He had barely started when he saw her openly skeptical expression, but powered on to the end of the story.

"So, you just happened to go right to the importer that was working for the Cadre?" she asked, her tone letting him know she didn't buy that at all.

"Sometimes, luck is bad," he admitted.

"Let's say that I believe everything you've told me—which I don't. That still doesn't excuse what you did. You and your men are going to Hoth for this, and you can take that to the bank."

"Hoth?"

"Our maximum security prison. It's way down in the ice under Ceres City. Only one way in and no prisoners ever come back out."

Brad certainly hoped that wasn't the case, but he supposed it was possible the Agency would wash their hands and let him go down.

"If you want any chance of avoiding that," the Lieutenant continued, "you'll tell me who else was involved. Even with your timeline, there are a lot of bodies that you couldn't have left behind, based on street cameras.

"There were a number of other people in stolen vehicles that ambushed fifteen people before vanishing back into Piazzi. Who are they and why did they get involved with you? Or are they your people and still on the loose?"

He was a bit at a loss as to explaining Fraser's people. He wouldn't give them up, though.

"Not us, as you say. I can't explain who they are."

Pearson leaned forward and poked her finger onto an image of the dead. "Can't or won't? That's the thread I'm going to use to unravel your entire series of lies, Commodore. That's the little detail that's going to see you on ice for life."

A sharp rap at the door earned the Lieutenant's wrath. She stood, strode over to the door, and yanked it open. "What?"

A gentleman in a suit stood between two security officers with lots of ribbons and various metal tabs that Brad suspected meant very high rank.

"This interview is over," the man said. "Commodore Madrid is being released into my custody and this case is closed. A pirate attack dealt with swiftly by a visiting mercenary and his company."

"Bullshit," Pearson growled. "I've got them cold and no one is covering this up."

"Let it go, Pearson," one of the security men said. "He had authorization to do this from the highest levels of the Commonwealth government. Legal authority to use deadly force here and capture or kill those pirates."

The suited man held out a sheet of paper. "This should cover things nicely. An order from the Belt Governor's office to let them go."

To say that Pearson was outraged might have been the understatement of the century. She looked as if she were about to have a stroke.

Her resistance to the idea was overcome when the senior security officers pulled her out of the room with perhaps more force than was warranted. Then again, seeing her snarling at them, it might have just been the minimum they could use to distract her.

The man in the suit stepped forward and extended his hand. "I'm Mark Perez with the Governor's office. I suggest we make haste and get out of the building before the good Lieutenant decides to shoot you and just accept the consequences. She's got something of a…reputation, if you know what I mean.

"Your men are already in a van outside, and we'll go directly to the spaceport from here. I hope that you'll take this the right way, but I don't expect that visiting Ceres again should be on your vacation plans for…oh, a century. At least. Shall we?"

CHAPTER TWENTY-THREE

Brad had visions of a baying mob of security people in hot pursuit of the van on the way to the spaceport, with Lieutenant Pearson in the lead wielding a torch in one hand and a pitchfork in the other, but they arrived without any issues. The vehicle took them right up to his shuttle.

Saburo was standing on the shuttle ramp and made sure everyone made it inside, including the injured trooper with the concussion. He waved at the suited man, who didn't bother getting out of the van, and followed Brad inside.

"I suggest you strap in," the Colonel suggested. "We already have your gear and they gave us a very narrow window to lift off. Once again, you've somehow managed to get us banned. At this rate, we won't be welcome anywhere in the system by sometime next year."

"You only think you're funny," Brad assured him as he took one of the open seats and started strapping in. "Did Commodore Fields arrange this?"

The Colonel shook his head. "Senator Barnes called and spoke with the governor and probably passed on that this was Agency business."

That did sound more likely. The Senator had a good amount of influence and the Agency had some muscle, too.

"We ran into a wall, but we might have gotten some data," Brad said as the shuttle took off. "Did you get everything we had or just the weapons and armor?"

"They said everything. Of course, they also cursed your name, so take the level of cooperation with a dash of salt."

That made Brad chuckle. "I had a data chip with some of the shipping records for the merchant ships that work for the Cadre. Turns out that the woman Fields sent me to talk with was their face here on Ceres."

"Awkward," Saburo said judiciously. "Do you think she had any classified info on them? Maybe we could go back and get the rest of her records."

"I wouldn't count on that, if I were you. I saw a picture of the import/export building burned to the ground. It wasn't us, so the Cadre hit squad torched it. They'd have purged the computers first.

"Even if we could, that would mean going back down to Ceres. I don't see us getting any cooperation from security, do you?"

Saburo smiled and shook his head. "I suppose not. Once more, you're a shining example of how to win friends and influence people, boss."

"It's a gift," Brad agreed. "How is Agent Watson?"

"Good news on that front. Kirabo was able to isolate the poison and thinks she'll recover some, but not all the way. The damage is too great for that and it was in her system too long, but enough that she could live a relatively-normal life somewhere.

"Not as an Agent, but maybe retired. I somehow suspect that's more than most of them get in the end, based on our experience."

"The laws of chance seem to get a negative tug around us," Brad said.

"When everyone is shooting at us, innocent people around us take hits," the Colonel agreed. "Still, she might have contacts down there that can get us more information."

Brad imagined she might. With Fraser plugged into the underworld, and them hating the ground the Cadre walked on, it might be possible to leverage more information now that they knew who had handled the cargos.

The Cadre kept their lips sealed far better than one would expect, but they had to tell people something. If anyone could find their scent, it was the criminals in competition with them.

On that note, he'd need to have the Agency make things up to Fraser and, through him, the people that had taken on the Cadre to cover his backside. They might be criminals, but they'd raised their profile with the pirates. There'd be payback and Brad hated leaving debts in his wake.

They docked with *Freedom* twenty minutes later and Brad got out before the shuttle headed back to *Oath*. One of their other shuttles must've already arrived, because Michelle was standing there beside the Fleet officer.

Throwing decorum to the wind, she rushed forward and hugged him. "I was so worried that they'd kill you down there. Or that security would lock you up forever."

"It was a damned close thing," he admitted, hugging her hard and giving her a quick kiss.

"Closer than any of us would've wished," Fields agreed as a grinning Saburo stepped behind him. "We need to get into my office and discuss what happened. Both your superiors and mine want some answers to some unfortunate questions."

Saburo held out the data chip that Brad had been talking about earlier. "Commodore Madrid told me that he had some shipping information here that might give us a clue. Perhaps Agent Watson or her associates will be able to assist as well."

"I sure hope so," Brad said as Fields took the chip and called for one of his subordinates. "The Cadre is up to something and we're still completely in the dark. That could end up costing a lot of innocent people everything. We need answers and we need them now."

———

After telling the full story of what had happened on the surface, Brad accepted a drink. Frankly, he thought he'd earned it.

"Why did the Cadre have so many people here?" Michelle asked, taking a drink for herself. "It can't be because they thought we'd be dropping by. Until we arrived at Earth, we had no reason to suspect we'd be coming to Ceres."

"That may not be completely accurate," Brad said, taking a sip of smooth whiskey. "Watson was sure that someone in the Agency had betrayed her before we got our orders. That same person—or people—could've gotten word of where we'd be in time to warn the Cadre. All it would take is them having a ship in good position and they'd be able to have a team waiting for us."

"In Piazzi?" she asked. "That's relatively specific."

"And I'm sorry for sending you into that, Brad," Fields said. "I thought she was a straight shooter."

"Thankfully not, since she tagged me in the armor a few times before I ended her," Brad said.

Seeing that his attempt at humor had failed spectacularly, he sighed. "It's better that we found her, I think. We got some data that we might not have otherwise gotten. The pirates were after tungsten in large quantities. I just have no idea why."

Sadly, no one else seemed to have any ideas why that was either.

"I sent a message back to *Oath* so that Agent Watson could contact her good friend on the surface," Saburo said. "With any luck, they can dredge up a few details about the cargo. Or perhaps speak with someone that was in a position to overhear where they were taking it."

"If they do," Brad said, "we can follow up and take out another group. With the price of the refined material, it has to be for something critical. They paid hard currency for it at the market value. That has to hurt their bottom line, and it means that it's something they simply had to have."

A rap at the door made them pause while Fields called for the person to enter. The hatch opened and the marines outside passed a petite Lieutenant Commander through. The woman had more than a hint of Japanese descent in her features and bright green eyes.

"Everyone, meet Commander Takahashi," Fields said as they all rose to their feet. "She's my staff intelligence officer. One of the perks of being a flag officer. What have you got for us, Heather?"

The woman closed the hatch behind herself and inclined her head politely to the group. "A mystery. My staff and I went through all the files you copied, Commodore Madrid. Each and every one of those ships took on a cargo of expensive refined metal and paid with physical currency rather than a transfer.

"That's rare enough that we were able to trace the funds to a bank on Mars. They wanted to be cagy about who withdrew the money, but I shut that down pretty quickly. It turns out all of those merchant ships are owned by the same person. Oh, various holding companies have the titles, but if one follows the chain back up, they all arrive at the same place: Western Hemisphere Holdings out of Earth."

"That doesn't sound so mysterious," Brad said as they all digested the news. "Lots of merchant ships are owned by a single company through dummy corporations. The key is figuring out who's pulling the strings. Who deposited the money."

The woman smiled coolly. "In this case, they are one and the same. The mystery comes in when I look at Western Hemisphere Holdings. It turns out that the Commonwealth itself owns that corporation. I can't get any more information without asking questions that'll send up a red flag, but it seems as if there's a hand somewhere back on Earth pulling the Cadre strings."

That revelation sparked some spirited discussion but no real answers. Whoever was controlling the corporation, their specific identities were concealed from Commander Takahashi.

They now had a new lead on the Cadre leadership on Earth that unfortunately left them no wiser when it came to the destination or purpose for the tungsten.

"I dug deep, looking for where the cargos were going," Takahashi said at last, "but none of the ships listed a destination that checked out. They filed flight plans for various ports of call, but none of them ever arrived there. It's as if they just vanished."

"What about Ceres Control?" Fields asked. "Did they note these ships all heading off in the same direction? That might point us to a possible target."

"Unfortunately, no, sir. They seemingly went toward their listed destinations and then disappeared. Nothing but a big dead end."

Brad's com sounded and he glanced at the screen. "It's *Oath of Vengeance*. Maybe Agent Watson's enquiries turned up something."

He accepted the call. "Madrid."

"We've received a response to the questions Colonel Saburo had for Agent Watson, Commodore," Xan Wong said. "She called someone on Ceres and they've been asking discreet questions."

"Did they discover where the merchant ships were heading?" Brad asked. "Or what they needed the tungsten for?"

"No, sir, but they did discover an odd coincidence in the incoming cargos. Except that we all know there is no such thing as coincidences in our business.

"The raw ore they delivered when arriving at Ceres all came from the same asteroid mining station. Not that the bills of lading indicated that, but the quality-control documents in the shipments did. The station is called Kobayashi Station and it's only about a day's travel from here at moderate speed. Less than twelve hours for us at flank speed."

"Good work, Xan. Pass my thanks to Agent Watson. Get the ships ready to move out. It looks like we have a target after all."

He killed the connection and raised an eyebrow at Commander Takahashi. "Any chance you can get us some information on this Kobayashi Station?"

"Use my desk," Fields ordered.

The intelligence officer stepped behind her commander's desk but didn't sit as she tapped on the controls. "It's small, but we have some data. They work a number of asteroids and harvest basic ore. They sell that to refineries like those here on Ceres."

"What would the Cadre want with something like that?" Fields asked, his brow furrowed. "What can it do for them?"

"It's less what it can do and more what a useful cover it would be," Brad said. "Just like the import/export business, no one would question the bona fides of a station like that. I have no doubt it's been around a long time, so people see what they expect to see.

"Then the Cadre could come in later and make additions to the station. No one that's visited in the past would know about them, and likely no one that visited in the future would be allowed to see the changes. If they were visible at all."

Michelle nodded. "We've seen that same pattern time and again. Usually right before the Cadre attacks us. I wonder if we might get the drop on them this time. That would be a refreshing change of pace."

Brad grinned. "Since it might give us a clue as to their eventual plans, I'm willing to give it a shot. If we sneak in under stealth, they probably won't see us until we're right on top of them."

"That's good, up to a point," Saburo said, "but we need a reason to inspect the place. *We're curious* just isn't going to cut it. Belters are a stubborn, irascible lot. Even the honest ones would tell us to take a flying leap."

"I might be able to help with that," Fields said. "It turns out that Fleet is authorized to inspect any facility we choose here in the Belt. Even if your ships weren't Fleet auxiliaries, I could contract with you to perform that duty for us.

"Normally, that would require me to pay you, but I think we'll let the Agency eat the bill this time," the Fleet officer said with a grin.

Brad rose to his feet and his officers joined him. "That sounds like a plan. We'll ship Agent Watson over to *Freedom* and head out within the hour. We'll pull one of their tricks and file a flight plan for Io. Then we'll circle around and go see what they're hiding."

CHAPTER TWENTY-FOUR

Brad's destroyers swept in from the darkness without warning, surrounding the unsuspecting mining station. They'd approached under stealth and seen nothing out of the ordinary with Kobayashi Station. Still, that was how the Cadre did business. Hiding their bases in plain sight until they needed them.

Not this time.

Once they abandoned stealth, it didn't take long for the station management to start screaming. Brad was certain that if these people weren't pirates in their own right, that's what they thought he was.

The burly black man on the screen looked like a miner. Hell, he looked as if he could chew stone and spit out refined ore.

"I don't care who you say you are; you look like pirates to me," the man said. "We've already called for help from Fleet, so you'd best clear away. Ceres is close enough to send people that'll ruin your day."

Brad smiled coolly. "You don't have to worry about that, Mr. Murray. We're officially sanctioned to perform this inspection by Fleet. That is part of your charter, to allow inspections like this."

The large man's eyes narrowed. "This is the first time anyone has sent mercenaries for anything like that."

"I'll send our contract and authorization. I suggest you don't make this into more than it has to be. Allow us to perform our inspection. If you fight us on this, someone might end up hurt but the outcome will be the same."

He killed the communications channel without waiting for a response. The screen went back to showing the mining station in the distance.

"What are you thinking?" Michelle asked. "Is he Cadre or a dupe?"

Brad considered the question before answering. "I'm not sure. He sounded sincere. Pissed off in the same way I'd be if the situation was reversed."

He rose to his feet and paced the bridge. "We'll go in like we were expecting pirates. If we're wrong, then I can apologize. It's not like we're going to come back this way any time soon. Not after Ceres gave us the boot."

"Be careful," she said. "If this ends up being a Cadre trap, I'd prefer you not get caught in the jaws this time."

"I'll do what I can. Keep an eye on the shipping around the area. No one in or out until we've cleared the station. Fire warning shots if someone tries to get past you and doesn't listen to reason. Use boarding parties if they ignore you."

———

Brad ended up taking about two-thirds of their available shuttles for the inspection. Saburo had plenty of troopers scattered into the mix, but he'd brought engineering specialists and other techs to look at equipment and materials of interest.

The station wasn't all that big, but it had several areas where raw material was delivered and from which the processed ore was shipped. Brad picked the largest outgoing shuttle bay for his landing zone.

For security reasons, he didn't tell Murray where to meet him. If the Cadre was around, that would be the perfect way to get a missile for his trouble.

It seemed as if they weren't going to open the hatch for a minute, but a series of increasingly insistent demands from him finally got them to allow his shuttles in.

Pitt chose a space clear of the cargo craft that had been in the process of loading processed ore. Brad rose as soon as they were down and met his troopers in the back.

"We're not looking for trouble, but if someone comes looking for a fight, don't hesitate. Physical force for physical force is acceptable, but only use lethal force if they fire first. Clear?"

They indicated their understanding, and Brad gestured the lead troopers to exit and followed them out. They had their rifles aimed low but could easily bring them up to firing position in moments.

The cargo loaders—he'd heard them referred to as longshoremen, which he didn't get—advanced on his people menacingly. They stopped only when his troopers started raising their weapons.

"You're not welcome here," an incredibly bulky man of Asian descent said with a growl. "Leave."

"We're not going anywhere until we've completed our inspection," Brad said. "Back up."

"Are you going to make me?" the man asked with a wide smile. "I think I'd like to see you try."

"Chang!" a man's voice called out. "Leave off."

Brad turned and spotted Murray hurrying up. Next to Chang, Murray looked small. They grew them big in the Belt.

Once the longshoreman had retreated a few steps, Murray turned to Brad. "I don't seem to have a choice about you being here, so I'd suggest you speed this along. I'd like you gone before someone tries to bash your head in."

"Has anyone told you that you're a bit touchy?" Brad asked as he gestured for the station manager to precede him. "You're making this a lot harder than it has to be."

The other man shook his head. "You don't know crap about Belters. We don't like outsiders telling us what to do. Hell, we don't like other Belters telling us what to do. Look at whatever you want and get off the hell off my station."

"I'll look at the loading facility first while my people look everywhere else," Brad said. "While I do, you can tell me about all the suspicious ships we've heard about in the area."

He'd decided to drop that as a potential line on the Cadre. They knew the station had supplied the processed ore the suspicious merchants had brought to Ceres, so why not see if he could shake some information loose?

Murray frowned. "The only suspicious ships I know about are yours, *Commodore*. Otherwise, my operations have been going along without any hitches. Who reported seeing strange ships near my station?"

"I don't have names. Even if I did, I wouldn't tell you, because you seem the kind of guy that would make sure they wouldn't make any other reports you didn't like."

The larger man didn't respond, so Brad let it go.

He'd seen his fair share of shuttle facilities over the years, so this one wasn't too strange. He could figure out what everything was used for and nothing seemed out of place.

Still, he wasn't here to assume anything. "I'll want to see the refueling station, too."

"Sure," Murray said. "It's on the surface, but we have an inspection port that you can see it from over here."

He led Brad to a small port that looked out onto the surface of the asteroid the station was built on. The fueling station was a fairly small affair for the number of cargo shuttles Brad had seen, but he supposed it would be adequate if refilled often.

He was about to turn away when the fuel feeds caught his eye. In microgravity conditions, a shuttle or ship could hover near the refueling station and the feeds would extend out to meet it. All fine and good.

Only, these lines were far larger in diameter than they needed to be. They were of a size to refuel one of his destroyers. Perhaps even something larger. Yet the tanks he was looking at wouldn't give one of his ships a quarter load. Why such much overengineering? What he saw made no sense.

Unless there was more there than met the eye. This was an asteroid station, after all. There could be additional tankage under the surface.

"We should be thinking about lunch," he casually said into his com over the general channel. That was the code phrase that told all his troopers there was trouble afoot.

His troopers immediately raised their weapons to threaten every Belter in sight. There weren't many, but a few were a short distance away. Those earned personal visits by his people, who herded everyone together as quickly as they could. They also confiscated everyone's coms.

"What are you doing?" Murray demanded.

"I think you're lying to me, so I'm making sure you don't run off or warn anyone while I see if I'm right. Take me to the underground refueling tanks. The ones under that little thing."

The man blinked. "Are you crazy? There are no other tanks. That's it."

Brad smiled. "I suppose we'll see. People, some of you spread out and find me the tunnel leading to the tanks. It'll probably be concealed, so look closely."

———

The access tunnel leading to the fuel tanks wasn't concealed, but the additional tanks that fed into it were. Someone had built side tunnels to additional tanks buried a short distance from the obvious one and placed a very convincing facade of sealed stone over the doors.

After his people found those, it only took a few more minutes to get to the tanks. They were huge and the controls said they were completely full. The sheer volume of fuel would be more than enough for a Cadre fleet, even one with a carrier.

It was also a sign that the Cadre warships hadn't been there recently. If they had been, the tanks would've shown use and needed refilling. That meant he had a chance to stop whatever the pirates were up to.

Satisfied that he was on the right track, Brad made his way back to the prisoners.

And that was what they were now. This kind of facility didn't just happen by accident, and everyone working there in a position of authority would have been aware of the hidden installation.

Murray glared at Brad as he stepped out of the access tunnels. "Satisfied?"

"If by that you're asking if I'm pleased to have found the concealed fuel tanks, I am. I'm less happy with you, Mr. Murray. How long have you been working for the Cadre?"

The man's eyes narrowed until he almost seemed to be squinting. "Trying to bluff me isn't going to get me to admit there's something there when it's not."

He'd been hoping Brad missed the clever doors. Or he'd hoped Brad would be gullible enough to think he knew nothing.

Brad brought up his wrist-comp and showed the man a brief clip of them opening the hidden doors. "Trying to bluff me isn't going to save you. As the manager here, you had to know about the concealed fuel tanks. Even an incompetent couldn't have missed the tankers that filled them. It would've taken quite a few.

"You're screwed. Flip on the Cadre and Fleet might have some mercy. What did the Cadre need all that fuel for? What was their plan?"

The other man shook his head. "Good luck proving that I knew anything."

"I'm sure your computer records have more than enough detail to make sure we can hang you," Brad said, stepping close. "The harder you make us work for it, the worse this is going to be for you personally. Tell me, do you really want to help those bastards kill innocent people?"

When the man stood there silently, Brad shrugged. "It's on you, then."

He turned toward his troopers. "Find a large set of rooms we can use to secure everyone on the station."

Then he activated his com and called *Oath*. "This is Madrid. We found a set of massive concealed fuel tanks. Bring some of our ships into close orbit to start assisting Colonel Saburo in searching this place."

He waited for confirmation of his orders, but when none came, he felt his gut tightening.

"Any Vikings ship, this is Madrid. Please respond." When that didn't elicit a response, he hit the command channel linking him with Saburo. "Be on the alert, Colonel. Something is going on."

It was only when he failed to get a response that he truly under-stood what was happening. They were being jammed. It was sophisti-cated enough that they hadn't realized it either.

Of course, it might only be his group. Everyone else could be screaming out warnings and he'd have no idea. The ships, too. He had to get a handle on what was happening.

"Secure the prisoners and fortify a place near here," he ordered the troopers. "The Cadre is on this station. Team One, with me."

He headed back toward his shuttle. He could lift away from the surface of the asteroid and get a feel for what was really going on. With luck, it was only the asteroid station being jammed.

Moving carefully, he and the troopers made their way back to where they'd left the shuttle. They arrived to find armored men entering their shuttle. Cadre commandos.

Brad came into sight just in time to see them toss Pitt out onto the deck. She groaned, so she was still alive, but he saw blood on her uniform.

"At them," Brad ordered, drawing his mono-blade. "Blades only. We can't risk puncturing a refueling line and igniting the fuel."

This was the kind of fight Brad had trained his people so hard for. None of the troopers were masters like he was, but they could hold their own in a fight.

The pirates heard them coming and turned. One of the men had his helmet off and Brad had no trouble recognizing Jack Mader.

The Phoenix—leader of the Cadre—was there on the station.

CHAPTER TWENTY-FIVE

"KILL THEM ALL," Mader snarled when he saw Brad and his troopers charging. "Blades only or you'll blow us sky-high."

The Cadre commandos quickly spread out, their mono-blades springing to life. The two forces were almost evenly matched numerically. Brad hoped his men's rush could carry the day, because if they got bogged down, they'd be in serious trouble.

"Fight me man to man," Brad shouted. "Let's settle this once and for all."

Mader laughed as he activated his own blade. "Not bloody likely, boy. The Terror was an idiot for agreeing to that nonsense. If you want me dead, you'll just have to take your chances with my men."

His troopers and the pirates had come together in a line of flashing blue blades with him at the center. That wouldn't hold once the fighting really got rolling. Blades were a weapon of individuals, not groups.

Keeping an eye on the pirates closest to him, Brad engaged Mader. If he could bring his skill to bear quickly, he'd turn the fight into a rout.

To his shock, Mader met his best attack with a laugh and a counter-strike that Brad only barely managed to deflect. The Cadre leader was better than he'd guessed.

The two of them exchanged blows until the tide of battle swept them apart. That pissed Brad off, so he took it out on the pirate that had separated them. The woman was good—damned good—but not up to his skill level.

It took half a dozen blows and twenty seconds, but he finally baited her into overextending herself and lopped her head off with a backswing. Bright blood shot into the air from her neck as her corpse fell, drenching the pirate right behind her directly in the face.

Brad followed up as the man frantically rubbed his eyes to clear them while wildly swinging his blade to defend against an attack he must've known was coming but couldn't see. Rather than aiming for a body strike, Brad settled for taking the man's weapon arm off just above his elbow, neatly disarming him. Literally.

He'd intended to finish the man, but Mader was abruptly next to him, furiously striking at his exposed side. The pirate leader's attack was so sudden that he might have killed Brad if one of his troopers hadn't chosen that moment to distract the Phoenix. As it was, Mader managed to cut deeply enough into Brad's shoulder armor to draw blood.

Brad threw his own blade into the counterattack, leaving Mader to defend on two fronts. That should've led to the man's speedy death, but the pirate adeptly parried both blades and counterattacked, striking low and taking the trooper's leg off just below the knee. He took a matching wound to Brad's in his own shoulder in exchange, but he didn't seem bothered even as his blood spattered the ground.

The pirate leader retreated a few steps and allowed two of his commandos to block Brad's advance.

"You're as good as they told me," he said with a nasty grin. "My uncle never knew what he was letting himself in for when he agreed to duel you. Too bad your people aren't as good as mine."

Uncle? Mader was related to the Terror? That might explain a few things, but Brad had no time to think about it now.

A glance at the fighting told Brad the man was right. His troopers were fighting hard, but they were losing. In all honesty, they'd already lost. Most of his men were injured or dead. Mader's commandos now outnumbered them handily.

"This is far from over," he shouted at the pirate leader. "I don't know what kind of sick game you're up to, but I'll stop you."

Mader threw his head back and laughed. "Good luck with that, considering you still have no idea what my true goals are. When this is all over, I'll hunt you down and get a critique out of you before I kill you."

He charged the pirates, but a new man stepped out of the shuttle with a shotgun raised. Brad barely had time to cover his face before the man fired into his armored body.

The impact of the pellets wasn't enough to move him, unlike what the vids always showed, but his unconscious reaction to the blast sent him staggering back off the ramp. By some miracle of either luck or skill, none of the fuel lines ignited or tanks exploded.

Mader cuffed the man across the back of the head and took the weapon. "Idiot! Are you trying to kill us?" He shoved the man back into the shuttle and smiled at Brad.

"This has been entertaining, but we have somewhere important to go. If you don't want to suck vacuum, you'd best run away like a good little boy."

Brad watched Mader turn his back and walk into the shuttle. He was so angry that his vision tinged red. It had been a while since he'd let that monster loose into his soul. He thought he'd beaten it, but this had proven him wrong.

Lacking options, Brad helped his men gather those of their brethren who were still alive, including the wounded Pitt, and retreated out of the loading bay. He had no doubt that Mader would use the weapons on the shuttle to blow the lock as soon as he was clear.

They were out of the bay about ten seconds before the indicator on the lock turned blood-red. Mader had gotten clear in Brad's shuttle and done exactly that.

"I have to get word to the ships," Brad told the highest-ranking survivor while one of the medics slapped a rough and ready patch on his shoulder. "Send a runner for Colonel Saburo and get what help you can for the wounded. Lock this place fully down and round up all the miners."

With that, Brad raced to one of the unloading bays nearby. They'd mapped them out before they'd landed, so it only took him a few minutes to get there.

He found the bay abandoned. There were three cargo shuttles that he could choose from, but all were only partly unloaded and had large bins of raw ore blocking their ramps. He'd have to clear one before he could take off.

Brad found a hand lifter and started moving the containers. The delay made him grind his teeth. With every passing second, it became more likely that Mader would escape.

After five minutes of backbreaking effort, almost as he was finishing, Saburo and several troopers came rushing in.

"Sorry I'm late," his friend said, panting. "We ran into some unexpected trouble with the miners. Seems they wanted to fight after all. I hear you ran into Mader. Where is he?"

"Getting away," Brad said, muscling the last container off the shuttle ramp. "I just hope he didn't snooker Michelle. Any luck finding the jammer?"

Saburo followed him into the cargo shuttle. "No, but we're looking. It's sophisticated. We never even had a clue that our coms were down. We need to come up with some way of detecting that, going forward—it fooled all of our existing safeguards."

Brad strapped himself into the pilot's couch. "Secure the station. Treat everyone as a potential pirate. We're going to turn them all over to Fields and let him sort this mess out. Now get everyone clear so I can lift."

The Colonel retreated and Brad heard the ramp close. When it registered as sealed, he brought the cargo shuttle to a hover and moved it into the lock. The controls to cycle the lock were built right into the console, so he was quickly out into space.

The sensors on this tub sucked, but he was able to see his ships well enough. The stolen shuttle wasn't visible, though.

It looked as if Mader might have escaped.

———

Brad kept trying to open a channel as he raced out toward *Oath of Vengeance*. The jamming field held until he was almost halfway there. It was more powerful than he'd expected and acted like a blanket that smothered all his signals.

"Brad?" Michelle asked, her expression confused when he was finally able to connect with his ship. "What are you doing on that shuttle and who was in yours?"

"Do you still have the other shuttle on sensors?" he demanded. "Jack Mader and some of his Cadre commandos stole it. We have to stop them."

Michelle stared at him for a few moments, her eyes wide. Then she spun in her seat to face Xan's console. "Get *Grant* and *Montgomery* after Commodore Madrid's shuttle. The Phoenix is aboard it."

She turned back toward him. "They're the closest. Your shuttle sent a message that you were going to check one of the nearby asteroids to follow up on a lead. We hadn't heard any warnings once you'd locked the station down, so I didn't think anything of it."

"They started jamming us," Brad said, his teeth grinding together. "Something I hadn't seen before. It locked our coms down but didn't give us any sign of jamming like we'd normally see. By the time I figured it out, he was already stealing my shuttle."

He checked the controls and saw that he had another five minutes until he docked. "Come meet me at max speed. I want to get after him before he springs any other nasty surprises."

That cut three minutes off his approach time and he was on *Oath's* bridge a minute after docking. Michelle had already started his ship in pursuit of the two leading destroyers.

"Have Xan signal *Bound by Law* and *Bound by Honor* to join us. *Horatio* can oversee the securing of the station. If I know Mader, he has at least one ship around here somewhere and probably others close by. If he's got that damned cruiser of his, I want to have the force to take it down. Captain Suzuki will just have to manage on his own."

Five minutes later, they were almost to the asteroid that Mader had been heading for. Brad spread his ships out to have better sensor coverage and came in looking for an ambush.

Instead, he found absolutely nothing: no shuttle, no ship, and no hidden base. The pirate leader had just vanished.

"How sure are we that he was headed here?" Brad asked.

"He *did* come here," Michelle said. "That doesn't mean he stayed here, though. I can see half a dozen other asteroids that he might be behind now. Or he might have kept going. Once we lost sight of him, he had a lot more options."

"Spread the fleet out a little more and get some probes heading for the potential hiding places," Brad said, trying not to snarl. "The sonofabitch is here somewhere."

Ten long minutes passed with no sighting.

"Contact!" Michelle said abruptly. "*Bound by Law* has your shuttle on sensors relayed from a probe. He's further away than I'd have expected, but we've got him now!"

That was usually when things went south for them.

"Where's he going?"

"There's a smallish asteroid not too far ahead of him," she said. "There's not much room behind it, so I don't think he could have a lot of firepower back there."

Assuming his wife was wrong wouldn't cost them much in the long run, so he'd be cautious. "Bring the other ships in close. If there's nothing back there, he can't escape us. If there is an ambush, we'll have a better chance of taking them down without being gutted."

They'd made up a quarter of the distance between him and Mader when the shuttle arced out of sight around the asteroid.

Twenty seconds later, a small ship came racing from behind the slowly spinning rock. It looked like a light frigate of the same class as the one Brenda Andre had commanded before she'd been discharged by Fleet. The little ships were small and fast but not strong enough to be a threat to any of the Vikings' destroyers out in the open like this.

"Range?" he asked.

"She's outside torpedo range," Narendra said from the tactical console. "She's really pushing her engines and we're losing ground. I might be able to hit her with the Gatlings, but that's a pretty difficult shot, considering her evasive maneuvers and the range."

"Maximum speed," he ordered Michelle. "Get us closer."

"We're going to be restricted in how much maneuvering we can do," his wife warned him. "That little ship is faster than us in a straight-line race. We have a chance to gain a little distance with her jigging around like that, but a stern chase is a long chase."

"Balance it with tactical. Narendra, let her have all our Gatlings. Maybe we'll get a piece of good luck and take her out."

It quickly became obvious this really was going to be a long pursuit if they didn't manage to close the distance. Even though the little ship was right there, it was barely getting closer. If they didn't take more of a risk, they'd be at this for hours. Hours during which other Cadre ships could intercept them.

And the Cadre had to have other ships in the area if they were planning an operation against Ceres. One that was far enough along for Mader to do a personal inspection. If the pirate hadn't come here in one of his big ships, he'd have expected he could get to one fairly quickly.

"Reduce our maneuvering," Brad ordered. "Get us into firing range sooner."

The closing rate increased, but now some of the enemy's Gatling fire was hitting them. Nothing their ablative armor couldn't handle. Not yet, but that would change.

"Got her!" Narendra exulted a moment later. "Lucky shot. She's losing a little speed. We must've clipped an engine."

"She can't escape now," Michelle said. "She's turning."

"Keep up the Gatlings," Brad ordered. "Launch torpedoes as soon as we come into range. Open a channel to the ship, Xan."

When the light on his console indicated the com circuit was live, he started speaking. "This is your last chance, Mader. Surrender now and you'll live a little longer. A little."

There was no answer, but then again, he really hadn't expected one. That was fine. He'd rather kill the bastard anyway.

Their victory was inevitable. The frigate didn't have a chance against even one destroyer in a head-to-head fight. Against five, the little ship was doomed.

The heavy mass drivers on *Bound by Law* found her first, ripping the pirate's hull wide open. Then one of the leading torpedoes slammed into what was left and blew the frigate apart.

"Yes!" Brad exulted. "Cut speed and we'll see if we can find any survivors."

Xan frowned. "Signal from *Horatio*. There's another ship approaching the Kobayashi Station at high speed. They think she's another frigate."

"Just one ship? It might be a lure to get them away from the station. Have them hold position. Signal *Grant* to search the wreckage while the rest of us head back."

"Fabia said it doesn't look as if they're heading for the station," Xan said a minute later. Then she cursed and turned in her seat. "She's stopping at the asteroid where this frigate had been hiding when we found her."

Instantly, Brad realized that he'd blundered. Badly. He'd assumed Mader had boarded the frigate and run for it. Instead, the pirate must've hidden his shuttle in a crevasse on the asteroid and let Brad hare off on this wild goose chase while he waited for another ride.

Now his enemy was escaping—for real this time—and there was nothing Brad could do to stop him. *Horatio* wasn't close enough to catch the second frigate and neither was he.

CHAPTER TWENTY-SIX

Brad fumed all the way back to the station. He couldn't believe he'd been such an idiot. He'd fallen for one of the most basic dodges he'd ever heard of. It was humiliating.

He'd been lost to his anger for the first time in years. So eager to get the bastard that he'd gotten tunnel vision and forgotten to cover all his bases. Now Mader was gone.

All Brad had accomplished was delaying the attack on Ceres. Hopefully, the lack of a stashed fuel supply really would make them abort or delay.

"You can't blame yourself," Michelle said, putting her hand on his shoulder. "None of us thought of it either."

"But I should have," he said bitterly, raising his eyes toward her. "That's what experience is for."

The corner of her mouth edged up. "You're a Platinum-rated mercenary commander, but you're not omniscient. Mader is *also* experienced, one of the craftiest opponents we've faced. I'd wager he never goes anywhere without an escape plan."

Brad snorted a bit before shaking his head. "I appreciate what you're saying, but he fooled me on the station and again here. I came swaggering in like I owned the place, and he used my overconfidence against me."

Xan cleared her throat. "We have a signal from *Horatio*. The frigate sent them a message before it got out of range. Video and audio."

Perfect. The bastard wanted to gloat.

"Put it on the main screen," Brad said, sighing.

An image of Mader appeared. He was sitting in the command chair on a frigate, grinning. "Well, I suppose you're right pissed now, aren't you, boy? Let that be a lesson to you never to underestimate your betters.

"You've set me back here in the Belt, but don't think this will slow me down long. You think you understand what I'm doing, but you're out of your league there, too. I have things in motion that you can't begin to fathom. By the time you do, you'll be screwed, blued, and tattooed."

He leaned back in his seat, his grin fading back to a smile. "Still, I'll admit you've done better than any of us expected. Particularly as ignorant of the…situation as you are.

"I won today, but I think I'll throw you a bone now that it doesn't matter. Word is that you've finally figured out that your little friend Falcone never made it where she was supposed to be."

Brad sat up, his jaw clenching, wishing he could respond.

Mader let the silence drag on for a few moments and then grinned again. "I expect you think I've killed her. My reward to you for almost catching me is to tell you that she's still alive. Better yet, from your point of view, the information about where she is can be found on the station you just captured.

"If you talk to the right person, you still might be able to save her. I kind of doubt you'll be able to, mind, but that's your business."

The pirate crossed his arms over his chest. "The people holding her aren't Cadre, by the way. More of a mutually disliked third party, even if you don't know them at the moment. I consider myself an excellent judge of character. Trust me when I say that you'll hate them.

"And with that, our business is concluded. For now. I look forward to crossing blades with you again, Madrid. For the last time."

The transmission ended and Brad just sat there, clenching his fists. The arrogant bastard. It burned his guts to be beaten so handily.

Well, they always said payback was a bitch. He'd have to make sure that he had all the options covered next time.

———

Brad's rage had cooled by the time he was once again back on the mining station. Thankfully, he had a much better handle on it than he'd had in the old days. Otherwise, he'd have been sorely tempted to shoot the station manager.

Murray was strapped to a chair when Saburo escorted Brad in to see him. They'd used binders to secure his arms at his sides and shackle his legs to the bottom of the seat. Then they'd wrapped a belt around him. It seemed they'd wanted to be absolutely certain the man didn't get any ideas.

Taking a moment to stand over the manager, Brad considered him coldly. "At best, you're a pirate sympathizer, Mr. Murray. At worst, you work for the Phoenix. What do you have to say for yourself?"

"You're the pirate," the man spat. "You seized my station and you're trying to spin some tale about the Cadre. No one will believe you."

Brad shook his head. "Sadly, you're going to need to do better than that. My word is good and yours is for shit. If there are any deals to be had, they'll go to the first person to tell me what I want to know. Is that going to be you, or should I put you out an airlock for piracy and talk to the next person in line?"

For the first time, the man's expression wavered a little. "What do you want to know? I'm not confessing to anything."

"Start with Jack Mader. The Phoenix. What did he tell you about his plans here?"

The large black man licked his lips. "He paid to upgrade the facility to have larger fuel storage. No crime there."

Brad grabbed a chair, spun it around, and straddled it. "Not a crime, no. Something suspicious, yes. Something you should've told the authorities about, yes. Why didn't you?"

"I said no confessions. Yes, it was unusual, but he offered me a lot of money."

"You know he'd have killed everyone here when he was done, don't you? The Cadre doesn't leave witnesses behind, if they can help it. The only thing that saved you was me showing up out of the blue.

"Mader even threw you under the bus when he called me to gloat after he'd escaped. Said information about one of my friends is down here. Either in a computer or someone's head. I'm inclined to believe it's in your head, because Mader is far too competent to leave that kind of thing just laying around.

"But if you're innocent, now is the time to prove it. Where might he have hidden a computer? If he had one here, you'd know about it. And don't give me any bull about being clueless. That only carries you so far before I start looking for an airlock."

The man considered him for a long while without speaking. When he finally spoke, his voice was a little deflated.

"He arrived here on a different shuttle than he took back out. It's down in one of the personal landing bays. Maybe what you're looking for is in there."

Brad considered that and then shook his head. "I'll look, but I don't believe he just left something like that lying around. If you want to save your life, now is the time to tell me where they're keeping Falcone."

Murray blinked and frowned. "I haven't heard that name."

"Saburo," Brad said as he stood. "Get him up. We're taking a short walk to the nearest airlock. Who's the next most senior prisoner?"

"Wait!" Murray said, suddenly looking terrified. "He was talking about a woman that someone had prisoner. Is that her?"

"It might be. Where is she?"

"I don't know, but I overheard him and his deputy talking about her. Some other people had her and were trying to get information from her back on Earth. Mader laughed and said that was a fool's errand, that she'd never talk and they might as well just keep her in their secret prison for all the good it would do them.

"The other man didn't like the sound of that, said he'd rather die than end up in a place like Red Diamond. Called it that by name, like it was a place."

"And he didn't care that you overheard him?" Brad asked. "Why would he blab secrets like that in front of you?"

"It wasn't like it meant anything to me."

That wouldn't have stopped Mader from making sure his secrets stayed secret. If he hadn't dealt with Murray, he'd already planned to slit his throat in the very near future.

He wished it meant something to him. He'd have to go through the Agency database he had to be sure, but he'd never heard the name before. He'd follow up on it as soon as he got a few seconds.

"Secure him somewhere away from the rest of the prisoners," Brad said. "Then we'll go find Mader's shuttle. Maybe something onboard will give us a hint what his plans are."

———

It took a few false starts to locate the Cadre shuttle, but they finally managed to discover its hiding place. It wasn't the same model as the one Mader had stolen, but Brad resolved to take it until he could get his own back.

The Phoenix had locked his up tight, of course. That meant it took Brad calling Mike Randall down from his engine room aboard *Oath of Vengeance* to bypass the locks, security systems, and probably traps.

The big man took his time and ejected Brad from the bay when he asked how much longer it would take one too many times. That paid off an hour later when the smug engineer sauntered out with a grin.

"Got it. I bypassed the security lockout, found and removed the explosive charge that would've blown the shuttle up, and removed the shunt that would've fried the electronics. I even found the jammer and shut it down. Can't wait to see what makes it tick."

"You found all that security?" Brad asked. "On a shuttle?"

The engineer shrugged. "Paranoid is as paranoid does. You can go inside now, but don't touch anything without me looking at it first."

Brad motioned for Saburo to join him, and the three men went inside the pirate shuttle. It was outfitted significantly more expensively than Brad's had been. It looked like a rich man's plaything, except for the weapons. Those were all business.

It wouldn't hold as many people as one of the Vikings' more utilitarian models, but it would do so in sublime comfort. The wood trim and gold plating probably cost more than everything in Brad's cabin rolled together.

The first thing that caught Brad's eye was the computer in the luxurious passenger compartment, but someone had taken the time to fry it. A quick check from the engineer confirmed it was unrecoverable. Pity, but not wholly unexpected.

Saburo and Brad went through the shuttle with a fine-toothed comb but found no incriminating devices they could break into. It was looking as if the shuttle was a bust.

He walked into the pilot's compartment and stared at the controls for a moment. "What about these, Mike?"

The engineer stuck his head in. "I already found the booby trap built into it and unlocked the console so that I could check the rest of the systems. It's clean now."

"Check the engines with your Mark One eyeballs. It wouldn't shock me if there was something back there that's set to go boom."

"Will do."

Brad sat at the controls and brought them to life. He then started with the piloting controls. Sadly, it only had records from once it left whatever vessel had transported it, probably the frigate they'd killed. No help there.

Next was the communications systems. It had also been wiped. For being in a hurry, someone had been thorough. Even having six destroyers unexpectedly show up hadn't stopped them from cleaning their tracks.

Damnit. They'd thought of everything.

Or had they? Yes, they'd wiped the com system drives, but it was possible they'd missed something in the buffer. He'd need to physically access that and hope that they hadn't thought to reboot the system completely.

It was a matter of only a few minutes to borrow the required tools from Mike and open the communications system up. Once the engineer confirmed there were no physical boobytraps, Brad connected his wrist-comp to the com system buffer and checked it.

There were two messages still in the buffer. He very carefully copied them off to segregated memory in his unit before any unlucky quirks of fate purged them from the temporary storage.

Only then did he try to bring them up on the shuttle's com. They had been encrypted, but someone—probably Mader—had unscrambled them when he'd viewed them. That left them wide open in the buffer.

The first one was the exchange between the shuttle and Murray welcoming the pirate lord to the station and directing him to the landing bay. That wasn't going to help the station manager when it came time for Commodore Fields to decide how guilty of collaboration he was.

The second was from Mader's ship, warning him of the Brad's arrival. The pirate's response was a curse.

"Keep this transmission on tightbeam," the pirate said in response to the unwelcome news. "It looks as if Fleet might have gotten wind of us after all. This station is no longer safe and I'm going to use my shuttle's jammer to keep them from communicating once they land. With any luck at all, I can steal one of their shuttles and get to you. Be ready to run when I do.

"Also, send orders back to the strike force that we're not going to be able to refuel after all. Have them move to the secondary location and await my arrival. We'll move on Ceres when I get there. Have them ready to move in fifteen hours.

"With half the Fleet strength out of position, we can execute Blue Lagoon in spite of the ships they still have there. We won't need to wait for any of them to leave on patrol, after all. Have our friend's ships transfer some of their fuel to us, since they didn't come as far.

"Take as much as you can get them to release and spread it around our ships. I want to have more maneuvering capability than our 'comrades' do when the time comes. Now, make it happen while I see about getting away from this rock. We'll come back later and blow it up to be sure no one knows we were ever here."

The transmission terminated and that was it.

Brad didn't understand why the pirate would want any of his ships to have less maneuvering capability, though. Especially when they had to fight Fleet to get to Ceres.

He'd really hoped the lack of fuel would deter the Cadre, but he should've known better. At least he had an idea of their strength. Enough to take a cruiser and six destroyers in face-to-face combat, but not enough to take down twice that number of destroyers without risk.

He needed to get this information back to Fields. Based on the time-stamp of the last call, he wasn't sure he could make it back to Ceres before the Cadre forces made their move. He had no idea how long it would take them to get from their secondary kickoff point to Ceres, but he had to bet he'd arrive too late to make a difference and plan accordingly.

Saburo had arrived while he was watching the transmission. "It sounds like we need to get moving, but I found something you'll want to see first."

The Colonel led Brad down into the bowels of the station, where it looked as if there was some kind of massive machine shop. One suited for forming and milling heavy metals.

He walked over to one of the work benches, picked up a glob of metal, and handed it to Brad.

"What is this?" Brad asked.

"Tungsten," Saburo said. "That made me have one of them show me the plans. Look here."

He gestured to a 3-D drawing on a nearby screen. It looked like a long, thin needle. Based on the scale at the bottom of the display, it was half the size of a shuttle.

"It's a weapon," Brad guessed.

His friend nodded. "One made to carry a nuke, based on the size and shape of the payload area. It's got some serious drives in the back, too."

That was definitely not good news. Brad considered the size and shape of the weapon. It wouldn't fit into a standard—or even over-sized—torpedo tube. It would have to be ejected from the ship carrying it before the drives lit off.

Then what? The long, savagely pointed tip gave him no direct clues. And why put a nuke inside something as expensive as tungsten? It was going to blow up anyway, right?

So, that meant the metal served a purpose before detonation. It didn't make the weapon faster, so it must make a difference when the thing hit the target.

That jarred a memory loose about some other weapon he'd read about that used tungsten. He tried to remember what it was, but nothing came.

Brad called *Oath* and Xan answered.

"I need a search of the databases," he said. "I'm remembering some kind of weapon that used tungsten. A large projectile, I think."

"Hold one," the communications officer said. "Got it. A hypothetical weapon proposed for use in orbital bombardment back on Earth. They called them Rods from God. They designed them to have the power of a nuke without a payload, using kinetic energy, and be able to penetrate the atmosphere all the way to the surface."

Brad blinked. How was that useful on Ceres? All they had to do was drop the nukes down on the dwarf planet. It didn't have an atmosphere at all.

Then it hit him. The metal in the projectile would keep the nuke intact while it penetrated deep into the crust and ice. Then the nuke would be much, *much* more devastating. With enough of them, the Cadre might be able to poison the drinking water for most of the Inner System.

Faced with that threat, finding Kate was going to have to wait.

"We're moving out," Brad told Xan. "We need to be back to Ceres as fast as Michelle can get us there."

He killed the connection and turned to Saburo. "I'm leaving you here with most of the troopers. *Horatio* will be your cover. Tear this place apart and hold everyone for Fleet. They just became willing partners in a terrorist incident in the making."

A terrorist incident he dearly hoped he arrived in time to stop.

CHAPTER TWENTY-SEVEN

ONCE HIS SHIPS were under way, Brad sat in his office and wrestled with how to warn Fields about what was coming without tipping his hand. With the risk to Ceres, he'd send an alert in the clear, if he had to, but that would certainly prompt the Cadre to attack even sooner.

Mader had been leery of attacking the full Fleet strength at Ceres before he'd realized the Vikings were the ships at Kobayashi Station. If he knew Brad was coming and Fleet was on guard, he'd fade away and strike when the odds were more in his favor.

The best outcome would be for Brad to discreetly warn Fields and then to place his destroyers where they could intervene at a critical juncture in the fighting. After all, they needed to stop the nuclear penetrators, too.

Based on the plans and manufacturing records they'd found, Mike Randall estimated the Cadre had a dozen penetrators to hurl at Ceres. Odds were exceptionally high that they'd target places like Ceres City and Piazzi. They'd likely also hit other places where significant human habitation was present.

It would take a long while to build water-harvesting facilities else-where on Ceres, because there was no infrastructure away from the established cities. That would be devastating to every off-Earth habitation in the Inner System, which was obviously the Cadre's intent.

That brought Brad back to the problem at hand. Mader could have access to Fleet codes. They weren't all that secure when one considered that someone was giving the Cadre Fleet-designed warships. They conceivably had access to even the most recent cyphers.

Then he smiled. He had access to a much more restricted group of people, and one of them was onboard *Freedom*: Agent Watson. She had the current Agency codes. Even if someone in the Agency had betrayed her, it was far less likely that Mader had Agency codes.

Based on the timeframe Mader had given his ships to be at their secondary gathering point, Brad could get back to Ceres about the time they started their move. The key would be getting there without being observed, and that meant coming in under stealth.

He opened a channel to his communications officer. "Xan, can we send a message to *Freedom* using a Fleet code while at the same time burying a separate message inside it for Agent Watson using an Agency code?"

"Making it completely hidden? No. Hiding it in plain sight, that we can do."

Brad frowned. "How does that work?"

"We send whatever you want in under the Fleet code and then insert a data packet containing whatever you want, using the Agency codes. Tell them you're attaching some of the recordings of the station we captured under a fictitious encryption code like 'Watson' or something leading them to ask her about it.

"Anyone that isn't in the know will spend a lot of fruitless time trying various Fleet codes on it without any luck, but Commodore Fields will understand."

Brad grinned. "That's brilliant. We can even give the Cadre misleading information about what we're going to do out here, and they'll think we're nowhere near them."

"Remember that when the raises happen."

With a laugh, Brad disconnected. He needed to record two messages and send them, one buried inside the other. First, the public message.

He activated the recorder and looked into the video pickup. "Commodore Fields, we've run into something worse than we expected on the inspection tour you sent us on. It looks like Kobayashi Station was involved with the Cadre in some way, and I ran into the Phoenix. We managed to blow up one of his ships, but he got away.

"We've got a lot of work here trying to piece together what they were working on, so we'll be staying for the next three or four days. Once we have more definitive answers, we'll bring the station crew back to Ceres for you to question. I don't see any reason to rush at this point. The horse already got out of the barn."

He smiled sadly. "One of these days, I'll get the drop on Mader and end him. He can't keep getting lucky like this forever.

"In any case, I'm sending you everything we're recorded under the Watson protocol to keep it to your eyes only. It's just a bunch of video of the station, but perhaps you'll notice something that I've missed. Madrid out."

Once he had the cover message saved, he started a second one. "Agent Watson and Commodore Fields, the situation is far more dire than I've let on. You're in imminent danger."

He proceeded to explain everything he knew and what he suspected, ending with the fact that he had five ships coming back to Ceres and intended to come in under stealth.

"We've really got two problems," he said in closing. "The nukes and the pirate ships. There are a couple of ways they could get the nukes on target, but it seems to me the best way is for them to come in under stealth of their own.

"If they pre-position the nukes, they can reveal themselves and pull you out of position. If you try to handle both problems, they'll cut you to ribbons. Mark, you have a lot more in the way of tactical resources to bring to the table, so I'll help in whatever way you need me to.

"Most of the human habitation on Ceres is in the same hemisphere, simply because it makes sense to have the cities supporting one another. That makes it unlikely they'll drop a nuke on the far side, in my opinion. With that in mind, I'm going to place my ships in a position to cover the places with the best shot at the cities."

He gave the video pickup a serious look. "No matter how we play this, it's going to be an ugly fight, but there's the possibility we can make it a decisive one with surprise and a little bit of luck on our side. We just need to make this opportunity count."

With that, he ended the recording and encrypted it with one of the Agency protocols. Then he sealed up the other recording and the one to Watson with a Fleet code, and forwarded the combined product to Xan.

That accomplished, he had time to brood. If things went poorly, he'd have to live with the consequences of his mistakes, and he'd rather not have something like that on his conscience.

———

"I have something on the sensors," Narendra Lewin said, hunched over her console. "I'm pretty sure it's a ship under stealth creeping into our containment area."

They'd been in the region near Ceres for a little bit more than an hour, their arrival being a mix of racing to get into position and slowly slipping into the final zone at a snail's pace so that they didn't give themselves away while under stealth.

Brad had been afraid they'd arrive too late to make any difference. After the initial exchange of data with *Freedom,* he hadn't dared to risk any further communication for fear of having the Cadre figure out he wasn't where they expected him to be.

Now all their care was paying off. Fields had sent half of his destroyers toward Kobayashi Station with orders to circle around and cover another angle of potential attack from the Cadre.

That had the dual benefits of reducing the obvious strength the pirates would need to attack and placing reserves that could strike the Cadre on an exposed flank when they made their move.

Depending on where the pirates launched the nukes from, either Brad and his Vikings or the second destroyer group would focus on stopping the weapons of mass destruction from reaching the surface of Ceres.

Now it looked as if he and his people might be playing nuke duty.

"Are there any other Cadre ships in the area?" he asked.

The tactical officer shrugged. "Not that I've seen, but that hardly means anything while we're using passive sensors. They have stealth as good as our own. The nuke is less well protected, and that's what I spotted first. Once I narrowed it down, I spotted the ship that had to have placed it.

"The vessel is probably a destroyer, but it might be a heavy frigate. We won't know until we can get a clear look. It's certainly not larger than a destroyer."

"Do you think you'll have much luck spotting other ships?" he asked.

"All we can do is look. If we don't, we'll just have the time from when the nukes light their drives to when they're about to impact to take them out. Even that is going to mean some nuclear material impacts Ceres. The closer the penetrators get, the most concentrated the fallout.

"But if we can prevent any of the nukes from penetrating the crust, that'll limit the effects of the radiation to something manageable. Particularly if we keep the devices from exploding."

He nodded. "Michelle, see if you can help spot any of the Cadre ships before they place nukes. Every little bit helps."

"I'm already on it. We all are."

"I just spotted a second ship," Xan said. "I'm forwarding the coordinates and heading to Narendra."

"Confirmed," the tactical officer said a moment later. "Good eye, Xan. The beer is on me once we wrap this mission up. The second ship hasn't deployed a nuke, but it's in a place where I'd expect them to place one. Once again, I think this is a destroyer, but it might be a carrier."

"How long after they place the weapons do you think they'll fire them?" Michelle asked. "Are they going to move the ships away from the launch zone first?"

"I would."

If Brad had been in charge of the attack, he'd reposition the attacking ships to come in at a different angle to maximize the chaos for the defense.

The choice for Fleet would then be to defend Ceres or themselves.

They could do both poorly, or focus on saving either the asteroid or themselves. If not all the nukes were deployed in the opening salvo, that might even ensure that a Fleet sacrifice was in vain, accomplishing both goals.

"The second ship just deployed a nuke," Narendra said. "Neither of them is moving away more than a couple of hundred kilometers from their payloads."

Whatever was going to happen, Brad expected it to happen soon. "Signal our ships with the findings. I don't know if this group is going to reveal itself, but we don't fire on them or come out of stealth until I give the order."

"Copy that," Xan said. "The other ships have acknowledged the order via tightbeam."

"Torpedo launch detected from both vessels we have on passive sensors," Narendra said. "There could be more from other sources, but we won't know unless we go active. It looks like the target is the Fleet station or the Fleet units in orbit near it."

"Signal *Freedom* as arranged but maintain stealth," Brad snapped. "The battle of Ceres is underway, but we're not giving up our surprise unless we have no choice.

"It looks like they're trying to get torpedoes onto target to disable or destroy any units they can before the fighting really starts. I'd expect some of the ships to charge in next, looking to draw any Fleet response out of position to shoot the nukes they intend to fire. Then the rest of the Cadre ships will enter the fray.

"Narendra, I want torpedoes targeted on the nukes we can see. The plans we found tell us what kind of speed they can manage. They were never designed for defending themselves, so let's make them pay for that mistake. When they start moving, I want to take them out, along with any we've missed."

"Copy that," the tactical officer said.

"*Freedom* has acknowledged our warning," Xan said.

"Now we wait to see how the battle plays out," Brad said, settling back in his chair. "One way or the other, we'll be fighting in a few minutes. Let's hope we're the hammer coming down on the Cadre and not the last-minute defense for Ceres."

———

"Drives detected," Narendra said. "Nukes, it looks like. Not the ones we detected, or even close to us, but a group of six set farther to the northern side of Ceres. *Freedom* and the attached destroyers are going to have to respond."

"Are any of the ships that fired them visible?"

"Negative. The Fleet station just lit up its active scanners at full power. They're firing at the nukes and the torpedoes we told them were incoming. The Fleet vessels are moving to clear the area around the station."

Since Brad and his ships hadn't been able to go active, he had no real idea how many torpedoes Fleet was dealing with. He hoped it would be a small number that they could brush aside easily enough.

Then the screen lit up with dazzling light before the automatic dimmers shielded the crew from the flash.

"Nuclear explosion detected," Narendra said grimly. "The Fleet station is gone. *Freedom* and the other ships got clear, but they have no supporting fire at this time."

"Eight ships just dropped stealth in the area the nuke penetrators came from, and they're accelerating in. I see four frigates, two run-of-the-mill destroyers, and two *Warrior*-class destroyers. They're firing at *Freedom* and her escorts."

Brad's guess had been right. The Cadre wanted to force *Freedom* and her escorts to choose between their own survival and that of Ceres. It was a good thing that Fields had a few cards hidden up his sleeve.

The scene ahead of them played out just like he'd guessed it would. The hidden detachment of Fleet destroyers fired a salvo of torpedoes at the enemy ships while *Freedom* and her consorts focused on the nukes.

Brad needed to wait until the ships near him were ready to commit. He wanted all twelve of the evil weapons in play before he revealed himself.

"A second enemy task force has come out of stealth," Narendra said, sitting abruptly straighter. "They were right behind the hidden Fleet destroyers! They're firing."

It only took Brad a moment to realize he'd made another mistake in underestimating the Cadre. Regardless of what Mader had said, he had more ships in reserve than he'd let on.

"What are we looking at?" Brad asked, leaning forward.

"Eight more destroyers. They have the drop on the Fleet units, and our allies are having to turn and face them rather than engage the ships firing on *Freedom*."

Two *Warriors*, ten older destroyers, and four frigates against a cruiser and a dozen destroyers. A close fight on a good day, but half the Fleet units were taking torpedoes from the rear, and the rest were splitting fire between a powerful attack force that could kill them and weapons that might destroy all life on Ceres.

And that didn't count the ships hidden near Brad, waiting for the right moment to open fire with weapons of mass destruction and then join the fray.

If the Vikings didn't act now, the tide of battle could turn and the Cadre would win.

Brad could commit his five ships to the fight, but he'd lose surprise. Then the remaining nuke penetrators would still be able to fire. He'd only spotted two of the damned things. There were four more and he was trapped in limbo until they went active, forced to watch the destruction of his allies.

CHAPTER TWENTY-EIGHT

"WHICH TWO OF our ships are farthest from Ceres?" Brad asked after a moment.

"*Grant* and *Montgomery*," Michelle said.

"Xan, order them to hold position and remain in stealth. *Oath*, *Law*, and *Honor* are going in to help Fleet fight off these bastards. Tell Fabia and Keala I want them to hit the remaining penetrators when the Cadre fires them and then disengage. This isn't a suicide mission, so I'd much rather them break contact and circle around than stand their ground."

Narendra growled like an angry animal. "*Freedom* is focusing on the incoming penetrators while her escorts try to protect her. She's taken out four of them, but they've lost three destroyers in the exchange. She'll get the last two, but the Cadre is going to be all over them by that point."

"What's the flight time for our mass-driver rounds to the nukes closest to us?"

"Thirty-five and forty seconds. The two destroyers are a little farther away, so add ten seconds for them."

"We'll fire our Gatlings at the two penetrators we can see. *Law* and *Honor* will fire their smaller Gatlings on the penetrators as well. In addition, they'll fire their larger mass drivers at the two destroyers we've detected. We'll hope they don't detect anything in time to react."

Seconds later, the tactical officer nodded. "Mass-driver rounds on the way from *Law*, *Honor*, and us. Thirty seconds until initial impact. Since the targets aren't moving, we've got a pretty good chance of getting hits at this short range. That'll be more than enough for the penetrators, but maybe not the ships unless *Law* and *Honor* get solid hits with their heavier rounds."

"Michelle, we'll go to flank speed as soon as the second penetrator goes up. Make sure *Law* and *Honor* are with us."

Brad watched the time slowly bleed away while he kept his other eye on the sensors. The penetrators wouldn't make that big a show when hit, so he was watching closely to make sure that they actually hit them.

The first penetrator came apart right on schedule, undoubtedly causing great consternation on board the Cadre ship tasked with firing it. The second penetrator burst apart a few seconds later.

That part of the operation had been pretty much foreordained. Detecting mass-driver rounds in flight on passive scanners was just about impossible. Even with active scanners, it wasn't all that easy.

"Going to full speed," Michelle said.

"Active sensors, Narendra," Brad ordered.

The repeater screen on his command chair blossomed with information. Since they already knew where two of the Cadre ships were, he was able to get confirmation on their class immediately: both were destroyers.

One of them must've realized they'd probably been spotted, because it went to full power and began evasive maneuvers that were only partially successful. They escaped the smaller mass-driver rounds but caught a burst of the heavier slugs from one of the *Bound*-class ships in the engineering section.

They didn't blow up, but they immediately lost thrust and began tumbling.

"Make sure someone on *Law* or *Honor* finishes them," Brad said coldly.

Heavy mass-driver rounds tore the second destroyer apart even as he gave the order. They ripped massive divots into the enemy ship's hull, and then it exploded.

By that time, his three destroyers were under full power and racing toward the area where Fleet was making their final stand against the attacking ships. His ships seemed to have surprised the Cadre ships they were hiding near, because no one fired at them for long seconds.

"Signal detected from behind us," Xan said. "It's using the same encryption scheme we got from the shuttle you captured, sir. It's a stand-down order. Instructions to hold fire, maintain stealth, and execute something called Jericho as soon as we engage the Cadre ships ahead of us."

Brad had no idea why they were holding fire, but it suited his plans just fine. "Jericho is probably firing the last of the nuke penetrators," he guessed. "Let's hope they don't go active before they launch them. If they see *Grant* and *Montgomery*, things will get very ugly for them very fast. How long until we can fire on the Cadre ships ahead of us with any realistic chance of hitting them?"

"We're inside mass-driver range already, even if the odds of good hits suck," Narendra said. "*Law* and *Honor* have already opened fire with their heavy drivers. Five minutes until we can fire torpedoes."

Five minutes was an eternity in a space battle. Brad hoped that some of the Fleet ships were still there when he was in a position to help.

———

Sixty seconds later, Xan detected a signal from the ships attacking the Fleet units. It was in a different code from the one the ships behind them had used, so they couldn't decipher the transmission.

What they could do was count the number of exchanges, of which there were several. While Brad couldn't be certain, it felt like there was some kind of disagreement between the two groups.

Whoever was still hiding in stealth got the last word, though. Five ships broke off from attacking the remaining Fleet units and raced to meet Brad's oncoming force: a *Warrior* and four lighter destroyers.

Fields and his people had suffered for splitting their attention. Even though they'd stopped all six of the penetrators, most of the friendly units were damaged or destroyed.

Out of the dozen destroyers Fleet had started with, six were destroyed outright and three more were combat kills. The final three were all damaged to some degree, though still fighting. *Freedom* was a wreck, but a fighting wreck.

Attacking them were five destroyers and a frigate. All the Cadre ships were damaged as well, but not as badly as the Fleet units. The only thing that had kept them from already sweeping the table was the skill advantage Fleet had.

And that wasn't going to save Brad's friends for very much longer.

"How long until we can fire on the task force coming our way?" Brad asked. "Torpedoes, not mass drivers."

"About a hundred seconds," Narendra said. "*Law* and *Honor* are firing mass drivers, but the other ships are evading our shots. They'll have to get a lot closer to be effective. We'll be exchanging torpedoes by that time."

Brad was about to order more speed, and damn the safety margins, when one of the destroyers ahead of them ran into a wall of heavy mass-driver slugs. It had to have been a fluke, but the angle was just about perfect, blowing the bow off the enemy ship.

That resulted in the other ships scattering a bit. No one wanted a *Bound*-class destroyer dialed in to their location.

That separation wouldn't affect the enemy's offensive power much, but it sure as hell had implications on their mutual defense against incoming torpedoes. It also evened up the firepower a bit.

"Target torpedoes on the *Warrior*," Brad ordered. "As soon as we're in extreme range, open fire. If we let them get too close, they'll rip us apart. They all have battle damage, so let's use our better condition to our advantage."

"The enemy isn't dodging as much as I'd expect," Narendra said. "That made the destroyer more predictable, I think. Could it be the fact that they didn't refuel as expected?"

Brad started to dismiss the idea but then remembered that Mader had ordered his ships to take extra fuel from some of the ships meeting his force. If they took enough, those ships could be extremely low on fuel and trying to conserve as much as they could.

"Plug that into your tactical calculations," Brad said. "Pass it on to *Law*, *Honor*, and the Fleet ships. We all knew it, but we didn't count on there being such a big effect from it. If we're wrong, we don't lose much. If we're right, we could flip this around."

They didn't get any other lucky mass-driver hits, unfortunately. The next big moment in the battle came when Narendra fired eight torpedoes at the *Warrior*.

His ships drew almost five times that number in return and went into evasive action while transitioning their smaller Gatlings to defense. The Cadre destroyers each picked one of his ships as a target, while the light cruiser split her fire between *Law* and *Honor*.

At least one of the *Bound*-class ships had focused on the *Warrior*, because that ship had the bad luck to catch at least one heavy mass-driver slug while the incoming torpedoes were on final approach, screwing with her defensive fire at a critical moment.

Rather than stopping most or all of the incoming torpedoes, they only managed to stop two. Two more missed the big destroyer, but four slammed into the ship at almost the same moment.

The *Warrior* exploded.

That didn't mean everything was turning up roses for the home team, though. *Law* stopped all but two torpedoes with defensive fire or reactive armor, but those last two got in solid hits, knocking the destroyer off course. They indicated they had substantial damage but were still in the fight.

Honor took one unlucky hit on a heavy mass-driver turret, cutting their offensive fire in half. They were otherwise undamaged.

Oath of Vengeance managed to avoid any crippling hits, but they had a lot of damaged systems. Nothing that couldn't be repaired after the fight, though. If they survived.

The enemy destroyers hadn't come out of the exchange unscathed. One of them had eaten a few heavy mass-driver rounds and was already veering away from the fight. With only a moment's hesitation, the remaining destroyers emulated their fearful sister and broke off the engagement.

Or they would have if Brad had allowed it.

"Fire on them," he ordered. "Add two of our torpedoes to *Honor*'s fire to help make up for their damage."

This time, the other ships' lack of evasive maneuvering took a heavier toll. The ship that *Oath* fired six torpedoes at stopped only one. Well, they stopped the rest with their hull, but that blew them up.

Law gutted their target without too much trouble. *Honor* must've been in worse shape than they'd admitted, because they missed. Or perhaps it was just bad luck.

Brad's precaution of firing two torpedoes at their target was only marginally effective. The enemy took out one of the torpedoes and the other only struck a glancing blow that didn't seem to slow them down in the slightest. In fact, they put on extra speed.

"Send *Honor* after that one, long enough to fire a few more salvos of mass-driver rounds, but don't let them get distracted from the fight around the Fleet units," Brad ordered. "We'll need them in a few minutes. Have *Law* end the crippled destroyer before it gets its act together and fires on us. How long to get to *Freedom* and what is their condition?"

"They're hurt bad," Michelle said. "And they only have one destroyer guarding their flank against those three destroyers."

"Take us in."

"The remaining Cadre ships just came out of stealth," Narendra said. "Looks like two frigates, four destroyers, and…and a cruiser. Sir, it's *Lioness*.

"The destroyers must've already placed the remaining four nuke penetrators. They're accelerating toward Ceres."

Here it was: the moment of truth. Mader had the drop on them and was going to come for them right now. Against all those ships and a cruiser to boot, they didn't have a chance in hell, but he'd do what he could to end the Phoenix before he died.

With that kind of overwhelming firepower arrayed against them, Brad wouldn't have blamed *Grant* or *Montgomery* if they'd held their fire, but the two destroyers came out of stealth virtually under the guns of the enemy ships. One fired at the nukes with everything they had while the other engaged the enemy ships that were already turning on them.

Moments later, *Grant* and *Montgomery* were gone, but so were the last of the nuke penetrators. His people had died, but they'd traded their lives for millions of innocent people. At this range, he couldn't tell if the Cadre ships were seriously damaged, but they still seemed to be in fighting shape.

It hurt him, but he knew that had he been in that situation, he'd have done the same as his people, no matter the personal cost, but their loss was a punch to the gut. Now all that was left was to play this charade out to the bitter end.

As if mirroring his thoughts, both *Honor* and *Law* finished their targets and moved back to join *Oath* in racing to *Freedom*'s defense.

The cruiser was now fighting alone, having lost the last of the destroyers defending her flank. There was no chance that Brad's ships would get there in time. He knew that, but he didn't let himself waver. They'd do what they could to save the Fleet cruiser and then turn on the new Cadre ships.

Only *Lioness* and her escorts just sat there, not accelerating toward Ceres at all.

That prompted several transmissions from the surviving Cadre destroyers, but Mader didn't respond. He just sat there as if he were watching the last of the fight play out, watching Brad try to snatch victory from the jaws of defeat.

Well, if he was going to play that game, Brad wouldn't argue.

"Engineering, I need more speed," he said over the com.

"I'm already giving you ten percent more than I should," Mike said, pausing at the end to swear at someone else in the compartment.

"Then give me more," Brad said. "*Freedom* is going to die if we don't get there faster."

"And we'll die if our engines go critical. I'll do what I can."

That turned out to be an additional few percent of speed and Brad was glad for it.

"Time to engagement range?" he asked Narendra.

"Ninety seconds," she said. "*Freedom* doesn't have that long."

That might've been true, but the surviving attackers lost their nerve before they managed to kill the cruiser. Seeing three mostly undamaged destroyers racing toward them with blood in their eyes was more than they could seemingly handle, especially after being hung out to dry by their leader. They broke and shot off in three different directions.

A mistake, as *Freedom* proved when she promptly destroyed one of them as soon as the pressure was off.

"Send *Law* and *Honor* after one and we'll take the other," Brad said grimly.

The Vikings' destroyers had a significant speed advantage on the enemy and blew past the crippled Fleet cruiser just as Brad's missiles found and killed his target. He immediately ordered *Oath* to decelerate hard and come around to protect the cruiser.

The *Bound*-class destroyers ended their target next, leaving only *Lioness* and her escorts to deal with. It would be a short, brutal fight that his people would lose, but if this was the day he died, he'd die well.

Only, the Cadre ships declined the engagement. They turned away from Ceres as a unit and moved off without even sending a transmission toward their enemies. Minutes later, they were accelerating hard and obviously not coming back to finish the survivors off.

The Battle of Ceres was over.

CHAPTER TWENTY-NINE

Freedom was a battered wreck. Brad had thought he'd understood the degree of her damage before, but as *Oath of Vengeance* tucked herself into a tight escort position on the cruiser's flank, he saw he'd underestimated it.

There were gaping holes in the big ship's armor. Entire sections of hull just…gone. She'd started with reactive armor over basically her entire exterior, and if any of the ablative strips were left, Brad couldn't see them.

And yet.

And yet she was still in the fight. She'd lost four heavy mass-driver turrets—but she still had four left. Dozens of her octobarrel gatling mass drivers were off-line, but dozens more remained. Half of her torpedo tubes were gone, but she retained over twice *Oath of Vengeance*'s torpedo armament.

The Commonwealth Fleet built their cruisers tough. *Freedom* was a wreck, but she and her escorts had held.

The Cadre had blinked. Brad wasn't entirely sure why—Everlit only knew, but the remaining destroyers and half-crippled cruiser couldn't have stopped *Lioness*, let alone the remaining escorts.

"*Freedom*, this is *Oath of Vengeance*," Xan Wong said into her microphone. "How can we assist?"

It took a few seconds before a response made it back.

"*Oath*, this is *Freedom* Actual," Fields's own voice answered them. "Good to see you're still with us. I think we have things aboard *Freedom* as under control as they're going to be, but our sensors just finally gave up the ghost."

The fact that Brad wasn't even getting a video feed from the cruiser was a hint as to the level of damage she'd taken.

"I'm about to kick all of my parasite craft out into space for search and rescue, but I don't even have local traffic control radar. Can I get you to handle coordinating SAR? Ceres's local space is a mess and I want to make sure we don't lose anyone we can save."

"We can do that," Brad told Fields instantly. "We lost two of our ships out here, too. Can I lean on your authority to get the locals to deploy to help out as well?" He grimaced. "While I suspect my name might be slightly less mud down there than it was yesterday, the people we need to talk to don't want to hear from me."

"They'll listen now," Fields said flatly. "I'll get in touch with space traffic control and let them know the situation. You're officially under a full combat contract with Fleet now, Madrid. In fact, we need to make that retroactive to at least twenty-four hours ago. We owe you death benefits and costs, at least."

"Won't bring back my dead, but I appreciate it," Brad said grimly. "We'll start getting our shuttles into space as well. I think I'm keeping my *destroyers* attached to your apron-strings for a bit. Consider it mutual security."

The Fleet Commodore chuckled, but it was a bitter tone.

"I appreciate it," he said sadly. "I've lost a lot of people today. I don't know why the Cadre ran, but I don't see a choice but to let them go."

"Unless you've got another cruiser or six in your back pocket that you didn't mention, I don't see us having a choice," Brad replied. "We'll find everyone we can, Commodore. You have my word."

———

Six hours later, the unending litany of escape pods, survivors, and prisoners was beginning to blur together for Brad. There were probably more Cadre prisoners today than in any other action with them to date, but price…the price was far too high.

Grant and *Montgomery* were gone. They'd engaged a cruiser at point-blank range, and their focus had been on saving Ceres, not themselves. There were no survivors from Brad's two lost ships.

Most of Fleet had been luckier, but that was a relative thing. Brad wasn't sure where their butcher's bill was going to end up, but they'd pulled something like five hundred Fleet personnel out of the debris.

If he'd only been looking at destroyer crews, that would have been half of the crews…but there'd been another four hundred Fleet officers and spacers on the space station, plus almost three thousand civilians.

There were a lot of names added to the list Brad owed the Phoenix today.

"Suit oxygen would have run out twenty minutes ago," Michelle said quietly. "Anyone who didn't make it to an escape pod is gone."

He nodded with a grunt. His people hadn't launched pods. They hadn't found any drifting Dutchmen, either.

"I hope that the locals appreciate what we did," he said hoarsely. "And what it cost us."

"We'll see," his wife replied. "If they don't, I think Commodore Fields will make sure they change their minds."

Oath of Vengeance still orbited beside *Freedom*, barely a kilometer clear of the bigger ship's starboard flank. *Bound by Law* and *Bound by Honor* made up the other corners of a triangle around the Fleet vessel. *Honor* was short a heavy turret, but his gunships were still a potent shield against future trouble.

"What about the nukes?" Brad asked.

"Locals have dialed in the debris from the penetrators and are tracking crash locations," she said. "None are looking particularly critical. Piazzi is going to get an ugly shower of radioactive isotopes, but nothing that will penetrate the dome."

"Thank Everlit. We did it."

"Yeah. We did." Michelle leaned her head on his shoulder. They tried to avoid public displays of affection on duty, but no one was going to say anything today.

"We're still running traffic control for over a hundred shuttles," he told her. "We're looking for pods and large chunks of debris now. That's…well, that's the easier part of this."

The hard part was looking for Dutchmen, loose suits like how he'd very nearly died once.

"We'll find everyone we can. The Phoenix doesn't get more victories than he earned," Michelle said fiercely.

"Agreed." Brad shook his head. "I'm looking forward to the interrogation reports from the prisoners, too. They're going to have a lot of data for us, but I'll admit I only have one real pressing question."

"Why they withdrew," his wife said with a nod.

"Mader handed us victory from the jaws of defeat. We probably would have beaten the crap out of *Lioness*, but he'd have taken us. Pulling out like that, abandoning his own people…"

Brad shook his head again, trying to clear the cobwebs.

"And with what we heard on Kobayashi? I feel like it adds up, somehow. There was a plan here…and I'm not sure it had *anything* to do with actually taking Ceres."

———

"I've got new engines on our scans," Lewin reported later that day.

She sounded tired. They were. Brad wasn't even sure when he'd last slept—or when he planned to next. A new threat, though…that could be bad.

"Where are they coming from?"

"Looks like Kobayashi Station," she told him after running some numbers. "Wait—the lead ship is *Horatio*."

"We are receiving a transmission from Captain Suzuki," Xan added as Lewin stopped. "Shall I put it on?"

"Of course," Brad ordered. He wiped his repeater screens of their current displays and turned his attention to the main screen.

Suzuki was a broad-shouldered man with near-black skin and pronounced folds to his eyes. Even among Brad's ex-Fleet officers, he was a rarity: an Earth native, born somewhere in China, Brad believed.

"Commodore Madrid, we are en route to provide assistance at Ceres," he said calmly. "We were relieved at Kobayashi by Fleet elements with an Agency warrant. I don't want to discuss further details on an open channel.

"Upon hearing the reports from Ceres, Commodore Boerefijn detached a significant portion of his forces to head to Ceres with us," he continued. "I have *Horatio* herself, two Fleet destroyers, and a dozen corvettes and frigates. I make it six hours until we are in position to assist."

Brad breathed a sigh of relief and activated a two-way channel.

"You had me worried, Captain," he told Suzuki. "We weren't expecting you back anytime soon."

With the problems on Ceres, even an Agency warrant didn't mean that Kobayashi was still in friendly hands, but there was nothing Suzuki could have done in the face of it—especially if this Commodore Boerefijn had enough ships to detach fourteen of them to relieve Ceres.

"The extra ships and hands will be more than welcome," he continued. "The situation here is a mess. It's as under control as it's going to get anytime soon, but..." He shrugged. "Like I said, more than welcome."

"That's what both Boerefijn and I presumed," Suzuki told him. "I'll need an in-person meeting with you as soon as we make it to Ceres. We learned more before we left—things I think you need to know."

"I may have to go fall over before then," Brad admitted, "but I'll make sure we're ready when you get here."

There was only one thing Suzuki could have learned that would have been that important. His subordinate knew where the Cadre had taken Agent Falcone.

The channel cut off and Brad leaned back in his chair, exhaling slowly.

"You need to go sleep," his wife told him. He jumped. He'd sent *her* to go nap after their last conversation, and that had only been a couple of hours before.

"And you don't?" he asked dryly, turning to look over at her. She was still clearly tired, with her hair in a ragged ponytail and bags under her eyes.

She was still gorgeous. He was probably biased.

"I woke up again," Michelle admitted with a grin. "Look, we both need a solid twelve hours of sleep, but if you need to talk to Suzuki in six hours, you need to be as ready as you can be. Go sleep. Narendra and I will hold down the bridge."

"Okay," Brad conceded. Rising from his chair, he looked around his bridge and grinned. "In that case, I see at least half a dozen *other* people who should go get some rest too, don't you, my dear XO?"

CHAPTER THIRTY

"THE GOOD NEWS is that it looks like Earth is taking this all damn seriously," Fields told Brad over the radio six hours later. The mercenary Commodore was watching with one eye as Suzuki's shuttle made its way over to *Oath of Vengeance,* and listening to the Fleet Commodore.

"That sounds like it's supposed to come with a side of 'bad news', Mark," Brad told the older man. "What's bad about Earth taking this seriously, beyond it being too late to make a difference?"

"Task Group *Immortal* just left orbit heading our way," the Commodore said flatly. "There is no way—none at *all*—that they got a battleship moving in thirty-six hours without prior preparation. Let alone a battleship, three cruisers, twelve destroyers, and thirty frigates."

Brad inhaled sharply.

Immortal. One of the Commonwealth Fleet's three battleships. The newest of them, not that any of the battleships were particularly modern. At six times the size of even the brand-new *Tremendous*-class cruisers, they didn't *need* to be. The sheer overwhelming firepower of their heavy fifteen-centimeter mass-driver turrets and torpedo batteries was more than enough—and that was ignoring the four *eighty*-centimeter super-heavy mass-driver turrets the ships carried.

But the battleships weren't truly mobile ships. They were too big to accelerate at the rates of the smaller Fleet ships, burned too much fuel. You could make up the difference by accelerating a bit longer and get there at much the same time in the end, but it cost a *lot* of fuel to move a battleship.

None of them had moved in Brad's entire adult life. And now one was heading to Ceres.

"Forty-six ships" was what he said aloud, however, summarizing Fields's comment. "That's definitely them taking the situation seriously, though I'm surprised they have that many ships to hand."

Hopefully, his tone was enough of a warning to Fields. With everything going on, he no longer trusted the Fleet's communications to be secure. Everdark, he barely trusted the *Fleet* anymore.

"Yeah," Fields said slowly, the long-drawn-out word showing he'd caught what Brad hadn't said. He shook his head, clearly thinking through something.

"We'll need to get copies of all of your sensor records, and I owe you at least a partial payment for your service," he continued, as if they hadn't just decided that they couldn't continue this conversation on a channel. "We owe you the price tag of two *Warriors*, and I'll admit I simply don't have that in my reserve, but I'll see what I can do.

"Would you be available for me to come aboard *Oath of Vengeance* and trade data for cash in person?"

And have the conversation they couldn't have over a radio channel.

"I am always at your disposal, Commodore," Brad told him. "I have a meeting with *Horatio*'s commander, but I'll be available after that. Say, sixteen hundred GMT?"

That would give Suzuki two hours to get through what he'd learned. Hopefully, that would be enough.

"That works," Fields confirmed. "I'll want to get your feeling on this whole battle as well, Commodore. Keep an hour or so free for me?"

"I'll do what I can."

———

Suzuki looked almost offensively rested and put-together. He saluted crisply as he entered the room with Brad and Michelle, then took a quick seat.

"Are you two all right?" he asked. "Everything I've seen says it was bad."

"We're fine," Brad said shortly. "I'm not going to get used to losing friends, but I have the sick feeling it will happen again. Until and unless we put an end to the Everdarkened Cadre."

"What happened at Kobayashi, Captain? I thought I left you orders to stay in place."

Suzuki snorted.

"That was my plan," he agreed. "We had the situation under control and the prisoners contained when the Fleet just showed up out of the night, about twelve hours after the attack on Ceres.

"From what Commodore Boerefijn told me, they'd been on a dark patrol through the Belt and responded as soon as you sent your report to the Agency." Suzuki grimaced. "I didn't get the impression that Boerefijn was entirely *enthused* with having his command coopted by the Agency, but it was pretty clear he works for Director Harmon. Not least because there were at *least* three Agents on the bridge of his carrier."

It took Brad a few seconds to process the several surprises in there. Antonio Harmon was the Director of the Agency, Brad's ultimate boss when he wore that hat. And, apparently, he had an entire carrier group swanning around at his orders.

"A carrier, Suzuki?" Michelle asked.

"Yeah. *Scorpio*," *Horatio*'s Captain confirmed. "Almost gave me a panic moment, but she's CV-03 and had all the right codes. They're Fleet, not Cadre." He shook his head. "And Agency. They had all of our people hustled off the station within an hour of arriving. Took possession of everything, even the Phoenix's shuttle and its computers.

"With a drone carrier and four destroyers watching me, I wasn't going to argue," he admitted. "That said, well, we'd already copied everything left of the Phoenix's computers. I don't begrudge the Agency their data, but I figured we had as much right to it as anyone."

Brad traded a glance with his wife. Suzuki knew they worked with the Agency a lot but didn't know that Brad was actually an Agency operative.

Director Harmon, though, *definitely* did. To shuffle Brad's people off like that...well, the right hand didn't seem to be talking to the left.

"Get anything useful?" Brad finally asked.

"I barely know computer code from great literature," Suzuki told them cheerfully. "Reece, however, cracked some of the key files before we left."

Tisha Reece was one of Brad's crackers, an exceptionally skilled group of experts he'd picked up to make sure computer security never got in his way. She was neither the first nor the best, but she was a close second-best. Assigning her to *Horatio* seemed to have broken in their favor.

"What kind of key files? Did she find out what 'Red Diamond' is?" Brad asked.

"No...but we may know *where* it is," the junior Captain replied. "The Phoenix had a communication channel open to Earth at two separate times while he was aboard the shuttle. They wiped the recordings immediately, but the com buffers still recorded the direction the transmitters were pointed."

"That's pretty slim to go on," Michelle pointed out.

"Yeah. And I'm not sure how Sergeant Reece pulled it off, but she pinged that *both* calls were directed from the same location. At Earth."

"There's a lot of crap in Earth's orbit," Brad replied. "That doesn't narrow it down."

"Even in Earth orbit, Commodore, there are only so many objects," Suzuki told him. "I don't know how Reece did it, it's outside of *my* expertise like I said, but she's flagged a small space station as the relay point."

That...that was more than he'd dared hope for. If it was a single station, he might be able to get access, find data.

"We have no sanction to operate in Earth space," Michelle reminded him. "The Guild, specifically, is banned from operating there."

The Agency wasn't...but it was also an established rule that the authority of the Commonwealth ended at Earth's atmosphere. Its *power* didn't, the economies of the Earthbound nations being utterly dependent on space-based resources now, but the Commonwealth explicitly had no authority on Earth.

Which meant even the Agency wasn't supposed to operate on the ground, and a station in orbit almost certainly wasn't the prison they were looking for.

"Good work, Captain," Brad said slowly. "I think we owe Sergeant Reece another promotion. We'll want her pulled over to *Oath of Vengeance* in any case."

"Commodore?" Suzuki asked carefully.

"If she's the one who cracked the data, she knows more than anyone what we're looking at, so I'm taking her with me to Earth."

Both his wife and his subordinate swallowed hard.

"I should also mention," Suzuki said slowly, "that Reece thinks she knows the name of the person Mader was talking to. They did something to double-delete the data, but she got a partial name: Andrews."

"Just Andrews, huh?" Brad asked. He didn't think he recognized the name, but it niggled at him with its familiarity.

"Jessica Andrews?" his wife demanded.

"We didn't get a full name," Suzuki replied. "Why?"

Now Brad remembered.

"Because Jessica Andrews is a supposedly dead Senator who's tied up with the Cadre," Brad told Suzuki. "And if Mader was talking to Andrews, then this just went from *urgent* to *yesterday*.

"Michelle—start getting the ship ready to move. Suzuki—thank you. I might be able to save an old friend now, and it's thanks to you."

The ex-Fleet officer saluted.

"I only know half of what's going on, sir," he conceded. "But I'm certain that's something I can feel good about."

By the time Commodore Mark Fields made his way aboard, *Oath of Vengeance*'s crew was in full hustle. They were going to be double-bunking the ground teams, bringing extra fire teams over from all three of the other ships to make sure Brad had the firepower for his mission.

If any of his officers or mercenaries questioned why he was making sure he had two full platoons aboard for a flight to Earth, it seemed they trusted him. Beyond all sanity, in his opinion, but it was a good thing regardless.

"You're looking busy," Fields said as he shook Brad's hand.

"We'll be shipping out shortly," Brad told him. "Something's come up. My office, please?"

Fields nodded and followed him silently, taking in the urgency around the ship.

"Where are you going, Madrid?" he asked as the door shut behind him. "I'm pretty sure there's nowhere in this star system more secure than your damn office, so tell me the truth."

"I now know where Kate Falcone is being held prisoner," Brad replied. "I may also know where what we believe to be a key Cadre financial supporter is hiding—and I have reason to think they're the same place."

Fields took a seat while thinking.

"You'd be more specific with me if it was anywhere in the Outer System," he noted. "Between the Guild and the Agency, there's only one place in the entire system you could be going that you wouldn't want to tell me."

Brad took his own seat, laying his hands on the desk and studying his old friend and sometime mentor across the plain plastic surface.

"And?" he asked calmly.

"What in Everdark are you planning on doing at Earth?" the Fleet Commodore said bluntly. "I'll stretch my oaths pretty damn far, but if you're taking a warship to Earth with intent..."

"Someone on Earth kidnapped Kate Falcone before she could testify to the Senate about Transplanetary Macro Fabrication supplying warships to the Cadre," Brad pointed out. "Someone on Earth has to be paying for those warships, too. Someone on Earth recruited the officers the Cadre is using to man their fleet.

"*Earth*, Commodore, seems to be the center of more problems than we thought."

Fields was silent again for several seconds, then sighed.

"You're not Fleet, regardless of your auxiliary status," he pointed out. "So, there's things you don't know, don't see."

"And?" Brad repeated.

"One of those is the readiness reports for the battleships," Fields told him. "Fuel is *expensive*. They're kept *combat*-ready, Brad, not *travel*-ready. *Immortal* shouldn't have had enough fuel aboard for even a two-day flight, let alone the ten days to get to Ceres.

"Missiles, troops, mass-driver rounds? She's fully stocked on all of those, but prepping her and her battle group to head out to Ceres? We're talking at least four days. Maybe a week."

"And she left, what, thirty hours after the attack?" Brad asked.

"Exactly. Someone knew, Brad," the Fleet Commodore told him. "Someone knew long enough in advance to start getting a battleship task group ready—which means we could have had an entire *squadron* of cruisers in place to meet *Lioness*."

"You were supposed to lose."

Brad's words hung in the room for a long time.

"Yeah," Fields admitted. "Someone wanted an incident, a clear atrocity against civilians that would provoke…I don't know what."

"War." Brad shook his head. "Senator Barnes said something about that, about a pro-war faction pushing to 'bring the Outer System in line.'"

"Look, Brad, I can't approve of you heading back to Earth with blood in your eyes," the Fleet Commodore said quietly. "I *can't*. But you're right that something's rotten back home. And if you are…how do you know who to trust?"

"I think I can trust Senator Barnes," Brad told him. "I know I can trust you. A few key people at the Agency. It'll be enough, Commodore. I'll *make* it be enough."

"And what happens when all the ducks come home to roost?" Fields asked. "Brad, this isn't using nukes against a pirate base without authority. This is Earth. You're talking about not just treason but… something close to *blasphemy*."

"Someone's already committed treason," Brad pointed out. "And they've got my friend. Nothing else really matters, does it?"

CHAPTER THIRTY-ONE

"Earth Orbital Control, this is the mercenary destroyer *Oath of Vengeance*, requesting orbital insertion slot," Xan Wong said into the microphone. "We have safed our weapons and will stand by for Fleet escort."

On their second trip to Earth, Brad's people could guess the drill. They had every intention of being fully cooperative—right up until the moment he had to launch a hostile boarding action against a civilian station, anyway.

His coms officer listened to the response from EOC, shaking her head where they couldn't see her.

"Same song as last time," she reported. "Hold position outside Lunar orbit and stand by for Fleet escort. They want to know our business here."

"Tell them it's personal, we're coming in to provide rest and relaxation, along with therapy for people injured in the Battle of Ceres."

That was news all over the system. Brad wasn't entirely enthused with his name being plastered across the news waves as a hero, but his people deserved the acclaim. The various news outlets were estimating they'd saved about three million lives, minimum.

Given that there weren't that many people on Ceres, he figured they had to be overestimating that number somewhere.

Other than watching the news, the trip to Earth had been almost boring. They'd made sure to pass Task Group *Immortal* at a good distance, but the kilometer-long warship had been a sight nonetheless.

Brad had never seen one of the battleships in motion, let alone accompanied by an entire fleet. They might *call* it a task group, but he'd only ever seen forty-plus warships in one place before—when the Cadre had tried to take Blackhawk Station out at Saturn.

Those ships had been almost entirely corvettes and frigates. The frigates of *Immortal*'s escort alone would have outgunned that pirate fleet. Now, though...now they knew the Cadre had carriers and cruisers of their own.

Probably not battleships. Brad had lost a *lot* of his people keeping cruisers out of the Cadre's hands, too, but he suspected they had at least another one on top of *Lioness*.

If they had a battleship, though, the Cadre would already control the Jovian Cluster.

"They confirm our intentions," Xan replied after a few moments, then chuckled. She activated her microphone. "Heard and received, EOC. I'll pass that on. Thanks."

She put the headset down and turned back to Brad.

"Apparently, the EOC operator's cousin is a VP at a company called Palace Resorts. They have resorts on the equator—plus hotels on Ceres. She's sending me his contact information, figures we could get a deal through them."

Brad wasn't actually there for R&R, but that still warmed his heart. He supposed being called out as a hero had some advantages—he hadn't expected deals on resorts to be among them!

"Well, it would look odd if we didn't try and take advantage of that, wouldn't it?" he asked. "Send the contact to Michelle. We'll see if we can get something arranged."

"Will do," Xan promised.

"As for our actual mission...get in touch with Senator Barnes's people. He and I need to talk."

"I appreciate you making time for me, Senator," Brad said as he was once again led into Barnes's luxurious station-board apartment. For a man as busy and important as the sole Senator for the Jovian Cluster to have seen him within the week—let alone within the *day* as he'd managed—spoke to the strength of their relationship.

Which, given how heavily Brad was intending to impose on said relationship, was a good thing.

"We have a common set of goals at the moment, I think," the Senator told him, filling two tall-stemmed wine glasses with purified water. "I'll admit I wasn't expecting to see you back at Earth yourself for a while yet, but your timing is impeccable. What have you learned?"

"I was hoping you'd learned a few things yourself," Brad admitted. "I have some key pieces that *should* be enough for me to locate Agent Falcone, but…I'm frankly terrified of where they point."

Barnes grunted.

"Home," he guessed. "Specifically, the homeworld."

"Yes."

"I've managed to track down a copy of Agent Falcone's evidence against TMF," Barnes told Brad. "That was…far harder than it should have been. Unfortunately, we've lost a lot of her validation and support, so a hand-picked team of people from the Agency is working on that as we speak—and another handpicked team is currently purging the Agency's Earthside personnel pool."

Brad winced.

"That's why I came to you," he admitted. "I have grounds to believe the Agency is compromised. The control for our operating agent on Ceres sent her into a trap—and then sent a Cadre kill team to her location when she called for extraction."

The Senator sighed and drained his glass of water. He looked at it with a disappointed face, as if he'd forgot what he'd filled it with, then sighed and refilled it.

"I don't suppose any report to that effect has made it back to the Director?" he asked.

"What channels would I trust?" Brad replied.

"Do you trust me?" Barnes said. "I'm meeting with Antonio in the morning; I can pass it on to him directly. It'll add at least one name to his list."

"How bad is it?" the mercenary turned covert operative asked.

"I don't know," Barnes admitted. "Antonio has told me more than he's told any other sitting Senator, and he hasn't told me much of anything at all. I know he's arresting Agents and support staff left and right, but he's keeping it on the down-low.

"I think he's worried someone *else* is moving in the shadows…and the Commonwealth is supposed to only have one covert agency."

"Damn," Brad murmured. "That lines up with what I've learned."

"Which was?"

"The Phoenix was in recurring communication with someone on Earth, probably Jessica Andrews. Often enough that even while he was on a shuttle to inspect a covert refueling station, he spoke to her twice.

"We located the relay station and confirmed the name *Andrews*—and the Phoenix himself told me that we'd find the answer to Falcone's location aboard Kobayashi Station."

Barnes was silent. He rose, poured his untouched water into the sink, and produced a bottle of wine from a cupboard. The Senator took only the barest of glances at the dark green bottle before grabbing two fresh glasses and filling them.

"Jessica Andrews is dead," he finally noted. "She died in a shuttle accident years ago."

"Not so much. That should have been in Agent Falcone's data," Brad told him. "We found footage of her aboard *Longbow*. She's been working with the Cadre, which suggests a connection back to Earth."

The Senator drained the glass of wine he'd just poured, coughing after he swallowed.

"Abuse of fine wine," he admitted, looking down at the empty glass. "I don't think you even begin to comprehend the level of problem Jessica Andrews being involved in this entails, Brad."

"Right now, I know that a friend and colleague is being held prisoner on Earth, where I have no authority, no sanction," Brad remined the other man. "How much more of a problem can we be facing than something that's going to require *treason* on my part to fix?"

"Treason," Barnes echoed, still staring into his glass. "That's a good Everdarkened word, isn't it? Jessica Andrews was an opposition Senator, yes, but she worked with both President Reynolds...and then-Senator Dave Mills."

Mills. David Mills.

Even Brad knew that name. *President* David "call me Dave" Mills was the head of the Commonwealth Senate, the leader of the Commonwealth. First among equals of the Senators, his power was relatively limited...but he was still the single most powerful man alive.

"But Reynolds and Mills were on opposite sides of politics, weren't they?"

"Parties are hardly as solid in the Senate as they were in many past similar organizations," Barnes reminded him. "The personal relationships between Senators are almost as important as any official political affiliation." He shrugged. "Left over from our days as the General Assembly, I suppose.

"But Andrews was Reynolds's go-between with Mills and his bloc. Then she died. Around when the Cadre first started being a real problem."

"Everdark," Brad breathed. "You mean..."

"It's entirely possible that she's still working for Mills, Brad. Which means we have a problem far beyond needing to rescue Falcone."

"What do you mean?"

"In thirty-six hours, Mills is scheduled to address the Senate. He's speaking to the aftermath of the Battle of Ceres and the Cadre actions, and I already had reason to believe he's going to ask for basically a declaration of war—with all of the additional powers for his office that entails."

"I don't even know what that would give him," Brad admitted.

"A lot. Enough, if he's ruthless enough, to make himself dictator. Emperor in all but name."

"He needed a war, so he created the Cadre." Brad swore again.

"Worse, it's entirely possible *Reynolds* created the Cadre," Barnes told him. "Because Reynolds died six months after he left office—and if I was stepping into another man's plan to be Emperor, I wouldn't want to have that man still around, expecting to *actually* be in charge."

"We need proof," Brad said quietly. "We need Falcone—and we need Andrews. Alive—and able to testify."

Much as he wanted to put the woman responsible for the deaths of so many of his friends out an airlock.

Barnes slammed his wine glass down on the bar, hard enough that the base and stem shattered.

"Everdark," he swore, but there was no heat to it. "What do you need from me, Brad?"

"There's a station in Earth orbit that was the relay for the Phoenix's communication with Andrews," Brad told him. "It's linked to somewhere on the surface. I need to identify that location, but if I board that station, I am in *so* much trouble."

"If anyone boards that station, we warn them we're coming," the Senator replied. "I don't think I have the resources to track that link, Brad—but I know who does."

"Senator?"

"Director Harmon. If the Agency can't track a tightbeam radio connection, even mid–witch hunt, we've given them *far* too much money over the years."

CHAPTER THIRTY-TWO

By the next morning, Brad was starting to go stir-crazy. He hadn't expected there to be a time limit on his operations on Earth—certainly not one this tight—but Barnes insisted on keeping to the timing of his appointment with Director Harmon.

He didn't think that Barnes had told the Director he was going to be there, but the squat goblin of a man who wandered into the apartment at exactly oh nine hundred hours GMT didn't seem surprised to see him at all.

Director Antonio Harmon was, frankly, ugly. He was short and broad-shouldered with a clear pot belly and unusually large ears and nose. The red tinge to his nose suggested a long-standing drinking habit, and he walked with a cane, his left leg clearly not working quite right.

"Commodore Madrid, it's a pleasure to put a face to the name," Harmon told him, offering his free hand.

Brad shook Harmon's hand carefully, somewhat concerned about the man's clear frailty. There was a glint in the Director's eyes, however, that suggested that underestimating this man was a dangerous game.

"I didn't think we'd told you I'd be here," Brad said delicately.

"Please, Commodore, if I can't keep track of the man who shows up in Earth orbit with a destroyer, the good Senator and his friends have given me far too much money over the years!"

The echo from Barnes's words the previous night suggested that this was a phrase one of them used a lot.

"Commodore Madrid came to me last night," Barnes told the Director. "He believes we've found Agent Falcone, but he needs help."

"You found Kate?" Harmon asked sharply. "Where is she? What do you need?"

He winced.

"I'm afraid I can't get you much in terms of resources. Normally, this would be the heart of our power, but today, I don't know who I can trust."

"I brought two platoons of my troops," Brad told the Director. "I can handle extraction. What I don't have is an exact location…or the authority to operate here."

"What do you have?" Harmon demanded. "We'll worry about authority later. We're the Agency; we ask *forgiveness*, not permission."

"The Phoenix was communicating with Jessica Andrews on Earth via a relay station we've identified," Brad laid out rapidly. "We've located the station, but the Fleet is keeping a close eye on my ship, so I can't board it without drawing a lot of attention."

"Don't need to," Harmon replied. "Give me the details; we'll find the original source."

Brad passed over a datachip that the Director plugged into his wrist-comp. He tapped a rapid email and fired it off.

"There are still people I trust completely," he told Brad. "We'll find out what we can as quickly as we can."

"The prison is almost certainly on Earth," Brad admitted.

"I know. Which means I fucked up royally," Harmon agreed. "I got the spiel on Andrews from Falcone before she went MIA."

"And you've done *nothing*?" Brad asked.

"Hardly. We may not have been able to officially move against TMF, not without the Senate authorizing it, but believe me, they haven't finished a ship since you intercepted those cruisers. Such an unfortunate series of accidents, delays, and material shortages."

Which meant, probably, that the Cadre at least had no *new* reinforcements.

"Andrews is almost certainly still working for Mills," Barnes said quietly.

Harmon was quiet for the longest stretch of time since he'd arrived.

"Damn, I didn't put that together," he finally said. "And His Eminence is pushing for war powers, isn't he?"

"What do we do?" Brad asked.

"I find that base," Harmon told him. "You kick in its doors and find our people. I cover for you with the police and the Fleet, and we drag all of our evidence in front of the Senate...and impeach that thrice-accursed madman."

———

"Control, this is Ghost-Eleven, we are continuing patrol, entering sector seventeen-kappa."

Harmon straightened up in his chair as the radio message played. Despite the seeming normality of the transmission, there was a reason it was being covertly relayed into Barnes's living room.

"That's the sector your station is in," he told Brad. "Ghost-Eleven is a Blackbird Six flying a regular recon operation in low orbit. Technically, she's USAF, but an old friend is doing us a favor."

"USAF?" Brad asked. The acronym seemed...familiar, but he couldn't place it.

"United States Air Force," Harmon replied with a shake of his head, then glanced over at Barnes. "This is what you keep talking about, isn't it? Entire generations raised off of Earth, to whom the politics of our teeming billions are completely irrelevant?"

"The Commodore isn't a perfect example," Barnes demurred. "Outside of his quite particular skill sets, he's rather uneducated by just about any standard."

Brad opened his mouth to object, then closed it. The Senator was hardly wrong. Brad could very nearly build a spaceship from scratch, could command a surface action or a space action with similar ease, and knew spacecraft like the back of his hand. His education aboard a Belt freighter, however, had been very focused.

And, well, he was only vaguely sure what the United States was at best.

"Ghost-Eleven, this is ground control," a new voice echoed in the room. "We have you off course and entering a no-fly zone."

There was a long pause.

"Control, please repeat. Who the hell is issuing *us* no-fly orders?" the pilot grumped. "I show us as on course, regardless. Check your instruments."

"That's strange," Harmon said. "Ghost-Eleven has it right—nobody should be issuing no-fly orders to that unit."

"Ghost-Eleven, check *your* instruments," the ground control replied. "I have you almost eight degrees off course and well into a zone marked as no-fly on your charts. Correct your course immediately."

Seconds ticked by, and Brad watched the icon of the surveillance spaceplane continue to dive into the space they were watching.

"Control, this is Ghost-Eleven. I repeat, our system checks out and we are on course," the pilot finally said. "Even if I wasn't, I don't show any no-fly zones on my charts. This is goddamned *Ghost Squadron*."

"Don't get full of yourself, Ghost-Eleven," the controller responded. "We have equipment discrepancy. I'm ordering you back to the barn for a full refit.

"We'll also want to check those charts, Ghost-Eleven. There are zones even we don't violate."

"Sir, I—"

"That's not discretionary, Eleven," the ground control barked. "You are to return to the Cheyenne Mountain Base *immediately*."

The controller's tone was such that Brad started to wonder just how they were planning to cover up shooting down a stealthed spaceplane.

"Understood, Control," Ghost-Eleven responded. "Adjusting course northwards, targeting CMB for landing procedures."

A few seconds later, Harmon reached over and turned off the speaker. He was checking his own wrist-comp—and then activated a holographic globe of the Earth.

"So, whoever was on the ground wasn't filled in on the favor the USAF was doing us," he said calmly. "And, fascinatingly, was clearly on the verge of trying to shoot down a billion-dollar spaceplane to try and keep the secrets we were after."

"And?" Senator Barnes asked carefully.

"And they failed."

A red icon, an old rotational pseudo-gravity platform, appeared "below" Earth on the globe.

"Your relay is in a medium polar orbit, circling the planet every eight hours," Harmon told them. "Ghost got their tightbeam all right, and flagged the no-fly zone, too."

A hazy red sphere appeared around the station.

"There aren't very many 'security no-fly zones' on the USAF's lists," he continued. "Most of the ones I know of are mine. Finding a new one floating around a decrepit station in a semi-decaying orbit… that's not good."

"Did they trace the tightbeam?" Brad asked.

A red line descended from the station.

"I'm guessing there's at least one more platform, or some hack on the general network," the Director replied. "I timed the Ghost flight to line up with the position in the orbital cycle of your transmissions from the Phoenix, though, so we got in while they were transmitting directly."

The line connected to the surface, somewhere in the southernmost continent.

"Antarctica," Harmon continued. "Still a barren waste few people visit. There are more-hostile places in the system, but they don't have nice beaches two hours' flight away.

"With Ghost's scans, our localization isn't perfect. The target could be anywhere inside an eight-kilometer circle."

"I can live with that," Brad said quietly. "If you'll excuse me, gentlemen, I need to go break the law."

"Be careful, Madrid," Harmon told him. "I can cover this if we win. If we lose…"

"Then I'm probably already dead. Keep my wife safe."

The little goblin of a spy director snorted.

"Done. Go save us all, Commodore. I'll see what I can pull together for backup, but the first wave is on you."

CHAPTER THIRTY-THREE

THE BRIEFING ROOM aboard *Oath of Vengeance* had been designed to handle more than the twenty-nine combat troops the ship carried. It had not, however, been designed to handle *double* that, which was what Brad was currently squeezing into it.

Fortunately, his troops didn't seem to mind.

"All right, people," he greeted them. "A lot of you were wondering why we crammed two combat platoons and their shuttles aboard *Oath* for this trip. The less polite of you have even wondered aloud why we seem to keep getting involved in Agency affairs.

"Well, the reason for both is simple: Agent Kate Falcone."

He owed his people honesty. Most of them had probably guessed that he worked for the Agency, and he was willing to let them know that. Outside of his bridge crew, though, he was trying to keep the number of people in the Vikings who knew he was also a spy low.

"Falcone and I go way back, as most of you know, so we're at the top of her list when she needs a combat force that doesn't get traced back to the Agency. Though, honestly, we've done so much work for her, I'm not sure we're that deniable anymore!"

That got him the chuckle it was meant to.

"You all know that we sent Agent Falcone back to Earth with all of the evidence we dug up on TMF and the rest of the bastards supplying the Cadre. If you were wondering why nothing seemed to come of that, so was I."

Brad shook his head.

"Agent Falcone was kidnapped. Not by Cadre but by someone working with the Cadre. We have reason to believe we're looking at a rogue Commonwealth operation, but we have confirmed where Agent Falcone is being held."

His troops leaned forward eagerly, and he traded a look with Saburo.

"She's being held in a secret prison buried in the Antarctic ice shelf. On Earth."

Brad let that hang in the air.

"Now, if any of you have forgotten, Guild mercenaries are explicitly forbidden from carrying out operations in the Earth planetary system," he reminded them. "What less of you know is that the *Agency* is theoretically prohibited from operating on Earth's surface. We've got a few legal fig leaves in place, thanks to the Agency, but I'll be frank:

"The operation I intend to launch is a blatant violation of Commonwealth law. Arguably, it's treason. Given a lot of people's view of Earth, it could even be blasphemy. But…I have a friend down there. So, I'm going in. The Colonel's going in."

Brad smiled grimly.

"I won't order any of you to come with me. I won't pretend I can pull this off without you, but this is a volunteer-only mission."

"Sure, and anyone who don't want to volunteer can meet me in the hallway to get your ass kicked!" Corporal Jimenez barked. The black-haired medic who supported *Oath*'s combat platoon grinned at her fellow troopers.

"It's the Commodore and it's Agent Falcone. Anybody *not* in, troops?"

"Belay that, Corporal," Brad told her, even as he smiled. "I mean it. Anyone who goes on this operation is risking their lives for the chance to be declared rogue by Guild and Commonwealth alike. If you want to step aside, it will not be held against you."

No one moved. Sixty elite mercenary commandoes looked back at him with grim determination, and his smile broadened.

"In that case, people, Colonel Kawa will go over what we know of the target."

———

They didn't know much, really. They knew there was a facility inside the zone that Director Harmon had identified and Brad was relatively certain they'd be able to identify in a close flyover.

That was it.

There were more questions afterward, of course.

"So, I'm in, but…this is *Earth*," one of the pilots pointed out. "Not only do we need to dodge the Commonwealth, but we also have to dodge the local powers, too. How are we doing that?"

"May I, boss?" Saburo asked. Brad gestured for him to go ahead.

"I've been coordinating our plans with some trusted people at the Agency," Saburo told them all. "The first part of this mess is that we're going to be running special transponders the Agency has given us. They switch over who we're supposed to be at random intervals, blending us in with civilian traffic.

"The second part is that Antarctica isn't actually part of any of the nations on the surface. It's international waters and territory—so it's UN jurisdiction."

Everyone, including Brad, gave the Colonel a blank look at the description, and he sighed.

"Commonwealth jurisdiction," he clarified. "Or close enough as makes no difference, anyway. There's no official overflight by anybody else, no radar towers, nothing. Just research stations and, apparently, someone's secret prison.

"So, the Agency's transponders will get us into Antarctic airspace, and once there, there shouldn't be anyone to see us."

"What about the people we're coming for?" Jimenez asked.

"Well, it turns out that the same stealth coating we have for anti-radar in space works just fine in atmosphere," Brad said brightly. "And the retractable wings are designed to keep our radar profile low. We're not quite as stealthy as, say, the recon spaceplane we had scouting this out for us, but if they're not expecting trouble, they won't see us coming."

"Thermal sensors should be enough for us to find the target, at which we come in hard and fast," Saburo told them. "We blow the roof in with explosives and hope like hell we come in somewhere near the cells. If Reece or our crackers can find a surface data access *before* we kick the door in, that would be fantastic, but we can't rely on it."

"We're going in blind, people," Brad warned them. "We're fighting in a full gee, which we train for but we aren't used to, and we're assaulting a fortified position.

"It is entirely possible that the people we're going after truly *do* have the legal sanction we don't. This is a crap job—but our friend is in there. And so is the evidence of just who is funding the Cadre.

"So, if we pull this off, we yank the rug out from under the bastards who've been screwing the System for years. We start the path to getting our justice. But it's going to be a crap job," he repeated. "You're my Vikings. The best. But I need to know, are you up for it?"

He shouldn't have worried. The roar of assent that came back nearly deafened him.

CHAPTER THIRTY-FOUR

"We're at our lowest point, twenty-five meters above the water," the pilot reported. "Coming in low and fast; we are approaching the ice shelf at six hundred klicks per hour."

Brad had underestimated just how heavy he was going to feel on Earth. He regularly worked out in full gravity gyms, but that was noticeably different from actually being permanently in a one-gee environment.

He could move in it, he could deal with it…but he was *heavy*.

If it was bothering his shuttle pilot, the man wasn't showing it. The spacecraft came screaming across the oceans of Earth and jumped slightly to stay twenty meters above the glaciers ahead of it.

"This is like nothing I've ever seen before," Saburo said over the radio. "Goes from near-infinite water to looking like an ice rock. Earth is weird."

"And yet it all feels kind of right, doesn't it?" Brad replied. Heavy as he felt, that sense was there. He wasn't used to this—and yet his body seemed to think it was right and every other weight he'd had his entire life was wrong.

"Yeah," the Colonel agreed. "It does at that. Almost feels wrong to be fighting here."

Brad snorted.

"You've read more history than I have," he pointed out. "Have humans ever *not* fought here?"

There was a long pause.

"No. Still feels weird to come home just to fight, though."

"Won't argue that."

"Two minutes to the target zone," the pilot reported. "Beginning slowdown for our first recon pass."

"Stay on passive scanners," Brad ordered. "We've already run into one bunch of assholes with antiaircraft systems where there shouldn't be any."

With their wings extended, the shuttles were lifting bodies and could fly in the air...to a point. Their *minimum* speed to avoid falling was apparently over two hundred kilometers an hour, though, which could be a problem for the survey.

If he wasn't trying to be stealthy, they could just hover. The shuttles had more than enough power and fuel for that, but they were actually sneakier in motion with their engines reduced.

The Commodore pulled up a repeater screen on his helmet, showing him the sensor sweeps his shuttles were completing. There really wasn't anything out there. They'd passed near a coastal research station—and that station's weather scanners probably knew *something* was wrong.

That was it. Even now, nobody lived there. Humanity had colonized even less-hospitable places across the Solar System, but those places didn't have nicer neighbors an hour's flight away.

"Recon zone."

Brad focused on the sensor display. The computers and techs were grinding through visual and thermal scanners alike, but there wasn't much yet. At their current speed, they'd cross through the target zone in just over seven minutes.

It wasn't long to try and find a concealed facility.

"No visual contacts," someone noted. "The surface is clear. Glacier looks like it moves about a shuttle length a decade; I'm not even seeing signs of a landing pad."

"At a guess, they wanted this place invisible from orbit and regular flyovers," Brad replied. "If we need to use radar, we'll do it on the second pass, but…"

"That won't be necessary," Tisha Reece's voice cut in. "They're clever and sneaky all right, but someone wasn't going to live without their internet connection."

Four red icons appeared on Brad's screen.

"Those are remote retransmitters," she reported. "They're probably linked to the facility by wire and kept well away, but with all four of them…"

A new target area drew itself on the screen.

"The base is almost certainly inside this area. Does that help, Commodore?"

"Keep this up, Sergeant Reece, and I'm going to stick a *commission* on you," Brad told her with a chuckle. Her new target area was less than two kilometers square, a fraction of the original recon zone.

It was also, interestingly enough, just outside the original recon zone. That zone contained two of her relays, which had probably been the recipient of the tightbeam transmission Ghost Eleven had traced.

"We've got them," a pilot reported. "They're buried hard, but we're looking harder. We've got the thermal signature of an underground facility in Reece's zone."

"Where in her zone?" Brad asked.

The speaker swallowed audibly, and a series of red shapes began to fill in on the scanners. The boxes and cubes of prefabricated structures, linked by tunnels and power facilities, stacked next to each other…and then more icons filled in. And more.

"All of it, sir. That facility is *huge*."

———

There wasn't enough time for Brad and his people to set down somewhere, transmit the thermal imaging they had to the Agency, and have a team of analysts in a more relaxed environment go over the layout and identify where they wanted to make their entry.

"There's the landing pad," Saburo pointed out, highlighting the closest set of structures to the surface. "Looks like a standard-opening dome from one of the asteroids, probably with some extra equipment to keep the ice attached and reseal it afterwards. We could go in there, make sure no one escapes."

"If we do that, we'll have to fight through the entire facility to get to the prisoners," Brad replied. "Consider what happened to Agent Mulroney on Venus. What are the odds any of their prisoners would still be alive by the time we made it to them?"

"Wasn't that Cadre?" his subordinate asked.

"We *thought* it was Cadre," Brad said. "What we *know* is that it was an outside force helping the pirates. What if it wasn't the Cadre? What if it was these guys, this Red Diamond?"

Saburo was silent.

"Then they'll murder their prisoners and set off a nuke if they can't get out," the Colonel finally said. "They won't have a lot of fanatics, most likely, but they'll have enough—and considering some of the crap the Cadre pulled, the nuke is probably activated remotely."

"So, we need to get to the prisoners ASAP—*and* make sure we have an exit they can't block," Brad concluded. "And if I had a super-secret hell prison hidden away inside my almost-as-secret base, I'd want to be absolutely sure no one escaped.

"If I'm locking up Agents, I'm locking up some of the best-trained infiltration and hacking experts in the Solar System, so I want to be sure I have as much time as possible to short-circuit any attempt at escape or rescue."

Brad highlighted a structure on the map.

"Which means I'd put it here," he concluded. "It's the deepest structure in the facility. There's nothing directly above it, and there's only one way in or out. It's as secure as you can get, and you'd have to go through the entire base to get into or out of it."

"Makes sense to me," Saburo agreed after several seconds' thought. "So, what's the plan?"

"We didn't take the guns off the shuttles this time," Brad pointed out. "Or the missiles."

"We did put *different* missiles on," the Colonel replied. "I signed for the Everdarkened things. Bunker busters, ground-penetrating weapons."

"Exactly. How rapidly can you sequence the twelve of them we've got to blow a hundred and fifty-meter-deep hole through the ice, big enough for us to take the shuttles down? Preferably *without* wrecking the bunker itself."

"Boss, if my gunners haven't been constantly updating something along those lines, I'm going to be hiring some new staff shortly!"

———

The snow swirling around on the surface of the Antarctic ice had been completely irrelevant to the Vikings' operations so far. If it had progressed into a true storm, it could have become a problem, but right now the clouds weren't even enough to help cover them.

Anyone in the storm would have heard a sudden cascade of thunder, as if the Everlit themselves had decided to unleash the fury of the elements in this desolate place.

Each of Brad's shuttles carried two bunker-buster missiles, designed to punch through asteroid crusts to shatter hostile facilities buried underneath. They flew over the target zone in a neat line, each shuttle deploying their missiles one at a time.

The ice beneath them shattered beneath the blows. The missiles themselves plunged through the ice without even noticing it, and then their warheads vaporized hundreds of tons of ice.

Then the next missile arrived, blasting the hole deeper and wider—and the shuttles came around for a second pass.

And a third.

The third pass, however, they weren't launching missiles. The hole they'd blasted was still filled with steam and superheated water vapor, but the shuttles could handle that.

Brad's spacecraft dove into the pit like avenging angels. Specialized plasma cutters mounted on the underside of the shuttles, intended to cut into starship hulls, hissed to life against the buried metal of the underground complex.

Forty seconds after the first missile hit the ice, Brad led his people through a still-steaming hole into the secret base.

CHAPTER THIRTY-FIVE

THE GUARDS in the prison block never had a chance. The few seconds' warning they had was hardly enough to account for the fact that they were armed with nonlethal weapons and wearing light body armor.

Brad's people swarmed over them in seconds, leaving the four men and three women trussed up like turkeys and thrown against the wall of their command center.

"Saburo, secure that entrance," Brad ordered. The prison block's one way in and out was great for keeping prisoners locked in. It was also great for turning this chunk of the base into a fortified position against the *rest* of the base.

"Reece, get into their computers," he continued, gesturing towards the console that clearly controlled the prison block. "Find Falcone, see who *else* is down here."

Troopers followed Saburo towards the door, yanking a heavy desk that had clearly been used for intake with them.

"Sir," Reece murmured as she took a seat at the console. "The wall."

She pointed at the sigil emblazoned on the wall in boldly colored paint.

He'd seen it. The same symbol was on the screens. On the guards' uniforms…and on every piece of Commonwealth Fleet and government gear he'd ever seen.

The sigil was a wreath made up of stars surrounding a polar map of Earth, all emblazoned in gold on a familiar pale blue. The emblem of the Commonwealth.

"We knew what we were getting into," Brad told Reece harshly. "Find those damn Agents."

One of the less-disoriented guards struggled her way somewhat upright and glared at him.

"Do you have any idea what you've done?" she snapped. "Do you know where you even *are*?"

Brad crossed the room in a handful of steps and had his rifle barrel under her jaw.

"I can guess," he told her. "But what I *know* is that this facility was in contact with the Cadre and you have prisoners here I'm tasked to rescue."

"The Cadre?" The guard laughed in his face, gun barrel or no gun barrel. "Are you *mad*? This is a secure training facility for the Commonwealth Secret Service!"

A chill ran down his spine. The *Secret Service*?!

"What's Red Diamond, then?" he demanded.

"This base. Red Diamond Division, logistics and infrastructure for the CSS," the guard told him.

"I've got her!" Reece barked. "And…*fuck me*. Looks like at least half a dozen other senior Agency types, two of whom my files are saying are *dead*."

"I appreciate your forthcomingness, Miss," Brad told the guard with a cold smile as he turned back to her. "It's going to make charging the right people with treason *so* much easier."

He pulled his gun away and walked back to Reece. "Where?"

"Cell B4. I can lead the way."

"I suggest you hurry up," Saburo told them. "I've got drones out along the hallway, and they tell me we're going to have company!"

"Hold the line, Colonel. We're getting our people out."

———

Brad and Reece made their way into the cells. There weren't as many as Brad had feared…but there were more than he'd really expected, either.

Six blocks of twelve cells. Seventy-two prisoners.

"Can we let them out?" he asked.

"Unlock codes are in everyone's wrist-comps," she confirmed. "Any of us can unlock any of the cells."

"Hear that, Saburo?" Brad asked.

"Yes, sir. I'll spare two troops to start checking who we've got and letting them out. I need the rest out here."

As if to underscore the Colonel's point, gunfire started to echo down the hallway behind them.

"This is B4," Reece told him. There was nothing on the door to separate it from the other cells. None of them were numbered individually. Presumably the guards knew by heart and had an augmented-reality overlay for new people.

"Unlock it," he ordered.

Reece complied, and the solid metal door slid upwards, revealing a comfortable, if small and utterly windowless, cell. Kate Falcone was standing next to the door in a combat stance, the sound of gunfire clearly having triggered her paranoia.

"Agent Falcone, report," Brad barked, relying on age-old boot camp training to bring his friend into the present.

She made it halfway out of the combat stance toward standing at attention—and then slumped in relief as she recognized his voice and face.

"*Fuck* you, Madrid," she replied after a moment, but there was only gratitude in her voice. "What took you so long?"

"Everybody thought somebody else knew what had happened to you," he told her. "Then we had to get your location from the Cadre and fend off a genocidal attack on Ceres. You know, the usual bullshit at the office."

"Speaking of bullshit, do you have any idea how deep we are?" Falcone demanded.

"Well, this is apparently a Commonwealth Secret Service facility I just invaded," Brad pointed out. "That fits with a bunch of other stuff

I've heard and leads back to only one man who can be behind all of this."

"Did you know the President's 'blind trust' is a major shareholder in TMF?" the blonde asked dryly. "Because I sure as Everdark didn't. Not until Secret Service agents showed up to 'protect me' prior to my presentation to the Senate."

"I'm sorry," Brad said quietly. "I'm so used to you going dark, it never occurred to me you'd gone *missing*."

"I'm not the only one here. They don't give us a lot of interaction with each other, but there's…"

"Another sixty or so prisoners, at least a tenth of them Agency," Brad confirmed. "We've got shuttles on the roof and you probably heard our doorknocker. We can evac everyone, though it'll be tight."

He glanced around.

"Any chance that some of these folks actually deserve to be here?"

"It's possible, but the only people I've met are basically political enemies of President Mills. I don't know how long this has been going, but it runs deep."

"Then we need to burn it out. We need to clean out this place's computers. Reece?" Brad turned to his hacker.

"Honestly, sir? I'm good…but the Agency types the Red Diamonds locked down here? They're as good or better—and seven of us will make a *hell* of a lot bigger dent than one."

"Kate?"

"She's right," Falcone replied. "Let me at these bastards' computers. I think I may even know what I'm looking for!"

"Let's do it."

———

"Incoming!"

Gunfire started up again as Brad led the collection of techno-geeks back to the security control center. Reece and Falcone had dug up the rest of the Agents held prisoner, all of whom were grateful to be released—and grimly furious at being imprisoned by their own government.

"Get into the computers," Brad ordered. He grabbed his rifle and stepped over the barricade, where his people were throwing a fusillade of fire down the hallway.

He realized quickly that it wasn't being a very effective fusillade. He'd never seen anything like what the defenders were throwing at him.

Three figures were proceeding down the corridor. Each was at least two and a half meters tall, black juggernauts wrapped in layers of armor that laughed at his people's weapons. They were equipped to deal with light body armor at worst, not...whatever in Everdark this was!

The suits clearly came with some kind of muscle augmentation as well, as no human could heft the massive heavy machine guns the three figures were carrying. Carefully aimed bursts down the corridor were keeping his people behind cover.

Even if their guns *could* get through that armor, they weren't firing with enough accuracy to manage it.

And the juggernauts advanced.

"Saburo?" Brad demanded as he reached their blockade.

"Power armor," the Colonel said with a shake of his head. "Fleet has something like, I don't know, maybe a dozen suits on each cruiser? You almost don't *want* them in space, as anything that can take them down will wreck the ship you're standing on."

"Not so big a concern down here," Brad concluded.

"No. I think the national militaries all have elite forces using them. Of *course* the bloody Secret Service has them."

"They're slow, at least," the Commodore observed.

"Yeah...and they want prisoners, which is the only reason any of us are still alive."

Brad had suspected as much. Those heavy machine guns could blow right through the cover his people were using. On the other hand...he was *much* less determined to take prisoners.

"Got a plan?" he asked.

"Working on one. You?"

Brad grinned and produced the toy-sized crossbow he'd used on New Venice from his combat gear. It had a far lower velocity than any of his "real" guns—but its monofilament-edged tip did not care about armor.

"How fast does that reload?"

"About a second."

"This is going to suck," Saburo noted.

"Got another plan?" Brad asked.

"Nope. Covering you."

Brad sprang out from behind his cover, taking careful aim. Every fraction of a second that he was visible was a risk, but the bow was a short-range weapon with no sights and a long reload time. He couldn't afford to miss.

The mini-crossbow *snapped*—and the bolt punched into the lead trooper's helmet. Its metallic fins were still protruding, but the point was at least three or four centimeters into the Secret Service man's brain.

Brad dropped as the two survivors focused their fire. The little motor in the crossbow reloaded, seeming almost glacially slow compared to a modern firearm, and he had to roll to the side as the HMG fire punched through their impromptu cover.

He popped back up and took aim again. This time, he barely got the shot off before a bullet hit him. His second shot was off target, but it still took his victim in the jaw. A crippling and life-threatening wound.

Brad, thankfully, was wearing his skintight armor under his armored vac-suit. Neither would have been enough to stop the heavy round at this range on their own. As it was, well, he wasn't using his right arm anytime soon—bruising and probably a cracked shoulder blade.

Unfortunately for the remaining uninjured trooper, Brad might not have felt up to using a mini crossbow with his left hand...but he was *definitely* up to using a mono-blade with it.

He was over the barricade as the trooper struggled to pull his friend back. With a curse, Saburo came after him...but he wasn't needed.

Brad bisected both of the troopers' weapons and whipped his mono-blade around to embed it in the neck of the third man.

He didn't take off the man's head. There was an electromagnetic field of some kind in the suit, one that would resist a charged mono-blade even if it couldn't stop the monofilament-edged crossbow bolt.

There was no way it would stop him a second time, and as Brad held the blade, he knew his opponent knew that as well.

"Shut down the suit and step out," he ordered. "Get your friend to do the same and we'll help you give him first aid. If you surrender. Deal?"

The hallway was silent and frozen for a moment, and then Saburo stepped up with the reloaded mini-crossbow and a truly vicious grin.

Then the Secret Service trooper carefully raised their hands and clicked a command on their helmet. She removed the heavy headgear to reveal a youngish woman with short-cropped copper hair and very, *very* scared eyes.

"Deal," she choked out.

"Out of the suits. Move!" he barked. "Your friends are coming, and I don't like my prisoners getting caught in the crossfire!"

CHAPTER THIRTY-SIX

BRAD ESCORTED the two half-armored grunts back behind his people's barricade, where Corporal Jimenez immediately set to treating the young man with a ten-centimeter crossbow bolt embedded in his jaw.

The mercenary commander couldn't help feeling guilty, even if the two young people he now had prisoner had been shooting at him. So far as they knew, they were legitimately working for the Commonwealth—and his people had just blown in the roof and started breaking prisoners free.

"There's no good news," Falcone told him as the medic took their new prisoners away. "We're locked out. I *think* the data is intact underneath, but all of our access has been cut. Without getting into the computer data center, we're not getting anything out of these people's files."

"Okay, so where's the data center?" Brad asked. So far, they had been letting the defenders come to them, but if he needed to assault deeper into the facility, he would.

He would lose people. He *knew* that. And half the people he was killing were basically innocents, too. But with the entire Commonwealth riding on the next few hours…he'd do what he had to do.

"Yeah, well, there may be no good news, but there's *worse* news," the Agent told him in a dry tone. "The one thing we *are* getting is a countdown timer. In about five minutes, this entire place is going to get blown sky-high—and unless I'm severely mistaken, the landing pad dome is sealed.

"No one is getting out, Brad. Someone, probably on the outside, pushed a button that trapped everyone in here and is going to kill them."

"We can get out," Brad replied. "But we need that data, Kate."

"Then we need to go," she told him. "Evac the prisoners, evac everyone. There's nothing here worth dying for."

"There might be," he said quietly. "Do you have enough to impeach Mills?"

Agent Falcone stared at him.

"No, but we have time and now we *know*. We can find the proof."

"In sixteen hours, President Mills will ask the Senate for a declaration of war and associated emergency powers," Brad told her. "Once he has them, I doubt he's going to relinquish them. The survival of our *nation*, Kate, depends on whether we can break him *today*."

"I can't," she admitted. "We don't have enough. I *might* be able to convince the Senate not to hand him emergency powers, to give us the authority to impanel a special prosecutor..."

"But if he's got the votes tied up enough that he expects to pass his declaration tonight, then we need a smoking gun, something sufficient to arrest him on the Senate floor," Brad replied.

"Then you need these people to surrender and I have no idea how you're going to do that," Falcone said. "There's a bomb at the deepest part of this complex, probably a fusion weapon of some kind, rigged to vaporize the entire underground base."

"So, they haven't told the grunts, or no one would be trying to fight past us," the Commodore noted. "Unless..."

It struck him like a blow.

"Kate, we're *in* the deepest part of the base. A roughly central part, too—and if they're running a secret black prison for the President's enemies, wouldn't you want to make damn sure those enemies never got out?"

"Everlit," Falcone breathed. "You mean we're sitting on top of the damned bomb?!"

———

Once they knew what they were looking for, it took them under a minute to find the bomb. The radiation levels hadn't been enough to trigger any alerts—they were effectively nonexistent, really—but the sensors on their combat vac-suits were more than capable of tracking it.

A floor panel in the center of the prison turned out to cover an access to a hidden compartment that contained a series of wires and blinking lights completely unfamiliar to Brad.

"Saburo," he barked into his coms. "Can we blockade the entrance so they can't get through inside the next few minutes?"

"Yeah, we were just keeping it open so we could get to the computer center," his Colonel replied.

"New plan. They're going to let us into the computer center. Seal the tunnel, whatever it takes, then get everybody aboard the shuttles. Leave one behind for me and Falcone, then get everybody else the *Everdark* out of here."

He looked over at the Agent.

"You can disarm this, right?"

She was studying the bomb carefully, poking at wires.

"Yes," she confirmed. "Not quickly, though. We may not have enough time."

"Get started," he ordered, then tapped his com. "Get out of here, Saburo. It's down to me talking and Falcone disabling the bomb. Anything else is just putting lives at risk. Go!"

"Wilco. And you said I'd never get any use out of these instant-concrete bombs."

"You *brought* those?" Brad demanded.

The "bombs" in question were more on the order of emergency reinforcement tools, designed to spray a foam all around them and then harden it in place. They wouldn't hold up anyone for long...but they'd buy ten minutes, at least.

The distinctive cracking and bubbling noise of the devices echoed down the hallway, and Brad switched his helmet radio to omnidirectional broadband.

"I need to talk to Jessica Andrews," he said calmly. "And I'd say we have about…oh, two minutes to have this conversation."

Several seconds passed.

"I'm impressed," the calm voice of an older woman finally responded. "Most people think I'm dead."

"I saw footage of you on *Longbow*, Ms. Andrews," Brad told her. "I'm guessing you didn't activate the bomb, so I have one very easy question for you: what are you prepared to do to get the man who did?"

"Who am I talking to? Madrid?"

"Bingo."

"Damn, you're a pain in my ass," she said. "Twenty years I gave this project, Madrid. Don't pity me because they decided I was expendable. I was in this for power and money. Willing to let me walk away?"

"No," he told her. "But right now, I'm sitting on a bomb that will kill you and everyone in this base—and we can turn it off. Do you want to live, Ms. Andrews?"

"Very much," Andrews snapped. "So, how about we stop playing games and you tell me what you *want*?"

"I want this base's files, intact and handed over to the Agency," Brad said. "And I want *you* with me tonight when President Mills tries to sell the Senate on making him dictator."

"I want full immunity," she countered instantly.

"You have sixty seconds or fiery death," Brad pointed out.

"And all of your shuttles but one have left," she replied. "If you don't disarm that bomb, you die with me. I'll give you everything you want, Mills just stabbed me in the back—but I want out and I want out clean. If you're not Agency, there's someone there who is and can make that promise."

Brad muted his mike and looked at Falcone.

"Are we going to die?" he asked bluntly.

She tore a chunk of wires out of the bomb and grinned.

"Not today."

"Can I actually offer full immunity?"

"Yes. I want that bitch to swing, but yes," she allowed.

He sighed, and turned on the microphone.

"All right, Ms. Andrews. You have a deal. You surrender this base and give me Mills's head on a plate, and we'll disarm the bomb. You get to live."

"Done," she said instantly. "Even if you probably already did disarm the bomb, I still want that fucker's *head*."

CHAPTER THIRTY-SEVEN

It was evening in New York City by the time they had everything in order. Brad, Falcone, and Andrews arrived at the spaceport on a regular civilian suborbital flight from Buenos Aires. Several of Brad's shuttlecraft remained in the city as well, but the two Agents, their witness, and the Vikings mercenaries he'd brought along for security filled the first- and business-class sections of the aircraft.

Harmon was waiting for them as they left the gate at the airport, a dozen burly young men in expensive black suits hanging around the squat Director of the Agency.

"Ms. Andrews," he greeted their witness. "It's been a long time. It's a pleasure to see you're still alive."

"Oh, shut up, Antonio," Andrews replied. "We've been sparring through the shadows at arm's length for a decade. You're allowed to gloat."

"I'll save gloating for when this is over," he told her. "I don't like the deal Madrid cut with you, won't pretend otherwise, but I'll honor it. When Mills is in jail, you get your pardon and immunity."

"I know you, Antonio," she said. "I was never worried. Now, I believe we have a Senate meeting to crash?"

"Are you trying to make me angry?" Harmon asked. "Because you'll have to try a lot harder."

She chuckled.

"Oh, I know. Shall we, my dear Director?" Andrews offered Harmon her arm.

He glared at her and gestured for the guards to fall in around her.

"This whole situation is getting messier by the second," he told Brad and Falcone, his gaze lingering on Brad. "Let's get this stage of it over with so we can deal with the *next* complication this disaster throws at us."

"Any more complications we can expect?" Brad asked.

"We'll need to borrow your troops," Harmon said, glancing at the mercenaries following Brad and Falcone. "At least some of the lictors at the UN building will defend Mills no matter what. We need to neutralize them, nonlethally if possible."

"That'll depend on what gear you can get us," Brad told him. "We didn't check bags full of hardware, if that's what you're asking."

"We'll sort something out," he confirmed. "Are you ready, Commodore? This is something new for you, as I understand?"

"I've argued my case in front of planetary governments," the gaunt mercenary replied. "This is just the next step up."

"I don't believe you've ever tried to arrest the leader of a planet, let alone the leader of the Commonwealth," Harmon said with a chuckle as a car pulled up to pick them up. "No one has."

"I just want it over," Brad admitted. "Full gravity is starting to get obnoxious."

His legs *hurt*. So did everything else. The subtle feeling of rightness was being overwhelmed by exhaustion at this point. Working out in a one-gravity gym for an hour a day at most didn't prepare you for spending a full day in that gravity.

It was a good thing no one was expecting him to do much more than talk at this point.

———

"It is a dark hour for our people."

Even as Brad and his companions were making their way through the corridors of the United Nations building toward the chamber where the Senate was in session, President Mills's speech was being relayed to his earpiece.

His people had scattered to the winds along with most of Harmon's bodyguards. There were just two of the suited grunts with them now, which was more than enough—with Brad and Falcone along, at least— to ensure Andrews didn't get any clever ideas.

"The attack on Ceres shows how daring, how bold our enemies have become. Cadre ships came within millimeters of destroying one of this star system's central sources of water. If the spacers of our brave Fleet had been one iota less capable, one iota less brave, one iota less *well equipped*…millions would have died."

"How long is he going to talk for?" Falcone muttered as they reached a security checkpoint.

Four lictors in decorative uniforms—but carrying very *non*-decorative assault rifles—blocked the way, and Harmon barged forward.

"We need to speak to the Senate," he told the guards.

"The President is speaking," the constable in charge of the lictors replied. "The Senate is in closed session."

"Do you know who I am?" Harmon demanded. "I am the Director of the Commonwealth Investigative Agency! I have not merely the right but the *responsibility* to interrupt a closed session if matters are important enough."

The constable looked unconvinced, turning back to his fellows and pulling up a document on his wrist-comp.

"Members of this Senate have urged a tighter hold on the purse strings of the Fleet," Mills's voice echoed in Brad's ear. "I refuse to contemplate ill of our wise compatriots, but we have weakened our only defense beyond all reason! We have only recently begun to undo the damage done by our peaceful intentions, and the worlds and colonies of the Outer System have taken advantage of our lack of will!"

The lictors were arguing now, and Brad could see Harmon starting to get itchy. If the Director ordered it, Brad and Falcone would disable the guards. He'd apologize later…but he understood the weight of the moment, too.

"We see the Cadre, but we also see this Independence Militia, and we must understand the truth: our Commonwealth is at war!" Mills was clearly building to his point already.

"We have blindly allowed a monster to grow at our border, to stand in the shadows and hold a club over our head, and I say to you: *no more!*"

The constable stepped back to them. He looked rebellious but resigned.

"You are correct, Director," he admitted. "That authority has never been invoked before. Given the circumstances of the President's speech…"

"It is utterly necessary that I speak to the Senate now," Harmon snapped. "The President's speech is *part* of that reason—and there is nothing in that document that says I have to wait for anyone!"

Brad shifted his weight, preparing to move.

"Fine," the lictor constable spat, standing aside. "On your head be it."

"That is exactly where the responsibility lies, son," Harmon told the officer. "You have done your duty. Everything after this is on me."

He turned back to Brad and the others.

"Come on."

———

Now Brad didn't even need the earpiece. The old United Nations building had incredible acoustics and he could hear Mills continuing his speech as the six of them approached the main Assembly Hall.

"In these dark times, as shadows loom over us and the future is in doubt, the Commonwealth—*humanity itself*—looks to us for leadership. We speak for Earth, for Mars, for Venus and Jupiter and every other colony out there."

The last barrier was the Senate Bailiff, who clearly hadn't been expecting anyone to arrive. The older woman scrambled to her feet as Brad and his companions approached, but she clearly recognized Harmon.

Brad supposed the Director was rather recognizable.

"It is our sacred duty to face the barbarians at the gate with a sword in our hands and a battle cry on our lips. It is our place to stand between the weak and the innocent and those who do them harm."

Harmon inclined his head to the Bailiff.

"I am here to invoke the right of my office to speak before the Senate," he told her. "*Now*. Before Mills is done speaking."

Either the woman owed Harmon something or she *really* didn't like Mills, because she nodded immediately and grabbed her staff of office with its built-in microphone.

"Follow me," she instructed.

"In this house, in this place, we must no longer be divided," Mills proclaimed. "In the face of the enemy, *we must not yield*."

The Bailiff's staff slammed into the floor with a sudden crash of thunder, the sound of the impact relayed through the entire building by the sound system.

The President stumbled to a halt, staring up the semicircular chamber and its rows of seats to the entrance. The staff slammed into the floor again, and the woman leaned on it.

"Esteemed President Mills, Senators of the Commonwealth of the United Nations of Earth, it is my duty to announce the presence of Director Antonio Harmon of the Commonwealth Investigative Agency.

"As is the right and duty of his position, he has requested and required the right to speak immediately. Under the rules and traditions that govern this chamber, I have no authority to refuse him."

She slammed the staff down again.

"Director Harmon."

Harmon led the way, with Brad, Falcone and Andrews immediately behind him.

Mills was frozen, his gaze fixed on Jessica Andrews as the party advanced down the stairs to the very heart of the Commonwealth.

"I apologize for interrupting, honored Senators," Harmon said loudly, projecting his voice to fill the chamber without any artificial aids. "But it is my duty to bring before you evidence of the greatest treason I have ever discovered.

"I must agree with President Mills. In these hours, in the face of the enemy, we must not yield. Where I must disagree with him, however, is where our enemy is."

Brad followed Harmon onto the stage, carefully looming over the short and stockily built form of President David Mills. Intimidating the theoretical ruler of the entire star system was surprisingly easy.

"Our enemy is not in the Outer System," Harmon told the Senate. "The Cadre's beating heart, the source of its motivation and its armies, is not hiding in the darkness outside our borders.

"Everything the Cadre has done has been directed from a single source. A single man, determined to use the Cadre to destroy all that we are sworn to defend.

"The true enemy of the Commonwealth does not lurk outside your borders. The true enemy of the Commonwealth is right here." Harmon pointed at Mills. "Your enemy, Senators, is the man who would use your fear to make himself *king*."

CHAPTER THIRTY-EIGHT

"THIS IS MADNESS!" Mills declared. "What kind of ludicrous accusation is this?"

Harmon grinned and calmly took the microphone away from the President. Despite his words, Mills was clearly still in shock, as he didn't even resist. The Agency Director passed the microphone to Jessica Andrews, who took it with a nod and faced the Senate.

"Esteemed Senators of the Commonwealth," she greeted them. "Many of you know me and are wondering how I come to stand in front of you today.

"For the rest of you, I am Jessica Natalia Andrews. Once, I sat among you as a member of this august body. Until eleven years ago, when, in the service of the man who now stands accused, we faked my death to allow me to serve as a conduit for resources and authority."

She smiled.

"But the story begins earlier. It begins over twenty years ago, in the aftermath of the destruction of the *Black Skull*. The Cadre's field commander, the man we know as the Terror, had escaped—but their leadership was shattered. The true patriarch and matriarch of the Cadre died with *Black Skull*.

"Our system breathed a sigh of relief that a long nightmare was over. But three men in our most august bodies and houses of power saw the opportunity present in everyone's fear. I and others were recruited to their cause, but the man at the heart of the scheme was Tyler Smith Reynolds."

That name brought the entire room to silence.

"Reynolds saw in the fear and terror of the Commonwealth the opportunity to change the world. Money and power are great levers, and he had vast quantities of both to wave in front of those he sought to recruit."

Andrews shook her head.

"Two other men were key to Reynolds's plan, one who stood at his right hand and one who was officially his opponent. Between them, they passed the Commonwealth Emergency Powers Act—passed in peace, when no one considered just what a sword they had handed their president."

Even Brad was hanging on her words now. He had guessed much of this story, but to hear it laid out quite so starkly was still horrifying.

"Those other two men? Sequoia Smith, then Chief of Operations for the Commonwealth Fleet—and the then leader of the opposition: Senator David Mills."

Falcone stepped between the President and the stage exit with a cold smile. Brad saw her movement and stepped over to block the other way out. No one wanted Mills to walk away just yet.

"For eight years, we built the fundamental structures of Reynolds's plan inside the Commonwealth. We funneled the Terror money and resources sufficient for him to secure control of the Cadre, to stabilize it and keep it present, a continuous threat in the back of everyone's minds.

"It became necessary to exert more direct control, so we faked my death and I took over the Red Diamond division of the Secret Service. Using the resources of the Secret Service's logistics division, we infiltrated and took control of Transplanetary Macro Fabrication, allowing us to channel more ships and more money to the Cadre.

"It was the Secret Service that funded the research at Blackhawk Station that the Cadre stole. It was the Secret Service that set up secret labs and manufactories for weapons of mass destruction across the star system.

"We needed an atrocity, an attack of such magnitude that no one could ignore it…and then the Terror got himself killed before we could execute our plan. Reynolds was too old, too stubborn…so we killed him.

"Age had already handled Smith for us, and all of this left one man at the heart of everything," Andrews told them all. "We needed a new figurehead in the Cadre, and the Phoenix seemed the perfect candidate. The designated heir of the first leaders, the Terror's apprentice and hatchet man. But still a minor player in the major scheme of things.

"We needed to feed him heavier ships to help him consolidate power. And again, the Mercenary Guild got in the way." She gestured at Brad. "Madrid got in the way. He found out much of this and sent a Commonwealth Agent to speak to this body.

"We arrested her…but didn't plan for Commodore Madrid to track her down."

Andrews wasn't quite glaring at Brad.

"Madrid found her. Found my base, my communications, my records. Everything needed to bring down the conspiracy…and so the man I've spent twenty years serving, the man who promised to raise me up to his right hand when this was all done, pushed the button to nuke me, my records, and my prisoners."

She turned her glare on Mills.

"Tell me, Dave, did you even hesitate? Blink? Feel a *moment*'s remorse for killing the people who had done so much to make you the ruler of humanity?"

"She's mad!" he replied. "You can't seriously believe this…this…*tale*."

"As Director of the Agency, I have no true authority in this chamber," Harmon told the Senate. "But I call on *you*, the men and women charged to guide our Commonwealth. I call on you not to hand this man a declaration of war.

"I call on you to impeach this man and hand him over to our justice system to face trial for his crimes. We cannot be divided and lost to fear while this conspiracy and its tentacles threaten our society, our nation.

"I cannot make a motion here. I can only beg you to."

Somehow, Brad wasn't surprised when Senator Barnes stood. The Senator for Jupiter was near the back of the chamber, showing the amount of importance the Commonwealth gave the Jovian Cluster... but he was still a Senator.

"When the Cadre came for my daughter, it was at your order, wasn't it?" he demanded.

Andrews faced him levelly and nodded.

"We needed your vote on key challenges," she told him. "Mills himself suggested holding your daughter hostage."

"It seemed his style," Barnes allowed. "I suppose you were promised immunity, Andrews?"

She raised her chin.

"That was the deal for my testimony, yes," she confirmed.

"So be it." Barnes looked around him and then slammed his hand down on the button on his desk that declared him to be making a motion.

"Senators of the Commonwealth, I have heard Director Harmon's evidence. I know his witnesses. While I wish to review the documentary evidence before we proceed with a full impeachment, I move that this body temporarily suspend David Mills's authority and immunity —and order the Commonwealth Investigate Agency to take him into custody pending that full impeachment proceeding."

The Bailiff slammed her staff down again.

"We have a motion on the floor," she announced. "Do we have a sec—"

The Senator for New Venice was already rising.

"There was a *nuclear weapon* detonated on my planet," the Venusian Senator reminded everyone. "If there is even the slightest chance that anyone, even our *President,* was involved, it must be investigated.

"I second the esteemed Senator for Jupiter's motion. We must detain President Mills to make certain he does not flee while we review the Agency's evidence."

"We have a second," the Bailiff declared. "Please record your votes."

Brad couldn't see the tally going up behind his head. He could see the light from the icons behind him reflecting off the gleamingly cleaned floor, however…and it was overwhelmingly green.

"The motion is passed," the Bailiff declared. "Director Harmon, please take Preside—"

The last thing that had crossed Brad's mind, given how shocked Mills had been, was that the man would be armed.

It wasn't a big gun, but the small pistol was enough to drown out the Bailiff's voice as Mills shot her. The man had been well trained, better than Brad would have expected, and put three rounds through the woman's center of mass in under a second. Before anyone could even begin to react to that, Mills turned and shot Andrews, the same neat three-round burst to the torso, then ran for the exit.

Even as the two women started to fall, Brad was moving. So was Kate Falcone, and she was closer. Neither of the two Agents was *armed*, nor had they been expecting Mills to produce a gun.

Falcone collapsed as Mills fired into her at point-blank range, falling against the President who shoved her aside. Brad's friend fell to the floor as he rushed toward her—and Mills was already on the floor, running up the stairs of the Chamber as pure shock froze everyone around him.

CHAPTER THIRTY-NINE

Harmon was already kneeling by Kate's side when Brad reached her, the Director producing a medical kit seemingly from nowhere. The two bodyguards were checking on the Bailiff and Andrews, and Harmon waved Brad away.

"She was wearing body armor; she'll live," the Director told Brad. "Catch that son of a bitch."

Brad gave Harmon a firm nod and took off after Mills.

He quickly realized that Mills was exiting the building as rapidly as possible—and while Brad was probably in overall better shape than the President, Mills was used to Earth's gravity. Brad wasn't.

By the time he was halfway to the courtyard, he was cursing both Earth's gravity and the security troops around the UN building.

Part of that was his fault, he knew. They'd sent in his mercenaries and most of Harmon's bodyguards to detain any of the lictors they suspected might be Mills's men, which meant that only about half of the security that was supposed to be there was actually present.

The rest, well. The order to detain the President of the Commonwealth might have been given, but that didn't mean everyone knew about it. He couldn't blame the men and women who'd let the President through when he'd barked orders.

Until two minutes before, after all, Mills had been their ultimate boss.

Earth's gravity tore on his muscles, but he kept going.

The guards at the front door, it seemed, had got the message in time to try and stop Mills—but not in time to realize he was going to be a threat. Two men were down, one definitely dead and the other grimly trying to patch up his own wounds.

The wounded man saw Brad coming and hit an override to open the doors.

"Sir, *catch*!" he shouted. Wounded or not, the lictor had one hell of an arm, and the submachine gun he threw almost hit Brad before the mercenary caught the weapon.

"Thank you," he replied, and charged out of the building. Weight told him there was a full magazine in the gun, but he only had one man to take down—and he really did want to take Mills alive.

Bursting out into the twilight, he was glad to see that Mills hadn't made it very far. The President was still in the middle of the main courtyard, pausing amidst the flags to check behind him while using the fountain as cover.

"Stop!" Brad shouted after the man, starting to charge across the pavement. Hopefully, Mills was out of bullets. The handgun he'd concealed couldn't have that many rounds in its magazine, after all.

The stockier man saw him, swore, and started running again. That gave Brad a perfect view of the President's head and back...as a pair of heavy sniper slugs blasted through Mills's upper chest.

The sniper had hit the traditional "sniper's triangle" perfectly, and whatever armor Mills had been wearing hadn't been enough to stop the bullets. His throat and chest disintegrated into a spray of blood and organs, and the man who'd tried to make himself king sprawled backward toward Brad.

Brad himself dove for cover behind the fountain, trying to locate the sniper in what he knew was a futile gesture. Even if he could find the sniper, he couldn't hit them with the light SMG he was carrying.

A third shot cracked; and a bullet slammed into the ground four feet from Brad. He had enough time to tuck himself further into the fountain before he discovered that it had never been intended to hit him.

A holographic image of Jack Mader appeared above the crater. The bullet was some kind of communicator.

Mader was looking away from Brad and tapped a command of some kind to align his gaze with where Brad was hiding.

"Commodore Madrid," he said brightly. "It's probably obvious that I'm watching you through a camera. Don't worry, though, my sniper is getting the hell out of Dodge. You weren't her target, and she doesn't want to get in any more trouble than she has to.

"I knew when I sent you after the Red Diamond that you were going to wreck Mills's day, though I don't think even I could have anticipated just how deliciously *epic* a stunt you would pull. Congratulations, Commodore, you've destroyed the President of the Commonwealth. You probably even have enough data to unravel his entire organization."

"You don't seem upset," Brad replied, wondering if Mader could even hear him.

"Nope," Mader confirmed cheerfully. "Mills became a liability the moment the Agency started short-circuiting our shipments from TMF. I never did need him as much as he thought, or as much as my uncle did." Mader grinned. "I was the Terror's declared successor, Madrid. I didn't need them to send me more and bigger ships to secure control of the Cadre and the Independence Militia.

"Those ships, though, they're going to be very useful. It was never my plan to make Mills dictator, Commodore Madrid. And since now everything is on the page, I will give you one last chance:

"Join me. Bring your fleet, your ships, and your alliances over to the Cadre, and when I am Emperor, you will be rewarded beyond your wildest dreams."

"Not a chance," Brad told him. "Everdark take you, I will fight you until my last breath."

"I figured. Know then, Commodore Madrid, that the Phoenix will offer you no further mercy. You cannot face the storm to come. The Commonwealth will fall...and like the name I chose, *my* empire will rise from its ashes."

Mader bowed mockingly.

"We will never meet again. Our only remaining speech will be by the gun and the torpedo. It's a shame, really…I finally worked out who you were."

The hologram cut off with a small bang as an explosive shattered the communicator.

———

Harmon came out of the building after him a couple of minutes later. Two of his suited guards came with him, but they weren't the ones they'd had on the Senate floor.

"Director," Brad said quietly. "I'm sorry. The Phoenix stole a move on us—he was expecting all of this."

"Damn." Harmon walked over to study Mills' body.

"Andrews is dead," he told Brad after a long moment. "The Bailiff and Falcone will live. Thankfully, Andrews has already testified." He shook his head. "Her files will give us a lot, but that woman knew more about the conspiracy than anyone except Mills himself, I think."

"The Phoenix…*mocked* me," Brad said bitterly, gesturing at the crater. "Bullet-delivered hologram."

"Did he say anything useful?" Harmon asked.

"That he didn't need Mills anymore," Brad replied. "That he'd intentionally sent me after him and had never planned to make Mills dictator. He thinks, at least, that he has enough ships and troops and firepower to conquer us directly. To make himself Emperor at the point of a sword."

Harmon was silent, then walked back over to Brad with his guards in tow.

"Then I hope to all that is sacred that the Fleet is ready. We've done all we can for now."

"Then it's over," Brad said with an exhalation. "For today, at least."

"Not yet." The Director of the Agency studied him like an eagle studying a mouse. "I have one last duty to discharge today, distasteful as I find it."

"Sir?" Brad asked, confused—until the guard he hadn't noticed stepping up to him slapped manacles on his wrists. "Sir?!" he demanded.

"Commodore Brad Madrid, you are being detained for the security of the Commonwealth," Harmon told him, his voice sad and quiet. "It took the forensics crew on Kobayashi days to work it out. They kept coming up with too few sets of matching DNA samples for the number of people they thought they had in the shuttle bay fight."

"I don't understand."

"It's because one of their sets was actually two people," Harmon replied. "Two people with almost identical genetics. Brothers. And since the Agency are the only people with a copy of *your* DNA profile, we could match one of the sets."

Brad stared at the Director. He had no idea what was going on.

"I wondered when I heard the name Mantruso, but the Mantruso and Riggio crime families were long subsumed into the Cadre, and it's not *that* rare a name," Harmon told him. "But now I know, and I can't risk you walking free."

"I don't understand," Brad repeated.

"Jack Mader was the designated heir of the founders of the Cadre, the leaders of the Mantruso and Riggio crime families. We thought he was their only child...except that *you* are his brother."

ABOUT THE AUTHORS

#1 Bestselling Military Science Fiction author **Terry Mixon** served as a non-commissioned officer in the United States Army 101st Airborne Division. He later worked alongside the flight controllers in the Mission Control Center at the NASA Johnson Space Center supporting the Space Shuttle, the International Space Station, and other human spaceflight projects.

He now writes full time while living in Texas with his lovely wife and a pounce of cats.

Glynn Stewart is the author of *Starship's Mage*, a bestselling science fiction and fantasy series where faster-than-light travel is possible–but only because of magic. His other works include science fiction series *Duchy of Terra*, *Castle Federation* and *Vigilante*, as well as the urban fantasy series *ONSET* and *Changeling Blood*.

Writing managed to liberate Glynn from a bleak future as an accountant. With his personality and hope for a high-tech future intact, he lives in Kitchener, Ontario with his partner, their cats, and an unstoppable writing habit.

OTHER BOOKS BY TERRY MIXON

You can always find the most up to date listing of Terry's titles on Amazon at author.to/terrymixon

The Empire of Bones Saga

Empire of Bones

Veil of Shadows

Command Decisions

Ghosts of Empire

Paying the Price

Reconnaissance in Force

Behind Enemy Lines

The Terra Gambit

Hidden Enemies

Race to Terra

The Empire of Bones Saga Volume 1

The Humanity Unlimited Saga

Liberty Station

Freedom Express

Tree of Liberty

The Fractured Republic Saga

Storm Divers

The Scorched Earth Saga

Scorched Earth

<u>The Vigilante Duology</u> with <u>Glynn Stewart</u>

Heart of Vengeance

Oath of Vengeance

<u>Bound By Stars: A Vigilante Series</u> with Glynn Stewart

Bound By Law

Bound by Honor

Bound by Blood

Want Terry to email you when he publishes a new book in any format or when one goes on sale? Go to <u>TerryMixon.com/Mailing-List</u> and sign up. Those are the only times he'll contact you. No spam.

OTHER BOOKS
BY GLYNN STEWART

For release announcements join the
mailing list or visit **GlynnStewart.com**

STARSHIP'S MAGE
Starship's Mage
Hand of Mars
Voice of Mars
Alien Arcana
Judgment of Mars
UnArcana Stars
Sword of Mars
Mountain of Mars
The Service of Mars
A Darker Magic
Mage-Commander (upcoming)

Starship's Mage: Red Falcon
Interstellar Mage
Mage-Provocateur
Agents of Mars

Pulsar Race: A Starship's Mage Universe Novella

DUCHY OF TERRA
The Terran Privateer
Duchess of Terra
Terra and Imperium
Darkness Beyond
Shield of Terra
Imperium Defiant
Relics of Eternity
Shadows of the Fall
Eyes of Tomorrow

SCATTERED STARS
Scattered Stars: Conviction
Conviction
Deception
Equilibrium
Fortitude (upcoming)

PEACEKEEPERS OF SOL
Raven's Peace
The Peacekeeper Initiative
Raven's Course
Drifter's Folly (upcoming)

EXILE
Exile
Refuge
Crusade
Ashen Stars: An Exile Novella

CASTLE FEDERATION
Space Carrier Avalon
Stellar Fox
Battle Group Avalon
Q-Ship Chameleon
Rimward Stars
Operation Medusa
A Question of Faith: A Castle Federation Novella

SCIENCE FICTION STAND ALONE NOVELLA
Excalibur Lost

VIGILANTE
(WITH TERRY MIXON)

Heart of Vengeance
Oath of Vengeance

**Bound By Stars: A Vigilante Series
(With Terry Mixon)**
Bound By Law
Bound by Honor
Bound by Blood

TEER AND KARD

Wardtown
Blood Ward

CHANGELING BLOOD

Changeling's Fealty
Hunter's Oath
Noble's Honor
Fae, Flames & Fedoras: A Changeling Blood Novella

ONSET

ONSET: To Serve and Protect
ONSET: My Enemy's Enemy
ONSET: Blood of the Innocent
ONSET: Stay of Execution
Murder by Magic: An ONSET Novella

FANTASY STAND ALONE NOVELS

Children of Prophecy
City in the Sky